INVITATIONS

Invitations

Carol Anderson

HEADLINE
Liaison

First published in 1996 by
HEADLINE BOOK PUBLISHING

A HEADLINE LIAISON paperback

10 9 8 7 6 5 4 3 2 1

ISBN 0 7472 5212 2

Typeset by Avon Dataset Ltd, Bidford-on-Avon, Warks

Printed and bound in Great Britain by
Cox & Wyman Ltd, Reading, Berks

HEADLINE BOOK PUBLISHING
A division of Hodder Headline PLC
338 Euston Road
London NW1 3BH

'Tis the most commonplace thing in the world, to love one man to distraction and to fuck frenziedly with another; you don't give your heart to him, just your body . . . There are two manners of loving a man: morally and physically.

L'Histoire de Juliette,
ou les Prospérités du vice (1797)
by Marquis de Sade

Chapter 1

The late afternoon sky was grey, joining seamlessly with the vast expanse of the North Atlantic ocean. A day out from England and the American liner, 'Northern Star', was a bright island of activity in a bleak endless ocean. On the main deck, Rebecca Hunt shivered and pulled her coat close around her shoulders; it smelt of home, a trace of her mother's perfume lingering on the fur collar.

'Miss Hunt?' Rebecca glanced over her shoulder as the voice was whisked off by the stiff breeze.

'Yes?'

'Message for you, miss,' said a uniformed steward.

Rebecca took the envelope reluctantly and turned it over and over in her fingers, fighting the temptation to let the wind carry it away. The steward hovered. Rebecca smiled mechanically and handed him few coins.

'Will there be any reply, miss?'

Rebecca considered for a second and then shook her head. 'No, I don't think so, thank you very much.'

She had nothing left to say to Oliver Cresswell and wondered why he had bothered to send a telegram after she'd sailed. Surely they had said everything the last time they'd met and the time before that – and the time . . . She sighed unhappily and as the steward hurried back down the gangway, stuffed the message, unopened, into her coat

1

pocket. It would just be much easier if she didn't love him so much. She stared blindly out over the metallic grey sea, fighting to hold back the tears and the feelings of heartache and sadness. Images of Oliver pressed up behind her eyes – his handsome face, its contours picked out by a day's growth of beard, his strong broad shoulders, the sound of his voice as he spoke her name – Rebecca shivered, remembering the little thrill of anticipation in her stomach every time their eyes met.

Turning away from the handrail, she tried hard to control the great wave of sadness that threatened to engulf her. 'It's over,' she whispered unsteadily under her breath. 'It's over,' and as she spoke, wondered for the thousandth time whether going to America was the right thing to do. Around her on the deck other passengers were taking the air. She lowered her eyes, anxious to avoid their gaze, and hurried back to her tiny shared cabin. Inside, once the door was closed, she threw herself onto her bunk and burst into tears.

Dinner was at eight. Rebecca pinned a coral brooch to the neckline of her evening dress and gazed coolly into the mirror. She turned slowly to check her outfit. The dress had been one of her mother's before the war, though no-one would guess, it had been beautifully re-modelled to fit her. The rich coppery tones flattered her dark hair and pale complexion. 'I really have to be more positive; this is supposed to be a new start,' she thought grimly, as she tucked a stray strand of hair back into place and clipped on a pair of earrings. Her reflection followed suit.

Touching the familiar fabric she wondered if there would be rationing in New York. Edith said not in her letters. It would be wonderful to be able to buy something new without counting coupons or having to make do and restyle something old. She added the lightest touch of lipstick; another little luxury that was all too rare in London.

The table lamp reflected for an instant in the coral brooch's gold setting. Rebecca stared at it; the last time she had worn it she'd been dancing in London with Oliver. She sighed and picked up her clutch bag. 'Why do I keep doing this to myself?' she said quietly. Oliver's face seemed to fill her every waking thought. It was over, behind her. Glancing back at her reflection the brooch glittered again, miserably she snatched it off and threw it onto the dressing table.

Upstairs the ship's bar was quiet. On the stage the band played a restrained medley of Glenn Miller songs, while a sprinkling of diners at the tables around the dance floor sipped cocktails and talked in low intimate voices. She hadn't quite got used to the luxury of the ship. British night spots and restaurants seemed so bleak and drab in contrast to the showy splendour of the 'Northern Star'.

'Good evening,' said a tall American man, stepping towards her as she walked across to the bar. 'Am I to take it that you've accepted my invitation?'

Rebecca looked round. The man, lightly tanned and elegantly dressed in an evening suit, smiled and extended his hand. She glanced over her shoulder; no-one else was even close by. 'I'm sorry, are you speaking to me?'

'My invitation?' he continued. 'I sent you a note this afternoon inviting you to join me for dinner.' His brown eyes sparkled mischievously as he pulled up a stool and waved the barman closer.

Rebecca bit her lip and felt herself redden. 'I'm sorry, you must have mistaken me for someone else.'

The man grinned and extended his hand again. 'I don't think so, Miss Hunt. My name's Callum, Callum O'Neill, and if that smug limey steward took my money and didn't give you my note I'll have to have a few well chosen words with him.'

Comprehension dawned and Rebecca blushed furiously. 'You sent me a note this afternoon—'

The man nodded.

'—Inviting me to dinner?'

'Right again, so can I take it you've accepted?'

Rebecca laughed uncomfortably. 'I'm most dreadfully sorry, I didn't read it. I thought it was from someone else.'

Callum O'Neill groaned theatrically and clutched his chest. 'Oh no, don't tell me, Miss Hunt – another admirer, a beloved husband, a fiancé waiting for you in New York? I should have guessed that a girl as lovely as you was spoken for.' He glanced around the bar. 'Or is he here, on board?'

Rebecca found it impossible not to smile. 'No, it's someone I'm trying hard to leave behind. I thought your note was a telegram from him.'

Callum grinned and pulled his wallet from his pocket. 'Wonderful, wonderful, well, perhaps not for you maybe, but for me things are definitely looking up. Would you care to join me for a drink before we have dinner?'

Rebecca sat down. 'That would be very nice, but I'm not sure I really deserve dinner after ignoring your invitation.'

Callum shrugged and waved her comment away. 'Don't worry, you're here now. Call it fate. Anyway, what'll you have to drink?'

She noticed the way his eyes seemed to rest like a caress on her face and she shivered under his undisguised interest. 'Whatever you're having,' she said softly, irritated by her own indecision.

'Okay.' Callum turned to the barman. 'The lady and I will have a martini.' He glanced back at her. 'I want to know all about you. I saw you come aboard, it's taken me all day to track you down.'

Rebecca sipped her drink. 'You're very forthright, Mr O'Neill.'

'Go on, tell me that's because I'm one of them goddamned Yankees.'

Rebecca laughed. 'If you insist. I was going to say how patient you were to have hung on all day—'

Callum laughed, revealing a delicate web of tiny lines around his dark eyes. 'Nooo, not really. I was just making sure there wasn't a Mr Hunt lurking aboard. So, tell me, Miss Rebecca Hunt, what are you doing aboard a liner heading for New York?'

She smiled, enjoying the banter between them. 'I'd rather hear about you—'

'How very flattering but there's not a lot to tell, I'm heading home.'

'Services?'

He sipped his martini and shook his head. 'No, I'm a foreign correspondent for the *New York Argus*. I've been doing a series on the brave limey warriors returning home.'

Rebecca snorted. 'And what about their brave, long-suffering wives and girlfriends?'

Callum grimaced. 'Ouch, do I detect the slightest rancour there, Miss Hunt?'

Rebecca stabbed viciously at the olive in her glass. 'You might do, I was a WAAF officer during the war, demobbed of course now—'

'And this man you're leaving behind?'

'Demobbed too, but things have changed a lot since we last met.' Rebecca sipped her drink and looked away.

Changed too much, she thought sadly.

Callum nodded sagely. 'Grown apart?'

Rebecca hesitated before she replied. 'You could say that. I may have to reconsider my views on your forthrightness, Mr O'Neill.'

Callum glanced around the bar. It was slowly beginning to fill up with diners. 'Say, Miss Hunt, do you like to dance?'

Rebecca nodded.

'How about joining me for a little lightening footwork on the floor, ma'am?'

She looked uneasily at the deserted dance floor.

Callum grinned. 'Oh come on, let's show these stuffed shirts how to have little fun – '

He took her hand gently and guided her onto the polished dance floor. As they stepped out under the subdued lights the band upped the tempo and Callum led her into a faultless fox-trot.

The dancing and dinner were a great success, Callum O'Neill made her laugh and ensured the wine flowed like water. By the time coffee was served Rebecca felt relaxed and a little tipsy. On Callum's arm Rebecca walked unsteadily to the luxurious smoking-room which adjoined the dining-room. The room was dimly lit and almost empty. Deep leather chairs were arranged around low tables which gave it the air of an elegant gentleman's club.

Callum called the steward over and ordered brandy and more coffee before leaning closer to Rebecca. His dark eyes sparkled mischievously. 'Right, no more small talk, Miss Hunt, I want to hear all about this broken tryst. What happened between you and your beau?'

To her embarrassment Rebecca felt brittle silvery tears press up behind her eyes. The memories were all too fresh,

'Are you sure you really want to hear?' she said softly, 'I'm sure all these stories are much of a muchness.'

Callum sat back. 'You have my undivided attention, Miss Hunt.'

'Well,' she began haltingly. 'I went down to meet the troop ship at Southampton. Everywhere was jam-packed. The city seemed full. It was like a huge carnival. On the quayside there were hundreds of people pushing and jostling with Union Jacks, banners, bunting – the atmosphere was wonderful but it was incredibly claustrophobic and so hot. I felt desperately alone; everyone else seemed to have brought their whole family with them.

'Anyway, the troop ship had docked by the time I got there, and was far bigger than I'd imagined. It seemed to cut out the sunlight. I remember staring at this endless drab khaki crocodile of men, so many anonymous grey faces. I was terrified that I wouldn't be able to pick him out amongst all the others or that somehow we might miss each other—

'As the men found their families, everyone got steadily more and more excited. People pressed closer together as people from behind pushed forward to catch a first glimpse of their lovers and husbands, fathers and sons—

As Rebecca spoke she could see the crowds in her mind. In amongst the great seething mass of people she had suddenly spotted Oliver on the gangplank, pale and haggard, his liquid brown eyes bright with fatigue. She'd felt herself being carried forward by the crowd and was sure that Oliver, in the same moment, had seen her. Instantly his expression had changed, suffused with light, love and relief. Pushing the others aside they had hurried through the teeming swaying singing crowd, never losing sight of each other as they came closer and closer.

Suddenly within arm's reach the rest of the crowd seemed to vanish; there were just the two of them, only their eyes, only their bodies. Oliver had opened his arms to embrace her.

For an instant Rebecca had hesitated, they had been apart for so long; almost all the years since 1939. It had seemed impossible it was finally over and that at last they could be together. Finally he was there in the flesh and she'd realised she was terrified. He seemed like a stranger. She'd taken a deep breath and for the first time been aware of his smell, hypnotic and distinctive above all the others, vaguely remembered from the heady summers before the war. A glistening flicker of anticipation had risen in her belly.

She'd whispered his name, her reticence suddenly swept aside as she flung herself into his arms. He had encircled her, lips pressing against her neck. She'd felt his heat through her blouse and moved closer still, letting the sensation of his strong muscular body engulf her. Hot tears pricked up behind her eyes, tears of relief, tears of longing – confused brittle tears that threatened to engulf her.

Rebecca blushed, realising that she had stopped speaking and Callum O'Neill was watching her face, waiting for the rest of the story. 'I'm so sorry,' she said nervously. 'I was just thinking.' She hesitated, collecting her thoughts and then began again. 'We'd written to each other for years, long letters, and slowly the tone of the letters changed from – well, we fell in love—' She looked up at Callum. 'I can't begin to tell you what it felt like when I spotted him in the crowd. There just aren't any words that can convey the feelings. He was home, he was safe. I daren't let him go. I just held his hand, afraid he might be an illusion, and led him through the crowd.' Her voice faded as she imagined Oliver's face and the feel of his hand in hers.

In the smoking room, Callum touched her shoulder, breaking her train of thought. Rebecca looked up, startled by the potency of her memories. She mumbled an apology.

Callum shook his head. 'No, it's me who should be apologising. I didn't mean to upset you,' he said gently.

'No, it's all right, I suppose I'm being silly. I should be looking forward to a bright new future not constantly looking back, but I'm finding it – ' she hesitated trying to suppress the tears that threatened to reappear.

Callum leant closer. 'Painful?'

Rebecca nodded.

'So, why don't we change the subject? Why are you heading off to the States?'

Rebecca laughed. 'Well, I suppose you could say I'm off to make my fortune. I'm going to stay with a friend of mine. Edith Hartman, in New York for a while, and then – ' she held up her hands, 'whatever takes my fancy.'

Callum took a sip of hot coffee. 'Sounds like a great plan, Miss Hunt.'

Rebecca picked up her brandy. 'You may call me Rebecca.'

Callum grinned easily. 'I know, but Miss Hunt suits you so much better.'

He leant closer, his lips brushed hers, the kiss was just the barest caress. Pulling back a little, his eyes sparkled. 'I've waited all day for that and it's been worth every second,' he whispered. His fingers stroked her neck, pulling her closer as he kissed her again; the combination was intoxicating. His lips tasted of rich red wine and brandy.

Rebecca blushed furiously, she could feel the pulse

beating in her throat and suddenly aware of where she was struggled to regain her composure. 'No,' she gasped softly and sat back into her chair.

Callum shrugged. 'It was just too much of a temptation, Miss Hunt,' he purred. 'You look so lovely sitting there with your broken heart and your bright, shiny new plans for the future.'

Rebecca sighed. 'It's hardly that, it's my new quickly-cobbled-together plan for the future. I'm still not certain if I'm doing the right thing,' she said, trying to quell the soft glow of pleasure that Callum's kiss had woken in her. 'But I couldn't stay in England, Oliver—'

'So that's my rival's name, is it?'

Rebecca shook her head. 'He's hardly a rival, Callum, he made it quite obvious that he didn't want me anymore, thought he didn't put it quite like that. So,' she said with false heartiness. 'I'm now footloose and fancy free.'

Callum took a long pull on his brandy. 'Forgive me, Miss Hunt, but I think we've missed something here. I don't understand, what about this wonderful re-union at Southampton? I mean, what went wrong? You waited for him during the war. Sounds as if you were made for each other – '

Rebecca nodded unhappily. 'I thought that too, but apparently I didn't wait quite long enough,' she said without thinking and then blushed scarlet.

Callum lifted an eyebrow. 'I'm not with you?'

'We'd been childhood sweethearts, then during the war we wrote and made promises and swore true love. You know how these things happen. Anyway, by the time he was due to come home we were in love and both were ready to settle down or so I thought.' Her voice tailed off. She stared into the brandy balloon, wishing she hadn't had quite so much to drink.

'And?' encouraged Callum gently.

Rebecca shook her head, still staring at her glass so that she didn't have to look at Callum's face. 'With hindsight it seems so ridiculous now, but the day he arrived home we made love. It seemed so natural, so right.' She shivered, thinking about the train journey home with Oliver.

Every carriage had been packed with returning servicemen. It had been impossible to find a seat so they'd stood shoulder to shoulder in the corridor, the movement of the train bringing them too close to each other and too close to those around them. It was such a relief when they'd finally got to London and changed onto the little branch line that would take them home to Norfolk.

Rebecca had found it difficult to know what to say and was annoyed that she couldn't find the words to tell him how she felt – it had been so much easier to write them. Oliver seemed equally uncomfortable. At Cambridge they'd finally found an empty carriage and she'd curled up beside him, longing to bridge the gap between them, 'I'm so glad you're home,' she'd said softly, looking up at him. 'We will find the words, don't worry—'

Slowly he had turned towards her and for an instant their eyes had locked with an electric and desperate longing. He pressed his lips to her and murmured, 'Rebecca, my love,' between hot sweet kisses.

Her body had responded at once, aching for his touch, for his warmth, for the smell of him. 'Oh, Oliver,' she'd whispered and returned his kiss fervently, feeling his tongue slip between her lips. She'd groaned as his hands lifted to cup her breasts, her nipples hardening under his caress, a tiny crystal ripple of pleasure coursing through her.

Something like a sob trickled from his lips and she'd

known then that they were lost. His fingers moved
frantically, fighting with her buttons, whilst his other hand
pushed eagerly between her thighs. Gasping with pleasure
she'd opened to him, letting his fingers slide across her
stocking tops towards her knickers, letting her desire guide
her. She'd lifted to let him have greater access and
suddenly, almost before she realised it, his fingers were
pushing aside the thin fabric and plunging into her.

She'd been wet for him, moist, fragrant – a wild longing
bubbled up inside her and her tongue sought his. She
remembered him whimpering and felt his fingers move
deeper, exploring every delicate crevice and fold.

Gasping, he'd moved nearer, his breath ragged and
excited. Rolling her onto the dusty carriage seats he'd lifted
her skirt and dragged down the thin material of her
knickers. She hadn't resisted him, in fact her hips lifted
unconsciously to meet his touch. His hand fumbled with
his flies and suddenly his cock sprung towards her,
aggressive, hot and needy. She hadn't hesitated, instead she
guided him back into the seat and mounted him.

The merest fleeting brush of his erect shaft against her
inner thighs sent a great coursing plume of desire through
her. She had waited so long for this moment. She'd knelt
over him and helped him guide the raging bulbous head
into the soft inviting heat of her inner lips. Sinking down
slowly she'd felt him slide home. For a few seconds her
body had resisted his assault and then he was there, filling
her, opening her. She'd cried out at the hot burning
sensation and pressed herself onto him trying to ignore the
deep hot ache she'd felt inside. She had wanted to possess
him, to reclaim him for herself.

He'd bucked against her, filling her to the brim. Tears
of pain and excitement bubbled up behind her eyes and she

whimpered as he began to move in and out of her – a slow smooth stroke – impaling her again and again. She felt a trickle of liquid on her thighs and looking down had seen a broad smear of blood but felt no regret, no fear at the passing of her virginity. She had waited so long for this wonderful special moment when Oliver would return safely. Her body was her gift to him.

The juddering, rocking movement of the train added to their fervour. Oliver thrust deeper, grasping her hips, dragging her closer. Instinctively she'd moved against him, enjoying the sensations of his fingers exploring the delicate contours of her sex where it wrapped around his shaft. His finger tips had brushed the swollen bud of her clitoris and she gasped. He'd stroked it knowingly, rhythmically, as if he'd totally understood what she needed to fan the glow of excitement between her legs into a roaring flame.

Against her neck he'd murmured soft, sweet words of love, whilst his other hand moved to her breasts, desperately trying to free them. Finally the buttons gave under his insistent fingers. Pulling her nearer, his lips worked over the sensitive areas of her shoulders and collarbone. His mouth pressed hot heady kisses into her tingling flesh, whilst the rhythm of his fingers and cock kept up a driving relentless force. Sliding her blouse down, his lips closed over her dark puckered nipples. Sucking one between his lips he let his tongue tease round it.

Rebecca had felt as if she was losing all control; between her legs the tiny glowing circles of sensation blossomed and grew. Her hips ground instinctively into Oliver's body, pressing down onto his fingers, pressing down on his cock, chasing the feelings even though they threatened to drown her.

Suddenly she had felt Oliver straining up under her, in

the same instant she'd felt the same desperate force within her, as her muscles tightened around his shaft. The intense circles of light shuddered up through her body and mind making her cry out in astonishment. Throwing back her head she let the great waves of pleasure and light engulf her again and again. Beneath her, Oliver bucked like a wild animal. Growling deep in his throat he pushed into her once more, joining her in an all-consuming, shuddering orgasm. Sobbing, Rebecca had collapsed down onto his chest and wept hot tears of joy and relief.

When Rebecca looked up, Callum O'Neill was watching her face with undisguised interest. She reddened, stunned by the vivid memories and the realisation that she had just confessed to a stranger something that she wouldn't have told even her best friend. She looked at him desperately, her voice was emotional and uneven. 'I really don't know why I'm telling you all this, it's so intimate, so secret – I mean, you're a complete stranger.'

Callum shrugged, topping up her brandy glass. 'I can't think of a better person than a stranger to tell your secrets to.'

Rebecca sighed uneasily, the images were still so new and exciting. 'It was so wonderful,' she said quietly, looking away, 'better than I could have ever imagined and at the same time it was awful. Oliver started to apologise the moment it was over. He wouldn't even look me in the eye. By the time we got to our stop he was sitting three feet away from me.'

Callum looked confused. 'Are you telling me this took place on a bus?' he said with astonishment.

Rebecca laughed inspite of herself. 'No, no, on a train. It was on the way home after meeting him off the troop

14

ship. During the next few days things got more and more uncomfortable between us. Everything really came to a head when we started to talk about our wedding. His mother desperately wanted me to borrow her wedding dress – it was a beautiful, white antique silk – her mother had worn it. She brought it down from the attic for me to look at and Oliver said I couldn't possibly wear it—'

Rebecca felt the anger and the unhappiness building up in her stomach, remembering Oliver's forlorn expression as he had stared out of the window in his mother's sitting room, refusing to look at either of them, his hands clenched into fists in his jacket pockets. 'He implied I'd prefer something more modern but the look he gave me said something totally different.' She stopped and took a hefty swig of brandy. 'I know he thought I wasn't fit to wear it—'

Callum leant back in his chair. 'But he was your lover?'

Rebecca nodded dumbly. 'Yes, my first and we only made love that once. After we got home he seemed afraid to be alone with me, as if I might bite him.'

Callum leant closer, the mischief flickering in his dark eyes. 'You bite, do you, Miss Hunt?'

Rebecca swung round to face him and said furiously. 'This is not funny.'

Callum held up his hands in apology, the glint not quite leaving his eyes. 'I'm sorry, but it's a long way from a white wedding dress to a decision to run away to America.'

Rebecca angrily slammed her glass down on the table. 'I am not running away. I did an important job in the WAAF. I don't want to stay home and play house. There's no work for me now the men are being demobbed and—'

'And what?'

She took a deep breath, trying to resist the temptation to use Callum as a sounding board for all the things she had

15

so desperately wanted to explain to Oliver. Oliver with his double standards and his story-book vision of her making jam while he ran his father's estate. She looked past Callum to the doors of the dining-room and tried to compose herself. 'I need a new start, my friend, Edith, is in New York. She wrote and invited me to stay with her for a little while.'

'There is no need to justify yourself to me, Miss Hunt. No need at all. Now, would you like to dance some more, or maybe after this,' he indicated the brandy balloons, 'you'd like to take a turn around the deck for a little night air.'

As he spoke he let his fingers linger for an instant on her wrist, his touch was soft, tentative. She glanced up into his dark eyes and saw understanding, and more – she saw desire. Quickly she looked away, out towards the windows. Beyond the glass the night was inky, stars glinting against velvet-black. She looked back at Callum and nodded.

Outside the wind had risen to a chilly bitter sting. Callum slipped off his evening jacket and draped it around her shoulders. She looked up at him and smiled. 'This is ridiculous, Callum, you'll freeze in your shirt sleeves and this dress isn't exactly designed for walking round the deck.'

Callum moved closer, for a second his hands rested lightly on her shoulders. 'I've got an overcoat in my cabin, why don't we go downstairs and collect it?' His voice was barely more than a purr.

Rebecca felt something stirring inside, recognised the invitation and knew Callum had more on his mind than a warm coat. She wasn't sure if she could trust herself to speak. 'I don't think . . .' she began, but instead felt herself being drawn towards him.

He pulled her close, encircling her in his arms, silencing her reluctance with a kiss. She could feel the heat of his body, smell his cologne and beneath it the dark heady musk of his masculinity. Her lips opened instinctively to his and she gasped as his tongue slid between her lips. His hands moved up over her back, kneading, touching. She moaned softly and returned his kiss, suddenly dizzy and excited by the prospect of his caresses. Slowly he pulled away, his eyes dark hypnotic pits. 'Let's get that coat,' he murmured.

She took his hand without a word and followed him back inside to the stairway. As they passed through the maze of corridors he looked back at her. She felt a fluttering mixture of excitement and panic in her chest as he spoke. 'Not all men are complete assholes, you know, Miss Hunt.'

Rebecca smiled thinly, not daring to speak.

He hesitated outside one of the state-rooms. 'Are you sure you want to come in here with me?' he asked softly, his eyes holding hers as he unlocked the door.

Rebecca looked surprised. 'You've got a state-room?'

Callum snorted and held up his hands. 'Here I am offering you a way out of being seduced and you want to know if I'm staying in a state-room?'

Rebecca blushed. 'I'm surprised that's all — '

As she spoke Callum pushed open the door, in the light from the corridor the room glinted richly. 'Why don't you come inside and take a look, maybe I'll even find my coat. Don't be too impressed by all the glitz. The *Argus* are paying.'

Rebecca followed him in. He closed the door behind her with a quiet click. She looked around, astounded. The room was enormous, furnished as a comfortable sitting room. Beyond a half open door she could see a large bedroom. Rebecca spun round to find that Callum had opened the cocktail cabinet. She held up her hand in protest. 'No more for me, I think I've had enough,' she said, as he held out a bottle for her approval. She bit her lip and added quickly, 'If I'm going to be seduced I'd rather know what I'm doing.'

Callum laughed aloud. 'You've changed your tune, what is it – my furniture convinced you?'

Rebecca shook her head and in doing so caught sight of herself in the mirror. Her attractive humorous face looked squarely back, eyes bright with drink and excitement.

Callum sipped his drink, a fruit juice she noticed. 'I really don't want to be used as an object of spite, Miss Hunt,' he said, moving slowly closer.

She shook her head, still concentrating on her reflection. 'You won't be, I'm a grown woman. I waited years to take a lover, someone I truly loved – and they didn't love me for it.' She hesitated and then said quickly, 'So, as you said earlier, why not a stranger now? It's less complicated this way.'

Callum grinned and stood his drink down on a side table. 'So what do you want then, Miss Hunt?' he purred teasingly, his approach cat-like, predatory.

She shivered, 'I'd like you to make love to me.'

He was beside her now, looking over her shoulder in the mirror, eyes bright. 'And how do you want me to make love to you, Miss Hunt?'

She glanced up at him, suddenly unsure and a little afraid, almost as much by her own boldness as by Callum's closeness. 'I don't know,' she said in a voice barely above a whisper.

He caught hold of her by the shoulders and pressed her back against the cold glass of the mirror. He moved so quickly that Rebecca let out a little squeal of panic. He kissed her roughly, almost brutally, his hands holding her face up towards him as his lips bruised her, pressing, probing. He pulled away breathlessly. 'Do you think you might like it rough, Miss Hunt?'

Rebecca fought to catch her breath, her stomach fluttered at the sensations he lit in her.

Now his kiss was light, barely more than a breeze on her lips, then over her throat, down onto her neck as he pushed his jacket back off her shoulders. 'Or perhaps like this; a soft sensuous seduction?' He looked into her eyes.

She swallowed hard. 'I don't know,' she murmured. 'I don't know what I want.'

Callum's hand lifted to her chin and he pulled her towards him. 'Then let's experiment, shall we?'

He drowned out her fear with his kisses, soft then brusque, wet then dry, hard then soft. She felt herself melting eagerly into his arms and did not protest as his hands slipped around to the zip on the back of her evening dress. 'Trust me, Miss Hunt,' he murmured as his lips pressed into her throat while from behind she heard the soft growl of the zip giving under his fingers. She stiffened as he pressed the silky fabric down to reveal her shoulders.

She pulled away for a second, glancing towards the bedroom. Callum caught her look and glanced up at her with twinkling eyes and an easy grin. 'Would you rather we went in there, Miss Hunt? This from a woman whose only experience of making love is in a railway carriage?'

Rebecca reddened. 'No, I just thought that, that . . .' Her mind was like a fog. All she could think of was the hot mellow feelings Callum's kisses were stirring in her belly. She shook her head. 'I don't know what I thought.'

Callum leant closer. 'We'll make it into the bed later, Miss Hunt. In the meantime I was going to take advantage of you here, in the light.' He lifted his fingers to the softly draped material of her dress. 'Why don't you slip this off?'

Rebecca gasped and then looked into his eyes. She saw the desire there and her own bright eyes reflected his hunger. She wanted him. She looked away and let the thin silky shift slip to the floor in a dark copper puddle round her ankles. Beneath she was wearing just a camisole top and knickers, with a pair of strappy sandals that she had bought in the summer before the war.

Callum stepped back with a look of undisguised admiration. She could feel her nipples hardening under his gaze, their puckered points pressing against the thin fabric of her camisole.

He let out an appreciative whistle, caught her eye and smiled. 'Your fiancé was a real fool, Miss Hunt. You are truly, truly beautiful. Turn around and take a look at yourself.'

As Rebecca started to protest Callum took her by the shoulders and turned her round to face her reflection. In the mirror Rebecca could make out the hard dark press of her nipples against the silk, the shadowy fullness of her breasts, the narrowness of her waist before her body curved out over full hips. Below she could see the dark mound of her sex, her knickers pleated in soft moist gathers around its outer lips. Glancing up she could see her glittering eyes, the pupils dilated and dark. Behind her Callum's face was open and encouraging.

'Lift your arms up,' he said gently.

As she did he caught hold of the hem of her camisole top and pulled it over her head.

'Look now,' he whispered.

Her breasts were small but round and even, flushed now with excitement, the nipples puckered into tight, dark, little arrowheads. She watched mesmerised as Callum's hands encircled them, stroking and teasing, drawing circles that set off glistening shards of sensation inside her head. Strange to be able to see it and feel it, she thought, as the expectation and excitement mounted in her belly.

One of Callum's hands slipped lower, as his lips pressed out eager wet kisses on the back of her neck and shoulders. She writhed under his touch as he made his way down over her belly and rubbing herself against him she felt the hard press of his cock.

His fingers found the waistband of her knickers and there they stopped. Over her shoulder he looked up and into the eyes of her reflection. 'Well, Miss Hunt, the choice is yours, tell me if you want me to stop. I really don't want to spend the rest of the voyage in the brig, so tell me if you're planning on yelling rape.'

Rebecca looked dumbly at his reflection, too excited, too afraid to speak. Finally she said thickly, 'What do you want me to say?'

He smiled, his fingers stroking the tender sensitive skin of her belly. 'I only need you to say you want me to make love to you, Miss Hunt, and be sure you know what it means. Just tell me that I have your express permission to take you to the pinnacles of ecstasy, dear lady.'

Rebecca laughed and then leant back against him, brushing herself against the hard bulge in his trousers, 'You have my permission, Mr O'Neill,' she said softly. As she spoke he lifted the thin fabric of her knickers and slid his hand lower, brushing across the dark curls of her sex. She whimpered and bit her lip. His hand moved lower, teasing, brushing against the swollen bud of her clitoris. She rubbed herself against his fingers, the electric pulse almost too much to bear.

'Beautiful,' Callum murmured, dipping lower to the engorged outer lips. 'My God, you are so wet, so ready, Miss Hunt.'

Rebecca could feel the tremor in her legs. Her whole body ached for the touch of his fingers, ached for satisfaction. Instinctively she moved to let him into her. She could hear a soft throaty chuckle behind her as Callum found the slick tight opening and gently slid a single finger just inside. She let out a shuddering gasping moan. His finger teased back and forth.

'Please—' she stammered throatily, shocked at herself for pleading for his caress.

'Slowly, slowly, Miss Hunt,' Callum said, returning his attentions to her clitoris.

Rebecca shivered and pressed herself against him as he stroked her rhythmically. Tiny waves of pleasure began to spiral out from the tight bud between her legs. She moaned softly and shivered.

'Why don't you take those off too?' he said thickly.

Rebecca hesitated and then gasped as another ripple of delight shuddered through her. With no more than a few seconds hesitation, her fingers slipped into the fabric of her knickers and slipped them down. The reflection glittering in the stateroom mirror shocked her. Her body seemed suffused by an inner light. In contrast to her pale shimmering skin, Callum's arm, still in his shirt, rested across her belly whilst his fingers opened her, revealing pink moist glimpses of her sex. The image was hypnotic. Callum caught her eye and could not disguise the look of anticipation on his face.

'That's it, enjoy, Miss Hunt. You look so damned lovely, drink it in, you are a feast, a banquet.'

She couldn't tear her eyes away from their reflection in the mirror, gasping with surprise as each move she saw echoed through her body. Callum began to move round her, his fingers wet with her juices touching her breasts and face. She could smell the musky oceanic smell of her own excitement on him.

His lips travelled down over her throat, down to her breasts. She gasped as his lips closed over her dark nipples, his fingers moving to play below. Rebecca found it hard to control her breathing. The sensations Callum was igniting within her were all engulfing, making her feel faint and heady. She shivered as she felt him sink onto his knees, his fingers still holding her open.

'What are you doing?' she hissed, as she felt his warm breath on her belly.

Callum looked up at her, eyes glistening. 'If you think I'm good with my fingers wait until you feel my tongue,' he said lightly.

'Your tongue?' As she spoke he lightly brushed her heavy outer lips with his mouth, the tip of his tongue prising her apart. 'Oh my God,' she gasped.

His tongue darted deeper now, seeking out her clitoris, lapping softly, nibbling, as his fingers slid gently deeper into the moist confines of her body. She knitted her fingers into his dark hair to hold herself steady as he probed deeper, his tongue keeping up a steady rhythm on the hard bud. The ripples of excitement grew more intense, coming closer and closer together until Rebecca felt her whole body would explode from the growing tension. Just as she felt there was no more, a great surge rolled up through her, taking her to the very edge of consciousness. She screamed out, thrusting herself on his tongue, her whole body shuddered, the muscles deep inside closing again and again on Callum's fingers as she reached her climax. Desperately she pulled away, seeing stars, feeling dizzy and breathless.

Callum looked up triumphantly.

Rebecca slipped her hands from his hair, trying to regain her balance.

He stood up slowly, a lazy smile on his face, slick juices around his generous mouth. He pulled her towards him and kissed her passionately. She gasped at the taste of her own body on his lips. He took her hand. 'Now for the bedroom you wanted so badly,' he whispered.

Without protest Rebecca followed him through the open door. Suddenly she was aware of the strange intimacy between them and felt self-conscious of her nakedness. As if sensing her unease he turned towards her. 'It's all right,' he murmured, 'there's nothing wrong with the way you feel. Do you understand?'

She nodded, dumbly.

'Get into bed if it makes you feel more comfortable,' he said, folding back the eiderdown.

She slipped quickly between the cool linen sheets. Callum switched on the bedside lamp, the soft light gave the luxurious room a delicate glow. She looked around uneasily and then closed her eyes while Callum started to undo his shirt buttons. She heard him laugh and looked up; he was still fully dressed although he had loosened his tie and unbuttoned his cuffs.

'Why don't you watch me?' he murmured. 'Aren't you in the least bit curious about what else I'm going to give you?'

She blushed furiously but opened her eyes and watched him as he slipped off his shirt. His muscular torso was lightly tanned with a dark swirl of black curls between his nipples, leading in a narrow line towards his navel.

'I don't know anything about you,' she said in a low voice.

Callum shrugged. 'Well, you know I have a penchant for beautiful lonely English women, I've got a hairy chest—' he paused and slipped his evening trousers down. His cock, broad and engorged sprung forward fiercely, he watched her reaction and then smiled. 'And I can take you to the edge of heaven,' he whispered slipping into bed beside her.

The heat and subtle masculine smell of his body made her shiver. She blushed as he turned towards her. His cock, like another person pressed between them, eager for attention. She looked at him helplessly. 'I don't know what to do,' she whispered.

Callum touched her face, brushing her hair away. 'I'll help you. Relax, this isn't a competition.' Taking her hand he closed it round the base of his shaft. Beneath her fingers she was stunned to feel how hard he felt, so alive, so fierce and yet covered in the silkiest smoothest skin. 'Now gently up and down,' he whispered, guiding her fingers, 'like this.'

She followed his guidance and was rewarded by a sudden quickening in his breath.

'Can you do this with your mouth?' she said, almost afraid to hear the answer.

Callum nodded. 'Yes, if you want to,' he said.

She shivered. 'I'm not sure I do,' she said. 'Not yet.'

Callum smiled, 'It's all right, take it slow, we've got the whole voyage.'

She let go of him in surprise. 'The whole voyage?' she repeated slowly.

'Look on it as an education, Miss Hunt,' he said in a deep voice as he rolled away from her.

'Where are you going?' she snapped nervously.

Callum swung back with a little packet which he waved towards her theatrically. 'Rubbers, Miss Hunt, American service issue. 'It's an education we've got ahead of us, not a shotgun wedding. Here, help me slip it on.'

She helped him and did not resist as he rolled onto her, his body pressing her back into the mattress, his hands gently pushing her legs apart. As the head of his cock brushed her thighs she shivered and froze.

'It's all right,' he murmured, 'I won't hurt you.' His fingers moved to the soft delicate lips of her sex, thumb pressing rhythmically on the bud of her clitoris that still throbbed from his kisses. 'Relax, Miss Hunt, we've got all the time in the world.'

For an instant she was afraid as she felt the bulbous head slip inside her and gasped. He eased in more slowly, as if he sensed her fear, stroking her, murmuring soft words of encouragement, until she felt she could take no more. He began to move, smoothly, evenly, and her body responded instinctively in kind, lifting to meet his stroke. He filled her completely, his lips moving over her breasts, hips grinding into her, his body rubbing hotly against hers. To her surprise she felt her excitement rekindling, the realisation made her call out.

Her cry was enough. Callum began to press deeper now, harder and faster. Her body matched him stroke for stroke as if it had a mind of its own.

Pinned beneath him she bucked, letting the rolling waves of light take her on and on. Suddenly it seemed as if the sun exploded deep inside her belly and at the same instant she felt Callum rear up, his breath wild and erratic as he joined her in a shuddering desperate climax that threatened to drown them both.

Their last few strokes were ragged and uneven until finally Callum collapsed down onto her. She shuddered; for an instant Oliver's unhappy face filled her mind. Even as she thought it Callum pulled himself up onto his elbows, his expression triumphant and suffused with delight. 'You really are amazing, Miss Hunt,' he said huskily, kissing her tenderly. 'Totally and utterly amazing. Come here, why don't we lay down and sleep for a while, I am totally bushed.'

Laying beside her, he wrapped an arm around her shoulders and pulled her close to him, his fingers stroking her hair gently. Rebecca curled close, relishing the smell and the heat between them and in seconds fell asleep in his arms.

When she woke there was an instant of panic. She struggled to remember where she was, though almost immediately her mind was full with the images of Callum's lovemaking. Beside her in the lamplight, her lover lay, sound asleep making soft child-like noises. She leant over and kissed his cheek before slipping from the bed. Glancing at the cabin clock she saw it was well after three. Collecting her clothes from the floor of the sitting-room she dressed quickly, only catching sight of herself in the mirror as she pulled her dress straight. She smiled at her reflection, realising that she didn't feel a shred of regret. She tidied her hair and let herself out.

The liner's corridors were silent except for the low throb of the engines as Rebecca crept through the ship to her small cabin. In the single bed nearest the door, Mrs Ross, the plump English woman who shared her cabin, was snoring hard. Gratefully Rebecca undressed quickly and climbed into bed, her body still aching from Callum's delicious assault. Pulling the bedclothes tight up round her she was asleep within seconds.

Chapter 2

The next morning Rebecca was relieved to find that Callum was nowhere in sight when she made her way to the dining-room for breakfast. She had no regrets, but needed time to recover from her night with him. Her body ached from his exquisite embraces and part of her mind was still stunned that she shared such intimate acts with a complete stranger.

Over breakfast and walking back to her cabin she wondered whether Callum would come to find her. She shivered; perhaps he would be like Oliver, the thought left her cold. As she opened the cabin door she was met by Mrs Ross, still in her curlers and dressing gown. The older woman looked surprised to see her.

Rebecca's greeting froze on her lips as she glanced round the little room and saw that all her personal possessions seemed to have gone. 'My things . . .' she stammered.

Mrs Ross shrugged. 'A steward came to collect them just after you went for breakfast, dear, I thought you must know you were moving to another cabin.'

Rebecca sat down heavily on the edge of the bed. 'There has to have been some kind of mix up, I'll go and see what's happened. Have you got any idea where they took my luggage?'

Mrs Ross shook her head. 'No, the man just said you were moving into one of the state-rooms, first class.'

Instantly Rebecca imagined Callum's mischievous handsome face. 'Thank you,' she said quickly and hurried out. In the corridor she found the day steward who serviced their deck, a middle-aged man with a laconic smile. 'Excuse me,' she said.

The steward turned round. 'Morning, miss, settled in all right, have you? We didn't miss anything, did we?'

Rebecca blushed furiously. 'No, no, you seem to have taken everything. What I need to know is where you've taken my things?' Even as she said it she knew where they had gone and was furious at Callum's presumption.

'State-room twenty-three, miss, Deck A.' The steward winked conspiratorially.

Rebecca hurried away towards the first class section of the ship and was met at the top of the stairs by Callum O'Neill. 'How dare you?' she snapped angrily before he had chance to speak.

He grinned. 'You don't want to move in with me?'

Rebecca was stunned. 'What on earth will people think?' she blustered. 'You had no right to assume that . . .' That what? Her mind raced; that they would meet again? Make love again? She felt her colour rising.

Callum leant against the wall, smiling. 'Why don't you come back to my cabin and we'll have some coffee. I assumed you'd like your education to continue face to face. It's not the kind of course you can take by correspondence.' His tone was light and teasing.

Rebecca let him take her arm, though her indignation had not abated.

'What will people say?' she said, as he opened the door to his state-room.

Callum laughed. 'Who the hell cares. Look, no-one is that interested, everyone knows about shipboard romances, they're famous. Come on, tell me you aren't just a bit flattered.'

Rebecca swung round and slapped him hard across the face, the blow cracked out like a pistol shot. To her amazement Calum threw back his head and roared with laughter. 'You little vixen,' he said, rubbing his cheek. 'I thought you said you bite, not slap. Come here and let me kiss you. What is it that guy says in the movies? "You're so beautiful when you're angry".'

Rebecca snorted. 'I'm not that kind of woman,' she began and then blushed furiously, thinking of his tongue on her body. She could see her angry expression reflected in the mirror, where – the night before – she had stood naked and the words died on her lips.

Callum moved closer. 'I know,' he purred seductively. 'But I think you would really quite like to be. Why don't you make yourself at home while I ring for another jug of coffee?'

Rebecca glanced around. In daylight the room was, if anything, more impressive than she had thought the previous night, with luxurious leather furniture and low gilded tables. The walls were painted in the softest cream and floor-length velvet drapes hung at the portholes.

She raised an eyebrow. 'How is it that a reporter comes to have a state-room? Surely your newspaper wouldn't foot the bill for all this?'

Callum shrugged. 'Caught me out on that one, Miss Hunt, I could tell you it's all down to smooth talk and a few bucks as a back hander—'

Rebecca thoughtfully stroked the arm of one of the leather chairs. 'I think I'd prefer the truth.'

Callum picked up the phone beside the sofa and ordered coffee before turning back to her. 'Actually, it isn't so far from the truth, that and the fact that my dad is Sam O'Neill.'

Rebecca grimaced. 'Sam O'Neill?'

Callum groaned. 'Don't tell me, that means nothing to you?'

Rebecca nodded. 'That's right.'

Callum threw himself casually onto the sofa. 'He's a major share-holder in the shipping line. Not that he'd approve of my free-loading on his name. He's a great one for saying we all ought to make it on our own merit, but well, a few words in the right ear and here we are.' He lifted his hands to encompass the state-room.

Rebecca sighed, feeling self-conscious. 'So, are you a poor little rich boy, looking for a new thrill?'

Callum pulled his face into an exaggerated expression of pain. 'Ouch, ouch, I was right, you really are a vixen, Miss Hunt. No, in answer to your question, not at all. I'm a very successful reporter, I've got my own column, a swish little apartment down in Greenwich village and am half-way through a novel that promises to make me as one of the great American novelists of the forties. Does that satisfy you?'

Rebecca considered for a few minutes then turned to face him. 'I'm still not sure that moving my luggage in here was a very good idea.'

Callum grinned. 'I was hoping that where your luggage went you might be tempted to follow.'

Rebecca laughed. 'You mean you've kidnapped my clothes?'

Callum patted the sofa beside him, eyes alight now with mischief and desire. 'You could look at it like that. Why don't you come over here. I've been thinking about what we could do for this morning's practical—'

Rebecca moved closer. Callum began to stroke her leg, his hand sliding slowly up over the swell of her thighs, tentatively, softly.

Rebecca sighed at the electric sensation. She might not be happy with his boldness but she knew she could easily become addicted to his knowing touch. As he brushed the contours of her sex, she flinched.

Callum looked up at her with concern. 'Are you okay?'

Rebecca nodded. 'A little tender after last night.'

He circled again, his touch was now feather-light lifting slowly over the mount of her sex, his fingers seeking out the bud of her clitoris. 'Don't worry,' he soothed, as he stroked his fingers against the fabric, I'll be oh so gentle.'

Rebecca let out a stifled moan and eagerly pressed herself against him. At that moment there was a soft knock at the door. Callum slowly pulled his hand away and called for the steward to bring in their coffee.

Rebecca stood self-consciously beside the sofa, furious at herself for feeling so ill at ease. Callum glanced up at her. 'Why don't you sit down, Miss Hunt,' he said lightly, 'I'd like to start dictation as soon as we've had our coffee.'

Rebecca stared at him in confusion.

Callum nodded towards the steward. 'My steward here has put your bags in your cabin.'

The steward looked up.

Rebecca frowned. 'What?'

Callum sighed. 'Maybe, steward, you'd show Miss Hunt her new room?'

The uniformed man nodded and moved across the state-room. In the far wall opposite Callum's bedroom was another door. The steward opened it slowly and Rebecca hurried across to look inside. Beyond the door was a small room with a single bed, lockers and a sink. Laid on top of the bed was Rebecca's luggage and a new shorthand pad and pencil. She swung round and pulled a face at Callum, who was grinning like a Cheshire cat.

'I hope you'll be comfortable in there, Miss,' said the man pleasantly. 'If we'd known Mr O'Neill had his secretary travelling with him we could have made the arrangements earlier.'

After he'd gone Rebecca threw herself, grinning, at Callum. 'Your secretary?'

Callum pushed her away playfully. 'As good a cover story as any. No one will believe it, whatever we tell them, this way at least we can pretend your reputation is intact. Now, where was I?' With the speed of a cat he grabbed her and kissed her fiercely. Rebecca gasped and then pressed her lips to his, relishing the taste of his mouth on hers. His hand snaked up over her thighs and began to brush rhythmically at the outside of her knickers. Rebecca shivered and then surrendered to his caress, knowing that she had found a teacher who took his very lessons seriously.

'There's the old Lady of Liberty,' Callum pointed through the sea mist as they approached New York harbour.

Below them the Hudson rolled, murky brown and grey, away from the cutting bow of the ship. Snuggled close to him, Rebecca found it hard to believe that they would soon be docking. Beyond the Statue of Liberty the Manhattan skyline was picked out dramatically against the morning sky. It was difficult to find words to describe what she was feeling.

She had spent the voyage making torrid, exciting love under Callum's eager tutelage. She turned away from the hand-rail and the dramatic skyline and looked back along the deck. 'What will happen to us when we leave the ship?'

she said softly, hardly daring to voice the words.

Callum slid his arm around her waist. 'That rather depends on what you have in mind, Miss Hunt. I don't want to stand in the way of your bright, shiny, new future.'

Rebecca shivered and not just from the cold. 'This voyage has been like a dream. Now I've got to wake up and get on with my life.'

Callum nodded. 'Right, so if you need me I'll be there . . .' His voice was low and even.

'But?' Rebecca said quickly, 'Were you going to say "but"?'

Callum shrugged. 'Not necessarily, I'd like us to stay friends but you're starting over. I'm the teacher not your husband, or your fiancé, not really even your lover.'

Rebecca snorted feeling a peculiar mixture of relief and pain. 'And are you saying you don't want to be any of those things?'

Callum laughed. 'No, but be honest, do you really want to start a new life with a ready made lover in tow? I'll give you my address and my phone number and if you're at a loose end then ring me and we'll spend a long lazy night in the hay. Is it a deal?'

To her surprise Rebecca nodded, she knew he was right. She had come to New York to be free, to begin again, not disappear straight into a new relationship. 'It's a deal, Mr O'Neill,' she said warmly and offered him her hand.

Walking down the gangway Rebecca was reminded of the day she had met Oliver at Southampton; the same sea of anonymous faces, the same sense of panic and isolation. Suddenly, beyond the barrier, she caught sight of a familiar face. Her friend, Edith Hartman, stylishly dressed in a crisp navy suit and a little pill-box hat, waved frantically.

Rebecca glanced back up towards the ship as she hurried across the quay to meet Edith; at the rail Callum O'Neill stood, as if he were watching her progress, and lifted a hand in farewell.

'Rebecca!' Edith's voice caught her attention and when she looked back Callum had gone.

'God, it's so good to see you.' Edith embraced her firmly and then held her at arms length as if to drink in the details of her face. 'I can't believe you're really here. We're going to have such a wonderful time. I think I may be able to get you a job at Berdys where I work. I've got so much to tell you. How was the voyage?'

Edith's cheerful voice and endless questions flooded Rebecca's mind, pushing away the pain of her parting with Callum and she was happy to find her luggage and let Edith guide her towards a taxi.

Edith's apartment was above a delicatessen in Greenwich Village and consisted of a strange arrangement of open rooms with just the bathroom completely divided off from the rest of the flat. Despite its open style it was cramped and untidy. Edith lit the gas and slid a kettle across onto the flame while Rebecca prised off her shoes.

Edith grinned happily. 'I'm so glad you came, it's glorious here, no black-out, no rationing, as much food as you can buy.' She laughed. 'You're really going to love it.'

Rebecca glanced round the tiny apartment.

Edith, catching her eyes, shrugged. 'I know, it's a mess but we're saving for something better but here there's the attic. Arnie uses it as a studio for his sculpture, it's included in with the rent. I'm afraid you'll have to have the sofa until you get yourself organised, if that's okay.' She paused. 'Arnie's out at the moment, he's helping his uncle down at

the market today, but he'll be back later. I'm sure you'll like
him, but – well, give him a little while. He's a bit quiet
around people he doesn't know.'

Rebecca grinned in surprise. 'You're living with him?'

Edith nodded. 'This isn't good olde England, my dear.
No-one bats an eyelid. Would you like tea or coffee?'

'Tea, please, now what's this about a job?'

A few days later Edith led an open-mouthed Rebecca
through the ground floor of Berdys department store to
Mrs Leinneman's office on the third floor. In the staff
elevator Rebecca grabbed Edith's arm. 'I've never seen
anything like this, it's like an Aladdin's cave down there.'

Edith grinned and pushed the button for the third floor.
'There are five floors of it, Berdys is only one step behind
Maceys. Now, for godsake, best P's and Q's for Mrs
Leinneman, she is a complete dragon, but you really do
need this job. The pay's not a fortune but there are all sorts
of staff perks.' As she spoke Edith glanced in the mirror and
straightened the skirt of her Berdys' store uniform. The silk
blouse and sharp grey skirt created a flattering and elegant
effect. 'The uniform being one of them, oh, and you get
shoes and nylons too. Here we are.'

The lift juddered to a halt and Edith slid the doors open.

Rebecca glanced out nervously into the corridor. 'What
is it you've told Mrs Leinneman I can do?'

Edith snorted, patting her hair. 'Everything, but most of
all just speak with an English accent, they think it's very,
very classy over here, that's why she's prepared to give you
an interview. They're looking for someone to work on the
lingerie counter, it's considered a very cushy job.'

Rebecca nodded and thought wryly of her own underwear,
most of which was made from parachute silk hastily run up

by her mother on their faithful sewing machine.

Mrs Leinneman's office door was slightly ajar. Edith pointed it out and then wished her luck. 'I've got to get down to perfumery, the chief assistant down there is like Ghenghis Khan in a frock, best of luck, see you later.' She waved with her fingers crossed. Rebecca grinned and then knocked on the office door.

Mrs Sarah Leinneman was a sharp-faced Jewish widow from Brooklyn, in charge of personnel at Berdys and queen of all she surveyed. She glanced briefly at Rebecca's papers and then back up at the young woman, with a jaundiced world-weary eye. 'Miss Hartman says you arrived from England a few days ago.' Sarah Leinneman's accent was heavy and metallic.

Rebecca nodded. 'Yes, that's right, Mrs Leinneman.'

'And you're staying with her at her apartment?'

'Yes, temporarily.'

As Rebecca spoke she thought about the cramped little flat and the dark hot noises she heard at night coming from the double bed in the room next door. During the day Edith's lover, Arnie, was almost silent, barely wasting a word on Rebecca, while at night his passionate cries were like a hungry wolf as he made long rough love to Edith. At first Rebecca had tried to block the noises out with a pillow, but it was impossible. In the end she had lay awake and listened with a mixture of embarrassment and envy to her friend's frenzied antics.

It seemed to Rebecca as if her presence added to Arnie's fervour. In fact Edith had almost said as much over breakfast, while, at the sink, Rebecca had caught Arnie staring at her with undisguised interest. The memory made her shiver; the sooner she found a place of her own the better.

From behind her desk Mrs Leinneman appraised Rebecca Hunt coolly. 'Well, your references and papers seem in order, Miss Hunt, and you have the right look for Berdys. We offer a high standard of customer service here.' She leant closer. 'You'll have to do something about your hair, but the girls upstairs in the salon will sort that out for you. We encourage our girls to wear make-up but keep it subtle and we have a very strict moral code. I'm prepared to take you on for a month's trial—'

In front of her, Rebecca, realising Mrs Leinneman was offering her the job, smiled broadly. 'Thank you.'

Mrs Leinneman shrugged. 'You won't be so quick to thank me when your feet are killing you and some rich old woman insists she can cram herself into a corset three sizes too small.'

She leant over and pressed a button on her intercom with long painted fingernails. A girl in Berdys livery scurried in. Mrs Leinneman barely looked up. 'Take Miss Hunt here to the stores and get her a uniform.' She glanced up at Rebecca. 'I want you here at eight-thirty sharp, Monday morning. Call in at the salon before you leave to arrange to have your hair done.'

Dismissing Rebecca with a wave, Sarah Leinneman lit up a cigarette and then picked up the phone. She had a friend who would be interested in the new English girl, a dear friend who had seen to it that her promotion from the shop floor to personnel manager had been swift and painless.

A secretary answered her call. Sarah Leinneman took a long pull on her cigarette. 'This is Mrs Leinneman here, from Berdys, can you put me through to Mr de Viton, please?'

★ ★ ★

'Or we could go to the zoo—'

'Look, Edith, I've already said I don't wanna go out. How many times do I have to tell you? I've got things I've got to do here—'

Arnie and Edith were arguing over breakfast in their cramped apartment, while Rebecca sat in the one decent armchair looking out at the colourful streets below. New York was an astounding, cosmopolitan place, full of new sights and sounds. So far she had barely scratched the surface.

Edith looked desperately at Rebecca. 'Say something, Becky, we ought to go out somewhere today. It's the weekend. You're new here, don't you want to explore?'

Rebecca pulled a face. 'I'm trying to make my money last as long as I can. I really ought to be out looking for an apartment.'

Arnie looked up at her with an expression that made her shiver. 'No need to rush away, babe. Edith likes having you here, don't you, kitten?' he purred, his eyes lingering on Rebecca's bare legs. She felt herself redden under his gaze.

He grinned and stroked Edith's face. Rebecca looked away. Arnie had dark brooding Italian features, that gave him a slightly sinister air, like a movie gangster. Sitting in a sleeveless vest his muscular torso reminded her of Callum. She swallowed and wondered whether she should give him a ring.

Edith slammed her coffee cup down angrily. 'I'm not going to be stuck in this place all day, what if we go for a walk instead?'

Rebecca eased herself out of the chair. 'All right, don't get so grumpy. I'm only trying to make my money last.'

Edith snorted. 'You start work tomorrow.'

Rebecca laughed. 'Hang on a minute. You're the one

that told me Berdy's don't exactly pay a fortune.'

She caught sight of herself in the pitted mirror above the fireplace. The girls at Berdys had persuaded her to wear hair shorter with the sides swept up in combs. It flattered the oval shape of her face and gave her a more elegant, feminine look. She turned a little to see the sides as Edith slipped from the table to get her coat from the closet.

Arnie moved closer, his hand resting lightly on Rebecca's waist. 'You look real fine, little lady,' he whispered.

Rebecca gasped as she felt his hands lift to cup her breasts and spun round to face him. 'Stop that,' she hissed.

Arnie shrugged lightly. 'Don't tell me you don't think about me,' he whispered. 'I know you listen to us making out at night. Wouldn't you like to feel me pressed hard up inside you?' He moved his body closer, rubbing himself suggestively against her.

Rebecca blanched; it was if he had read her mind.

He moved away as Edith stepped back into the room. 'Are you coming with us, Arnie?' she said, seemingly oblivious to the sexual tension between the two of them.

Arnie shook his head. 'Nope, I'm going upstairs to the studio and get a few hours work done in peace without you two gabbing on.'

He gave Rebecca a strange penetrating look which made her flinch.

Edith handed Rebecca her coat. 'Come on then, looks like it's just you and me.'

That night Rebecca found it almost impossible to sleep, from the room next door she could hear the compelling sounds of Arnie taking Edith again and again. Her friend called out in ecstasy as Arnie drove her to the edge of madness. Arnie's voice was gruff and thick as he reached out for his own climax. Rebecca desperately wrapped her head under her pillow to shut out the noises. Her mind, teetering on the edge of sleep, sought out comforting images of Callum O'Neill and his smooth sure touch.

She didn't hear Arnie's soft padding feet as he headed towards the bathroom in the early hours of the morning but in her dreams she felt the softest brush of a hand on her breasts. The caress transported her back to the long steamy nights on board ship. She moaned softly as the hands moved down over her nightdress to the moist swollen lips of her sex. A finger slipped experimentally inside her and in her dream she opened willingly to Callum's eager touch but was shocked by his brutal probing.

Suddenly she was awake and came face to face with Arnie's dark brooking eyes. She gasped, realising that it was his hand firmly clamped between her thighs.

He smiled lazily. 'Tell me that you don't like the way it feels,' he said huskily.

She tried to push him away, fighting her own body's aching dream memory of Callum as much as Arnie's lust.

His fingers brushed against her clitoris. She tried to wiggle away from him but the pressure was relentless.

'I'm going make you sing, baby,' he whispered and grabbed hold of her arms. 'Come with me.'

'No,' she hissed, 'please, Arnie, don't.'

He laughed without humour and pulled her to her feet, dragging her towards the door of the studio.

The stairwell was bitterly cold; her body stiffened, rapidly losing heat through her thin cotton night-gown. In spite of her protests Arnie pushed her roughly up the stairs in front of him.

Above the apartment the whole roof space was empty.

Dark forbidding shapes, draped in dust sheets, stood under a single sky-light. Dragging her across the room Arnie grabbed both her wrists with one hand, crushing her into a frenzied embrace. She gasped as his lips found hers, startled by the intensity of his passion. His rough hands pawed at her breasts, his lips bruising hers as he pushed her down onto the floor. He knelt astride her, pinning her down, his breath reeking of beer and – more disturbing – the subtle, deep oceanic musk of Edith's body.

'I'll scream if you touch me again,' Rebecca sobbed.

Arnie laughed thickly. 'Go ahead, babe. Edith sleeps like the dead and no-one else is going to take a blind bit of notice. No, sweetheart, it's just you and me. Don't tell me you haven't imagined what it would be like with me, I've seen it in your eyes.' He glanced around the room and snatched up a length of rope from the floor, crushing the breath from her as he looped it round her wrists. Rebecca was so stunned she couldn't move.

Grabbing hold of the rope he pulled her back onto her feet. 'I know I've been thinking about you,' he said darkly. He breath came in laboured excited gasps. 'Every night I think about you lying there in the dark, all on your own. Seems such a waste—'

She stared at him dumbly, caught somewhere between fear and shock.

He looked at her from behind his heavy, hooded lids. 'I want you,' he whispered, pushing her back against the attic wall. The vicious bite of the plaster against her back brought her to her senses.

'Stop it, Arnie,' she said, her voice uneven and emotional.

He grinned. 'I don't think you want me to,' he said in a low hypnotic voice.'

'Please—' she whimpered, as he tightened the rope and slipped her hands over a hook set into a one of the low roof beams. Her feet barely touched the floor. The fear and sense of vulnerability flooded through her, making her struggle, fighting wildly against the fiery bite of the rope. Her frantic struggles made him smile. She watched his face, her heart beating wildly in her chest.

What unnerved her was that at some level, Arnie was right – her body was electrified by his brutality – the knowledge stunned her.

Arnie's breath came in short laboured gasps as he stepped back. 'Now you're all mine, babe,' he purred, as she twisted against the rope. Her arms screamed out in protest as she turned and pulled away from his invasive touch.

He caught hold of her chin. She tried to look away, afraid that her eyes might betray the tiny glint of excitement she felt in her belly. Arnie laughed. 'You want this, don't you? You don't fool me.'

She started to protest but was silenced by his mouth on hers, bruising, crushing the breath out of her, as his hands lifted to the thin cotton of her night-dress and ripped it away. The material bit into her shoulders and she screamed out at the indignity and exposure.

Arnie stepped back from his prize and stooped to light a lamp on the floor. The golden arc threw her naked body into sharp relief, highlighting the soft orbs of her uptilted breasts and the dark points of her puckered nipples. He moved closer and bit softly at one of the sensitive buds. Rebecca cried out at the pain and at the same time gasped as she sensed the jagged flickering excitement building between her legs. He grabbed hold of her hips, pulling closer, his fingers plunging into her, feeling for her pleasure zones, pressing back into her hot moist quim. She let out a little sob; a dark cry of pleasure and shame. He pulled away in amusement, fingers still buried deep inside her.

'You're wet,' he snorted. 'Maybe you're like Edith. Do you crave a little bit of rough?'

At the mention of her friend's name the tears welled up behind Rebecca's eyes, 'Arnie, no,' she stammered, 'Edith—'

But he ignored her, slipping his fingers from her body he undid his flies to reveal a thick, angry-looking cock that jutted towards her like a dark curved snake. He caught hold of her legs and pulled her onto him, impaling her on his thick phallus. He drove his cock home with frightening ferocity. Rebecca screamed out, feeling as if he would split her open in his frantic attempts to press deeper into her.

'Do you want me to stop?' he hissed, between clenched teeth. His fingers bit into her buttocks pulling her onto him while she struggled against the rope, her shoulders screaming out in agony as she bucked against his strong hot body. He grabbed hold of her hair and dragged her face up to meet him. 'Tell me, do you want me to stop?'

She bit her lip as she stared intensely into her eyes. 'No,' she whispered on a thick emotional sob. 'No.'

His expression was triumphant as he kissed her again. She could smell and taste Edith's passion on his lips as he forced his tongue into her mouth.

'Move with me, baby,' he murmured darkly, and to her horror she realised her body was doing just that, matching him stroke for stroke as he pressed home with his great meaty cock.

In her belly she could feel the dark circles of pleasure building, in spite of her shock and repulsion. Arnie's mouth moved down to her breasts, his teeth nipping at her engorged nipples, closing again and again on them, sending her to dark dizzy heights of ecstasy. Just as she thought she was lost Arnie pulled out of her, leaving her body feeling raw and empty.

He reached up and lifted the ropes over the hook. She looked up at him with a sense of relief, but the expression she saw on his dark features convinced her her relief was misplaced. He let go of the ropes suddenly, she stumbled and fell onto her hands and knees on the rough board floor. She looked up again at him in desperation. He smiled, his fingers circling the base of his cock.

'Come here,' he purred.

She started to clamber to her feet.

'No, stay on your hands and knees.'

She crawled towards him, bright tears of humiliation coursing down her face. When she reached his feet she knelt in front of him. Catching hold of her hair, her jerked her head back and pressed his cock between her lips. 'You know what I want,' he hissed.

She gasped as he thrust into her mouth and then began to work on him with her tongue. Instinctively, hands still tied, she lifted her fingers to cradle his heavy distended balls while above she heard him moan with pleasure.

His cock was slick with her own juices and the smell of Edith's body. She closed her eyes, trying to imagine that it was Callum with her, tender, gentle, guiding Callum, who would take her eventually to the heights of ecstasy. Between her legs she could still feel the seeds of the dark submissive passion Arnie had lit in her. Grunting, he locked his hands in her hair and arched his back as she took him deeper into her mouth.

She could feel his excitement building, his breaths coming in wild eager snorts as she brought him closer and closer to the edge. Suddenly, just as she thought he wouldn't be able to hold back he stepped away from her, eyes glistening like jet.

He stared at her, naked, crouched on the floor, and smiled. 'Lay down,' he said. She complied without a word, not daring to look at him. She could feel his eyes moving over her, eyes as invasive as his fingers and cock. He made a sound of satisfaction and pleasure. 'I've been thinking about this since you got here,' he said in a low voice. 'I've been watching you, there are so many things I want you to do—'

She shivered, trying to imagine the fantasies he had woven as she had slept in the room next to him. Kneeling beside her he explored her slim body with his fingers and tongue, making her tremble and writhe under his touch.

'Open your legs,' he whispered as his lips brushed hers. She let her thighs slide open, watching the excitement on his face. 'You're good,' he murmured as he untied her hands, 'real good.' He took one of her hands laid it over her sex, then guided her head into his lap and pressed the broad threatening arc of his cock to her lips.

'I want to watch you touch yourself,' he hissed as she began to suck and stroke along his engorged shaft. 'Touch yourself, show me what you like, baby — ' She pulled her hand away in surprise, but he held her fingers tight, pressing them against the tight button of her clitoris.

'Stroke yourself,' he muttered, 'make it feel real good —'

Rebecca closed her eyes and began to stroke the moist aching peak, moving rhythmically in tight circles until she felt the little bud glow beneath her fingertips. Arnie grunted in satisfaction.

She could feel the growing ripples of excitement building deep in her belly and the raw electric throb of Arnie's desire as he began to move his cock more fiercely between her lips. She tried to conjure Callum's face. The sensations grew stronger, more intense. She began to writhe to be rewarded by Arnie's fingers sliding deep inside her. Instinctively her body tightened around him and he groaned with pleasure. She gasped as the intense waves of her climax crashed over her, tighter, harder. Above her, Arnie snatched his cock from her mouth and spurted great hot waves of semen onto her flushed breasts. For a few seconds the only sound was their wild gasping breaths.

Finally, shuddering, Rebecca pulled herself away from Arnie and sat up.

He looked at her, eyes dark and unnerving. Picking up the remains of her night-dress from the floor, he threw it to her. 'Here, clean yourself up,' he said.

'What are you going to tell Edith?' she whispered.

Arnie ran a finger around the tender aureola of her swollen breasts. 'I was going to tell her how much her old friend likes it a little rough, baby. How do you think she'll take that?

Rebecca gasped. 'You raped me—' but knew, even as she said it, that it was a lie.

Arnie's fingers nipped teasingly at the contracted peaks of her nipples. 'Tell me you didn't like it. Tell me being tied up and screwed didn't turn you on.'

Rebecca grabbed hold of him. 'You bastard . . .'

Arnie leant closer, his lips, wet and slack, pressed against hers and to her horror she responded, letting him slide his tongue between her bruised lips. He pulled away and looked into her eyes. 'You and Edith are both the same.' He eyed her thoughtfully. 'I wonder how she'd take to you joining us for a little three in a bed?'

Rebecca clambered to her feet, dragging her night dress

up around her to cover her nakedness. 'No,' she hissed, 'please, Arnie, don't—'

He smiled and turning away made his way slowly back to the apartment and Edith.

Rebecca sat for a while amongst the ruins of her night-dress on the rough cold floor, dark images of Arnie's passion flooding her mind. In one respect he had been right, despite her fear she had enjoyed his dominant roughness, but she didn't want him to take her again. She valued her friendship with Edith too much to risk losing it for a man like Arnie.

The next morning, Edith had commented on how quiet Rebecca seemed. Rebecca pushed away her breakfast, untouched, and said she hadn't slept well. Behind Edith, leaning against the sink, Arnie smiled archly and sipped his coffee.

Edith glanced at her watch. 'Time we weren't here. Can't have you being late on your first morning.'

Rebecca shivered when Arnie gave Edith a goodbye kiss; all the time his lips and hands worked on Edith his eyes were on Rebecca.

The lingerie department at Berdys store was on the second floor. The sales floor was arranged around a wide U-shaped counter, backed by half a dozen plus changing rooms and small island displays. Rebecca arrived at half-past eight to meet Lily Reubens, the chief saleswoman in charge of lingerie.

Lily smiled and held out a hand of welcome whilst Rebecca tried to overcome her amazement at the wealth of goods for sale. The display cabinets and stands were full of frothy lacy confections of every colour and style. Lily grinned and took her on a guided tour around the sales floor.

Lily spoke with a soft southern drawl that gave her an air of sleepy sexuality. The impression was heightened by her tiny elfin features framed by mass of soft, almost white, blonde curls. 'Don't worry, kid, you'll soon get the hang of it. The punters here fall into two types; men buying frothy nonsense for the women in their lives and the women bringing it back to get something warm and sensible.'

Rebecca laughed.

Lily picked up a tape measure from her desk and hung it around Rebecca's shoulders. 'There you go, sweetheart, your new badge of office. This week you'll be helping me or one of the other girls and then next week, you're out on your own. Competition round here is real fierce, everyone is on commission on top of their basic wage, so it pays to work hard. Only rule is, don't go poaching anyone's regulars. The customers usually ask for an assistant by name, if they do – until you know the ropes – keep your hands off. Okay?'

Rebecca nodded and then set to work with Lily tidying and sorting a new arrival of stock. Other girls, all smartly dressed in Berdys distinctive grey livery appeared, taking up stations behind the various counters and stands. By the time the store opened at nine-thirty Rebecca was relaxed and happy with Lily showing her where things went and how the elegant sensual underwear was to be displayed. Nothing prepared her for the loud bell, rung a few seconds before the store opened. She jumped back from the counter in surprise. Lily grinned and glanced at her watch, then looked round to make sure all her staff were in place before smiling at Rebecca, who was still recovering from the shock of the bell. 'If you think that's bad wait until the customers roll in,' she joked, taking up her position behind the counter.

She was right, Berdys store seemed to have only two states – full or empty. Even though Lily had said that for the first week she was only to assist the other staff, Rebecca found herself serving and more to the point, enjoying herself. Customers expected their purchases to be beautifully wrapped and their orders were whisked away by uniformed pages to appear a few minutes later tucked in elegant gift boxes, tied with extravagant bows.

The luxury and the sheer opulence of Berdys made Rebecca dizzy. Women thought nothing of buying a dozen pairs of stockings at a time, or delicate confections in pure silk that were priced at more than Rebecca expected to earn in a month.

It was just before lunch-time that Lily waved her over. She smiled easily. 'You're doing real well, Miss Hunt, you're a natural.'

Rebecca thanked her graciously, fighting back an unbidden urge to tell Lily just what she had been through during the war; in charge of a group of harassed tired WAAFs on whose accuracy men's lives depended. By contrast, selling lingerie to idle self-indulgent women was like a holiday. Instead she smiled politely and turned back towards the sales floor.

At one of the far island displays, an elderly, distinguished-looking man in an expensive black coat stroked a diaphanous night gown and peignoir. As Rebecca approached he looked up, his face was handsome, with strong chiselled features that belied his age. He smiled; Rebecca shivered under his searching gaze. He was appraising her much in the same way as he was the nightgown.

'Good morning, sir,' she said softly. 'Do you have a regular assistant to help you with your purchases?' Lily

Reuben's parroted little speech rolled off her lips.

The man smiled, soft lines forming around his dark brown eyes. 'I see Lily has been training you. You do it very well—'

Rebecca nodded politely. 'I'm sure she'd be pleased to hear that, sir. Would you like me to get her for you?'

He shook his head, smiling still. 'No, I don't think so. Tell me, does this come in cream?'

Rebecca hesitated and glanced back towards Lily who was now busy with another customer. 'I'm not sure, but if you'll excuse me for a second I'll find out for you.'

The man fingered the thick lace at the hem. 'It's very lovely, don't you think?' he murmured, catching her eye. His deep even voice made her feel uneasy, stirring something inside her. He seemed to sense her discomfort and let his eyes move slowly over her body. 'Do you think it would fit you? I mean, is it your size?'

Rebecca picked up the discreetly hidden label, the price was astounding. 'Actually it's a size too big,' she said briskly, struggling to maintain control of the flutter she felt in her chest. She took a deep breath and turned to face him, squaring her shoulders. 'Is your wife my size?'

The man laughed aloud. 'Oh, I'm not buying it for my wife, my dear. I thought it would suit my mistress better.'

Rebecca flushed crimson. 'I think I'd better fetch the chief sales assistant to help you,' she said quickly.

The man winked. 'Just tell Lily it's Leo de Viton.'

Rebecca practically ran over to where Lily was just handing a small package to one of the page boys as an imperious woman strode off towards the lifts.

Lily looked up. 'Why, honey, you look as if you've seen a ghost. What is it?'

Rebecca looked towards the island stand where Leo de

Viton was still standing, smiling. Lily grinned. 'I see you have met the infamous Le de Viton. What did he do, proposition you?'

Rebecca shook her head, realising her reaction to his comment had been ridiculous and undoubtedly she'd done exactly what he'd expected.

Lily patted her wrist. 'No need to tell me, just humour him. He's got more money than you can shake a stick at and he's got a real thing about shop girls, so you'd better watch your step. Come with me, I'll help you sort him out.' Lily led Rebecca back to Leo de Viton, who at once took Lily's hand and pressed it delicately to his lips. As he did Rebecca felt his eyes on her.

Lily smiled easily. 'Well, how can we help you, Mr de Viton? Are you shopping for your wife or one of your courtesans today?'

Leo lifted his hands in mock surrender. 'You know me too well, my dearest Lily, both actually. I wonder if you have this set in cream.'

Lily glanced at the label and nodded. 'We do and also in dove grey, black and red.' She winked conspiratorially at Rebecca. 'Would you like me to order you one up in every colour?'

Leo grinned. 'Oh, Lily, no, just one in cream in a size smaller than this.' He glanced at Rebecca. 'And be so good as to introduce me to your new assistant.'

Lily turned to Rebecca. 'Mr de Viton, may I introduce Miss Rebecca Hunt, who has recently arrived from England.'

Leo stepped forward. 'Charmed, I'm sure,' he purred and lifted her hand to his lips. Rebecca shivered. At the very last second Leo turned her hand in his and sucked one of her fingers into his mouth. Rebecca, astonished, jerked her hand away.

Lily sighed theatrically and said, 'Actually Miss Hunt has to go for her lunch now, Mr de Viton. Maybe I can help you?'

Leo de Viton pulled his face into an exaggerated little moué of displeasure and then shrugged. 'Oh well, Lily my dear, if you insist.'

Lily nodded. 'Let me go and get some of the new night-gowns we had delivered this morning, they've just arrived. I'm sure there'll be something to your taste—'

As she turned she waved to Rebecca to follow her. 'Go up to the stock-room until it's time for your lunch break, I'd eat off the premises today, if I were you,' she whispered out of the corner of her mouth as they walked towards the lift. 'And don't look back.'

Rebecca nodded dumbly, but her expression held a question.

Lily touched her wrist as the lift doors closed. 'Leo de Viton can be big trouble, honey. Take my advice, stay upstairs until one o'clock and then get your coat and go out for lunch.'

Even wrapped inside her coat Rebecca felt the cold as soon as she stepped out of the warm confines of Berdys. Midday uptown traffic pipped and hooted all around, while above her the huge buildings appeared to touch the sky. Everything seemed bright, alien and desperately noisy. Rebecca suddenly felt completely disorientated and homesick. For the first time in days she thought about England and Oliver. Tears welled up inside her, so raw and painful that they took her breath away. 'Lunch', she murmured firmly under her breath and headed off along the busy sidewalk.

From his chauffeured limousine Leo de Viton watched her

hurrying along the pavement and smiled to himself. Sarah Leinneman had been right; Rebecca Hunt was extremely interesting. He glanced at the elegantly wrapped package at his feet; she would look wonderful in cream silk, he thought.

Chapter 3

Oliver Cresswell, Rebecca's ex-fiancé, drained his glass and glanced around the interior of his godfather's study. The older man looked at him from his armchair. 'Well?'

Oliver grimaced as the spirit hit his empty stomach. 'I think I've made the worst mistake of my life letting Rebecca leave.'

George Winterton snorted. 'Then for godsake, put it right, man. You've got her address in New York, haven't you?'

Oliver nodded. 'Yes. But I'm not sure it's as simple as that,' he sighed. 'I behaved very badly. I'm not sure she will forgive me.'

George laughed. 'You won't ever know unless you ask. Now, are you up for dinner at my club?'

Oliver nodded and then sat down, thinking about Rebecca's slim body, so needy and compliant. As beautiful and desirable as he could ever have possibly dreamt of.

George looked at him. 'Well?'

Oliver poured himself another scotch from the tray beside the chair. 'You're right. Of course you're right. I'll write to her—' He looked at his godfather. George Winterton had guided Oliver through the niceties of choosing good wine, using a shotgun, taking him to his own tailors and, when he had been barely more than a boy, it

57

had been George who had taken Oliver to his first brothel. They had few secrets, for this Oliver was inordinately grateful and why he had come to London to talk to George about Rebecca Hunt.

Oliver couldn't quite come to terms with what Rebecca had made him feel; he had wanted her so much and yet been shocked, almost horrified, when his longing had been reciprocated, when his fantasies had stepped into reality. And he knew that afterwards he had behaved like an insensitive fool. Why couldn't he have seen that she had given herself to him because she was in love, alight for him because she wanted him more than anyone else? He could almost smell her, see her bright flashing eyes as he had eased himself into her tight wet sex. Losing her was like a physical blow. He shivered.

When he glanced up from his thoughts George Winterton was studying him thoughtfully. 'Most men would sell their souls for a woman like Rebecca, Oliver. If you love her you have to find a way to make your peace. I'm sure it's not too late.'

Oliver sighed unhappily. 'I wish I were as certain.'

Late on Saturday afternoon Rebecca walked into the rest room at Berdys, eased off her shoes and winced. Her feet and legs throbbed unbearably, her back and shoulders felt almost as bad. From the corner of her eye she caught a glimpse of Edith Hartman dressing her hair in the mirror above the sinks.

'Edith?'

Her friend turned and smiled. 'So there you are. How does it feel then? First week's always the worst.' She spoke with hair grips in her mouth, tucking stray curls back into place. 'I thought we'd go out tonight and celebrate your first week's wages. There's a great club down on the square. We could go dancing—'

Rebecca groaned theatrically and slipped on her soft sandals. 'I don't think I'll ever be able to walk again, let alone dance.' She paused, choosing her words carefully. 'Now that I've got a job I'll be able to get out of your hair and look for an apartment of my own.'

Edith looked hurt. 'Oh, but Becky, there's really no need. I love having you around. Even Arnie—'

Rebecca barely heard the words as Edith tried to dissuade her; Arnie was the reason she was determined to leave. Rebecca could feel his eyes on her whenever they were all in the apartment. She had been careful never to be there alone with him since the night in the loft. He hadn't touched her again – instead he let his eyes move across her body. They felt almost more invasive than his fingers. She knew it was part of a game he was playing. He was making her wait, teasing her, perhaps even trying to lull her into a false sense of security, but she knew he would be back for more. She could see it in his face. Worse still she knew some part of her longed for his rough arrogant attentions. She shivered. It was time she found a place of her own.

Over her thoughts Edith was still speaking. '—And what's all this about your new gentleman friend, then? The whole of Berdys is buzzing with it.'

Rebecca blushed. 'He's hardly a friend.'

Edith snorted. 'Hot-house flowers, chocolates, perfume? What more does a man need to do for a girl to let her know he's keen?'

Rebecca pulled her coat out of the locker. 'He's just a customer, he's married and, apparently, Mr Leo de Viton is notorious for having a passion for shop girls. My supervisor told me to ignore him, he'll soon get bored.'

Edith grinned and rolled her eyes heavenwards. 'Seems such a shame—'

As she spoke a uniformed girl appeared around the rest-room door, 'Rebecca Hunt?'

Rebecca looked up. 'Yes?'

'Mrs Leinneman would like to see you in her office before you leave.' The girl hesitated before adding. 'As soon as possible. You know what she's like, doesn't do to keep her waiting.'

Beside Rebecca, Edith pulled a face. 'Oh God. Now what have you been up to?'

Rebecca buttoned up her coat. 'Nothing as far as I know, but we'll soon find out.'

Edith glanced at her watch. 'Would you like me to wait for you?'

Rebecca shook her head. 'No, it's all right. I don't know how long I'll be. Besides I thought I might ring Callum and see if he's free tonight.' She smiled. 'Go on, I'll be all right.'

The department store was all but deserted. On the ground floor cleaners were beginning to arrive as Rebecca made her way up from the basement rest-room to the third floor offices of the personnel officer. She wondered what Mrs Leinneman could want; she'd worked hard. Her supervisor, Lily Reubens had said she had done really well for her first week. Outside the office door Rebecca glanced in the glass panel to make sure she looked neat and tidy before knocking.

Sarah Leinneman's distinctive voice called her in. The older woman was seated behind her desk as Rebecca stepped into the office. 'Thank you for coming up, Miss Hunt,' she said stiffly. 'If you'd like to take a seat.'

Rebecca pulled out a chair. 'You asked to see me?'

Mrs Leinneman nodded, her expression made Rebecca apprehensive. 'Is there a problem?'

Sarah Leinneman peered over her glasses. 'Not with your work generally, you seem to have made a very good start, Miss Hunt. You're the sort of girl Berdys is looking for. Lily Reubens has already been up to see me, singing your praises—'

Rebecca nodded but knew there was more; this wasn't a pat on the back. Mrs Leinneman leant forward. 'But we have had a complaint.'

Rebecca felt her colour drain. 'A complaint? Who from?'

Sarah Leinneman picked up a folded sheet of paper. 'One of our most influential and valued customers, Mr Leo de Viton.'

Rebecca looked up in astonishment. 'Mr de Viton? I don't understand. I've been extremely courteous to him, I—'

The older woman held up her hand to silence the girl. 'I don't doubt you have but I believe you've returned various gifts that Mr de Viton sent you here at the store.'

Rebecca nodded, feeling uncomfortable. 'Yes. I didn't want to encourage him, Mrs Leinneman. You said yourself the store has a very strict moral code amongst its staff.'

The older woman sighed. 'Yes, yes I did, didn't I? But we're prepared to make allowances when someone of Mr de Viton's stature expresses—' she paused as if searching for the right words, '—an interest in one of young ladies. Mr de Viton has asked me if you would consider joining him for dinner tonight.'

Rebecca was so stunned she stood up. 'He asked *you* to ask me?'

Sarah Leinneman nodded. 'Yes and I've told him you will be delighted to accept.' Rebecca flushed scarlet with a mixture of fury and disbelief, but before she could speak Sarah Leinneman continued. 'We have an obligation to humour our most valued clients. It's just a dinner invitation, Rebecca, nothing more. Mr de Viton had told me to tell you that you may choose any evening dress from the store, matching shoes – a complete outfit.' She paused. 'And a car will collect you from here at eight.'

Rebecca was speechless. Sarah Leinneman got up. 'I'll help you choose something suitable. You can use the bathroom in the executives suite to get ready.

'And what if I say no?' Rebecca said in an unsteady voice.

Sarah Leinneman sighed. 'Of course you can say no if you want to, but take my advice, accept. The longer you refuse him the more obsessive he'll become. He'll find your home address, bombard you with flowers, invitations – He's not a man to be put off easily.'

Rebecca looked steadily at Sarah Leinneman, seeing the woman's attractive face beneath the lines of passing years. 'Did he do that to you, too?' she said softly.

Sarah Leinneman laughed at Rebecca's perception. 'It seems a very long time ago now.' She looked steadily at Rebecca, woman to woman, the veneer of boss and shop girl gone. 'Leo de Viton is very influential, very promiscuous and a very generous man. He is obsessed with his own power – you're his perfect prey; a beautiful, newly-arrived emigre. He'll wine you and dine you and attempt to seduce you. Whether or not he does is entirely your affair. He tires of his conquests quickly, but while you are with him you will have only the best.' She indicated the door of her office. 'Now, are you going to choose an evening dress or do you want me to ring him and say you've said no?'

Rebecca stepped towards the door. 'Am I supposed to be flattered by all this?'

Sarah Leinneman shrugged. 'That's entirely up to you, a lot of girls in your position would fall over themselves to be Leo de Viton's latest object of desire.' She smiled. 'Why don't you just enjoy the dinner, drink his wine. Let him flatter you a little. He's great company—'

Rebecca nodded, thinking about the way Leo de Viton had looked at her in the lingerie department. He had consumed her body with his eyes.

On the top floor, under the subdued lighting of the empty store, Sarah Leinneman made her way between the displays, letting her professional eyes move back and forth between the sumptuous dresses and Rebecca Hunt. The English girl stood nervously by the lift doors. Sarah selected half a dozen gowns that she was certain would flatter the girl's slim frame and at same time delight Leo de Viton.

Twenty years before someone had done the same favour for her – and her life had changed for ever because of it. Rebecca Hunt didn't know how lucky she was to be chosen by Leo. Sarah Leinneman appraised the girl's ripe but slim figure appreciatively. As she folded the gowns over her arm she imagined Leo eagerly undressing the girl, his knowing hands caressing her pert, upturned breasts, his fingers seeking out the slick depths of her quim. Sarah shuddered with a mixture of pleasure and envy. She guided Rebecca to sit on the sofa reserved for the most favoured customers and held out the first dress, a bias-cut tissue confection of rich blue silk with a thread of silver in the weave. Rebecca Hunt looked astonished and murmured, 'It's so beautiful.'

Sarah Leinneman nodded. 'It'll suit you perfectly. Why don't you try it on?'

She waited outside the dressing room listening to Rebecca getting changed, resisting the temptation to step inside and help. Leo de Viton had lit a symphony of desires in Sarah Leinneman that she now had few opportunities to indulge. She imagined stepping inside and finding the English girl naked. She could imagine the soft swell of her hips, the delicate rise of her pale breasts. Just as Mrs Leinneman stepped forward to open the heavy drapes that fronted the dressing room Rebecca stepped back into the light. The evening dress fitted her like a second skin, cut off the shoulder, with a wisp of sheer silk around the bodice to soften the plunging neckline.

Sarah Leinneman swallowed hard; Rebecca Hunt looked like an angel. 'It's perfect,' she said thickly. 'We'll find you some lingerie and shoes to wear and I'll help you to dress your hair when you've had a bath.'

Rebecca nodded dumbly as Sarah Leinneman discarded the rest of the dresses on the sofa and hurried back towards the lift.

It was a few minutes to eight when a black limousine drew up outside the rear entrance of Berdys store. Rebecca looked nervously at Mrs Leinneman who kept to the shadows of the foyer. Rebecca bit her lip and then turned to check her reflection in the plate glass door. The dress accentuated her narrow waist and rounded hips, before swooping up in a sensual curve to the swell of her breasts. Mrs Leinneman had found her a short fur cape and high-heeled sandals. In the gentle lighting faux-pearl earrings glinted against her dark hair, which was softly folded into a sleek chignon. Rebecca smiled at her reflection – barely recognising herself. Mrs Leinneman waved her towards the door. 'Don't keep him waiting.'

Rebecca felt a little flurry of nervousness in her stomach. She stepped out towards the car with a confidence she didn't feel and allowed the chauffeur to guide her into the back seat. To her surprise the back of the car was empty. The chauffeur regarded her with cool disinterest. 'Mr de Viton is expecting you to join him at his apartment for dinner, Miss.'

'I thought . . .' she began, glancing at the empty seats, but her words were lost as he closed the back door with a quiet click. From behind the tinted windows she saw Sarah Leinneman turn and walk back slowly into the shadows of the store. Suddenly she felt afraid and desperately alone. What had she agreed to?

The limousine purred noiselessly through Manhattan out through the elegant streets and avenues of the Upper East side. With every passing block Rebecca felt more and more apprehensive and almost cried out when the car pulled up outside an elegant town house. The chauffeur accompanied her to the door where a uniformed footman waited to take her cape. 'Mr de Viton is expecting you, Miss,' he said in an obsequious voice as he guided her into the elevator. She felt a growing sense of unreality as the ornate doors slid closed on silent runners.

At the top, when the doors opened again, Rebecca found herself in a luxurious hallway that wouldn't have looked out of place in a French Chateau. A chandelier hung from the tall ceiling, the walls were panelled in deep polished wood, and in the open double doorway to the room beyond, Leo de Viton stood watching her with undisguised pleasure. She shivered as he stepped towards her.

'Good evening, Miss Hunt,' he said softly. 'How very nice of you to join me. May I say you look stunning.'

As she murmured her thanks he stepped closer and took her hand in his. This time there was no disguising the desire in either his tone or his expression. 'I'm so glad you decided to accept my invitation.' He pressed her hand to his lips, running his tongue slowly along each finger. The intimacy of his caress made Rebecca gasp.

She looked at him dumbly unable to trust herself to speak. She swallowed hard, struggling to find her voice. Finally she said, 'I had a choice?'

Leo de Viton allowed himself a narrow smile. 'Why of course, my dear. You always have a choice when you are with me.' He paused, his eyes alight. 'I expect nothing from you that you wouldn't give me willingly. Why don't you let me guide you? Let me show you what it is you have to give. Let me teach you how to play my game—'

He stepped closer still. His handsome features couldn't quite disguise the hint of menace in his eyes. Rebecca felt like a mouse caught in the hypnotic gaze of a snake. Leo de Viton ran a finger lightly across her lips and then down over her throat. His lips followed an instant later. It seemed as if he was tasting her flesh like some exotic dish. His kisses lit dark plumes of desire inside her.

She shivered as his fingertips strayed down over the tissue-thin material that covered her breasts. She felt her nipples harden under his attentions and blushed furiously. Leo laughed with delight. 'Oh, this will be such a pleasure for us both, Miss Hunt.' He stepped back, letting his hands linger over the outline of her tight nipples, as if to admire her before saying very quietly, 'Lift up your skirt.'

She was about to protest until she saw the look of animal hunger in his eyes. She could feel the throb of excitement low inside and knew she wanted to play the dark intriguing game that Leo de Viton was inviting her to join. She slid the silky sheath up to her knees. He raised an eyebrow. 'Oh, a little higher, I think, Miss Hunt. I want to see what else I've bought from Berdys.'

She slid the fabric up to her hips revealing the soft white

underwear Sarah Leinneman had chosen for her. He nodded. 'Very pretty,' then glanced over his shoulder into the shadows of the opulent hallway. Rebecca flushed scarlet as she realised that hidden in the velvety darkness stood the uniformed bulk of Leo de Viton's chauffeur. She let out a little sob of horror and went to step backwards; a glance from Leo de Viton stopped her in her tracks.

'Stay where you are, Miss Hunt,' he purred. He beckoned the chauffeur closer. The uniformed man was large and imposing with a wide Slavonic face. He still wore the cool impassive expression that Rebecca had seen when he had collected her from Berdys. He glanced at his employer before kneeling down slowly in front of Rebecca. She shivered, her fingers closing tight around the silky fabric of her dress as the man's hands lifted to the waistband of her knickers. Leo de Viton looked at her, his expression offering her an escape. Instead she bit her lips and moaned softly as the chauffeur's fingers slid inside the lacy fabric. Gently he slid her panties down, she didn't resist as his cool fingers lifted her feet, guiding them over her sandals and dropped them on the floor beside her.

Exposed in front of the two men her mind raced, part of her was afraid and shocked. The other half, a dark animal that roared in her belly, relished the sensation of exposure and desire she felt, a little plume of anticipation flickering through her.

Before she had time to resolve the paradox Leo de Viton stepped behind her. His arms slid around her waist and caught hold of the hem of her dress. She could feel his hot breath on her shoulders while, below, the uniformed lackey leant forward and eased his long tongue between the lips of her sex. She gasped as he found her clitoris and in spite of herself leant back against Leo de Viton's strong body.

The chauffeur nuzzled at her like a hungry dog, nibbling and lapping with desperate passion. She opened her legs to him, relinquishing all control, shuddering as she felt Leo's fingers slipping down over her cool belly to hold her sex open for the man's eager tongue.

'Open yourself, give yourself to him,' Leo said softly in her ear.

Rebecca moaned and whimpered as she felt the chauffeur's strong probing fingers seeking out the sensitive contours of her inner lips, seeking entry, plunging deep inside her when he found the wet tight opening. Behind her she could feel Leo de Viton's growing excitement. She closed her eyes and let the pleasure take her, each invasive caress of the man's lips brought her closer and closer to the edge. Her apprehension and sense of vulnerability added to the growing spiral of sensation.

She let out a long soft moan as the chauffeur smeared her juices down onto her thighs, whilst Leo slid one hand up over her ribs. His fingers circled and nipped at the engorged excited buds of her nipples and she found herself straining back against him, drinking in the delicious attentions of them both. Just as she felt the swell of her orgasm rolling up from deep inside, the chauffeur pulled away. Rebecca gasped, her eyes snapped open. 'Oh no, please,' she whispered huskily. 'Please, don't stop.'

Behind her she heard Leo de Viton laugh, 'This is just the hors d'oeuvres, Miss Hunt.' As he spoke he snapped his fingers and the chauffeur rose to his feet. Rebecca could see the slick silvery traces of her excitement on his lips. The man's face was still expressionless. In his first he had a knot of white fabric, it took a few seconds for Rebecca to realise it was her panties. Before he turned and vanished into the shadows of the hallway he pressed the thin silk to his nose, drinking in her scent, his eyes not leaving hers. She found it hard to suppress a shiver.

Leo de Viton let the silky fabric of her evening dress fall to the floor. 'Come with me,' he invited, slipping his arm through hers. 'Let's eat. My wife, Isabella, will be joining us for dinner.'

Rebecca flushed crimson. 'Your wife?' she stammered uncomfortably. Between her legs she could still feel an unfulfilled ache glowing like a raw wound.

'You haven't met her, have you?' he said conversationally, as if they were meeting at a cocktail party. 'She is a most charming woman, I'm sure you will get along wonderfully well.' As he spoke he guided her through the double doors into an elegant dining room. The room was dominated by a long walnut table. In the centre stood a huge ornate candelabra, its candles making the linen and crystal on the table glitter richly in the flickering light.

As Rebecca walked across the room she was aware of the soft moist sensations of excitement between her legs and shivered. A uniformed servant appeared with a tray of champagne cocktails. Rebecca took a glass gratefully, though she couldn't help noticing the slight tremor in her fingers as they closed around the crystal. For a few seconds there was silence. Rebecca wondered what she could possibly say to Leo de Viton when another door opened in the far wall.

Isabella de Viton stepped into the dining room and smiled warmly at Leo and Rebecca. She was several years younger than her husband; small, barely reaching Rebecca's shoulder, with Italian colouring and classic features. Her sleek coal-black hair was cut into a short bob, diamond drop earrings accentuating her long neck. Rebecca took a deep breath to steady herself and smiled nervously as Isabella de Viton crossed the room with her hand extended. The smile on the other woman's face did not falter for an instant as she folded Rebecca's hand into her own. 'Good evening, Rebecca, my husband tells me you have recently arrived from England.' Her voice was low and musical with the slightest trace of a foreign accent. Rebecca couldn't help wondering why Leo de Viton found it necessary to entertain other women when his own wife was so stunning.

Isabella directed Rebecca to the table. 'I thought we would all sit together at this end,' Isabella said lightly. 'I hate it when I have to shout along the table to join in a conversation.' She laughed at her own joke. Her accent was clipped and she dropped consonants from the words at random as the footman helped them to their seats.

Leo sat at the head of the table with the women on either side of him. Rebecca watched his face as he unfolded a linen napkin. He looked like a distinguished business man, grey highlights accentuating his dark, almost black hair. In his youth he must have been stunning, now well into middle-age good living had softened the chiselled line of his jaw but it didn't detract from his aura of authority. He looked up at her and smiled. She doubted that the look in his eyes had changed; in the candlelight she could detect feral sensuality and dangerous tempting strength. He was a predator—

While the first course was being served Isabella kept up a light flowing conversation about her own visit to England, which Rebecca suspected was to put her at ease. Whatever she had expected Leo de Viton's wife to be like, Isabella certainly wasn't it. The tiny, dark-haired woman laughed easily, helping herself to wine, teasing Leo, plucking grapes from an arrangement of fruit at the table centre. Although she was elegantly dressed in an exquisite black evening dress, perfectly made up and coiffured there was a strange underlying coarseness about her, a rough edge at odds with the overall image. Leo smiled at her indulgently and then back at Rebecca. As he did Rebecca felt his hand snake across her thighs. She gasped, feeling her colour rising, while across the table Isabella poured herself another glass of wine. 'I am hoping now the war is over I can persuade Leo to take me to Paris. Have you ever been, Rebecca?'

Rebecca shook her head, as Leo's skilful fingers began to gather up the silky material of her evening dress. 'No,' she said unsteadily, 'No, I haven't.'

Leo moved his hand higher, seeking out the contours of her quim, parting her thighs, sliding down into the silky wetness — she shuddered, while across the table Isabella began to describe a trip she had taken to Paris before the war. She talked with her hands, making expansive gestures of delight while beneath the table Leo's fingers caressed Rebecca, seeking out the throbbing bud of her clitoris. She looked across at him in horror, her eyes pleading for him to stop. Her excitement hovered beneath his fingertips, still glowing from the attentions of the chauffeur. Leo appeared to be entranced in his wife's recollections, all his concentration apparently on her words. Rebecca wanted to scream, feeling the waves of pleasure bubbling up through her, spiralling out from deep inside her belly. Just as she thought she couldn't take any more Leo slipped his fingers away. She sighed, blowing out a soft stream of air as she struggled to regain her composure.

Across the table Isabella's story was coming to an end and the servants came in to serve the next course. Rebecca watched with a horrid fascination as Leo slipped his fingers between his thin lips and licked them.

During the rest of the meal Rebecca found it impossible to concentrate, expecting at any second to feel the soft brush of Leo's touch against her thigh. When finally coffee was served Isabella was the first to leave the table, inviting Rebecca to join her by the fire whilst Leo poured them liqueurs.

'Were you born in America, Mrs de Viton?' Rebecca asked conversationally as she sat in the armchair Isabella indicated.

The older woman smiled. 'Please, you must call me Isabella. I was born in Naples but my parents came over here when I was no more than a little girl.' She paused, sipping her coffee.

'So you grew up in New York?'

Isabella de Viton's face hardened slightly and she fixed Rebecca with her dark eyes. 'Yes, but that is a long time ago now.'

For the first time since meeting her, Rebecca sensed Isabella de Viton's discomfort. Where she had come from and what she had done before marrying Leo was obviously not a subject Isabella was comfortable with. Rebecca glanced across at Leo who was standing by the side board, opening bottles. He turned and came across to them with a tray of glasses, smiling warmly. 'Why don't you tell Rebecca about our beach house, Isabella?' he said pleasantly. 'Perhaps we can persuade her to spend some time with us there while she's in New York.'

Isabella de Viton immediately launched into a full blown description of the house she and Leo had found out on the coast, a fading mansion, that they had resurrected from certain decay. Rebecca listened with interest to the woman's enthusiastic descriptions. When the liqueurs were finished Isabella suddenly stopped, almost mid-sentence and glanced up at Leo who was standing by the hearth. 'I hope you won't think me rude, Rebecca, but would you please excuse me?'

Rebecca looked puzzled. 'Of course.' She hesitated. 'Are you all right?'

Isabella nodded. 'Of course, how sweet of you to ask. Yes, I'm just feeling a little tired.'

Rebecca began to get to her feet, wondering if this was an indication that she should leave too. 'Perhaps I ought to be going—'

Leo de Viton stepped forward. 'Not at all, Rebecca. My wife is not a night owl. I'd be very pleased if you would stay a little longer and keep me company.'

As if it had been pre-arranged, Isabella got to her feet and said brief pleasant goodbyes to Rebecca before disappearing back through the door from which she had appeared. As soon as she had gone Rebecca felt uncomfortable. Leo went to the sideboard and poured them both another drink. 'I told you my wife was charming, didn't I?'

Rebecca nodded. 'Yes and she is very beautiful. Are you sure you wouldn't prefer it if I left as well?'

Leo de Viton laughed dryly as he handed her her glass. 'I would be devastated, besides I've got so much more I want to show you.'

Rebecca took a long pull on her glass, wondering what else he had in mind for her. He stepped closer and looped his fingers through the thin fabric around the top of her evening dress. 'I'd like you to take this off for me,' he purred.

She gasped, looking towards the doors at the far end of the dining room. 'But your wife?'

De Viton smiled. 'Has gone to bed, she won't be back.

Now will you take this off or would you like me to rip if off you?' As he spoke his fingers tightened around the delicate fabric. Shivering Rebecca lifted her fingers to the zip and pulled the catch open. The dress slid down over her body like a breath of silken wind, dropping in liquid folds around her ankles. Leo extended a hand and she stepped out of it.

In the subdued candlelight her breasts were touched with gold. All that she had left on were her sandals, stockings and silky suspender belt that hugged her lips, framing her sex and lower belly like an invitation. Leo looked at her appreciatively and she felt her pulse quicken. 'You are very beautiful,' he murmured on an outward breath. He stepped nearer to the fireplace and tugged at the bell pull.

Rebecca's first instincts were to run. She crossed her hands defensively across her breasts, eyes bright with alarm and stopped to pick up the discarded dress.

Leo's eyes flashed with amusement. 'Oh please, don't worry, Miss Hunt, I have nothing in mind but our mutual pleasure. Don't tell me you're not excited, remember I have touched you—' as he spoke he licked his fingers provocatively. 'You taste divine.'

Across the room the doors into the hallway opened and the chauffeur reappeared and beside him a uniformed man carrying a covered tray. Neither seemed in the least bit non-plussed by Rebecca's nakedness. The chauffeur stepped close, in his hands he held a long silken cloth which he tied around tightly around Rebecca's eyes. Plunged into darkness she let out a tiny squeal of panic as she felt his hands tracing across her body. His cool touch lit a bright fire inside her. The subtle mixture of fear and desire was a heady cocktail. She whimpered as she felt him stroke a finger from the pit of her throat down to the rising of her sex. 'Please,' she murmured huskily, really not knowing whether she was begging him to stop or continue.

Leo de Viton watched with delight as his chauffeur gently guided the delicate English girl back towards the dining table. He could sense her fear and the bright enticing scent of her curiosity. She moved hesitantly, as if she were trying to guess what lay ahead. He hadn't dreamed that she would be so compliant, so eager to submit to him. Sarah Leinneman had recognised Rebecca's potential – he should trust her judgement more. He poured himself another drink and watched the tableau unfold. The girl was spread-eagled over the end of the table now. The edge of the cool wood tilted her hips, making her mount of Venus lift provocatively. His chauffeur was exploring her, kissing her, allowing his lips and hands to seek out the rise of her breasts, the moist open folds of her quim. She moaned deliciously, writhing under his man's touch. As she moved under him he firmly but gently pressed her hands back above her head. She made only a token resistance. The uniformed servant took each of her wrists in turn and tied them with silken scarves to the little rings Leo had had concealed beneath the table top. The uniformed lackey worked without expression, tying knots. He knew his employer's tastes only too well. He moved silently around the table taking hold of the girl's ankles and tying them to the table legs. Although she did not resist, Leo could detect the little flutter of fear in her throat. Leo de Viton smiled. Rebecca Hunt was theirs now. Above the dining room, secreted in her bedroom his wife would be watching with interest through the spy hole he had installed. The knowledge that Isabella was observing them added to his pleasure.

When Rebecca Hunt was tied securely he stepped

closer, watching his man's tongue flick across her dark erect nipples. The girl bit her lip, lifting herself enticingly, whimpering softly with delight. His chauffeur's kisses worked lower now, pressing into the basin of her belly, the scintillating mound of her quim. She strained against her silken restraints, lifting towards him, seeking fulfilment. Beads of sweat began to rise in the delicate valley between her breasts as the chauffeur's clever lips took her to the edge of ecstasy and then cruelly moved away, bringing her pleasure so tantalisingly close that Leo could almost see it forming in crystal waves, the tide ebbing and flowing in time with his chauffeur's caresses. Her body arched, pleading for release. She mewled and groaned like a little wild cat. As she strained higher, lifting her hips up off the cold table, Leo touched his chauffeur on the shoulder and the man stepped aside without a word.

Leo de Viton stepped between Rebecca Hunt's legs and slid his aching cock from the fine material of his evening trousers. Without a second's hesitation he plunged into the open gaping depths of Rebecca's body. The girl beneath him screamed out in pleasure and surprise and at once he felt her orgasm closing around him, driving away his control. He pressed himself home, letting her suck him dry. Gasping she thrust herself up again and again until he thought she would suck the very life from him. Finally, sated, she collapsed down onto the table, sobbing with exhaustion and delight.

Leo de Viton looked up into the steely blue eyes of his chauffeur and smiled. 'She's yours now, I must go upstairs and see Isabella,' he whispered thickly, sliding his exhausted member from inside Rebecca's pulsating quim.

The tall man smiled narrowly and unbuttoned his uniform trousers. His thick engorged cock sprung forward in an aggressive salute to the girl's excitement. He leant forward and sniffed at Rebecca's moist sex. A thin animal whine trickled from between the prone girl's lips as the uniformed man stepped up to take his employer's place, his fingers already working into her tight throbbing opening. Rebecca snorted and then lifted herself again. Leo de Viton turned away. Rebecca Hunt was a magical find and one that he would have no hesitation in savouring.

When Rebecca woke she was in a bed, in the dark and alone. For an instant she was afraid, wondering where on earth she was. Recollection came on the heels of the fear; she was somewhere in Leo de Viton's luxurious apartment. She sat up, thinking about the events of the evening. The compelling sensual freedom she had felt when tied astounded her. Rendered anonymous by the blindfold, her lovers had taken her again and again, bringing her to the pinnacle of pleasure, using her, caressing her, rough and tender by turns until she had felt she would go mad.

She stretched, ignoring the complaint of her muscles, relishing instead the wanton enjoyment her submission had given her. She had no idea whether it had been Leo alone, his chauffeur, the uniformed lackey or all of them who had taken her. Her body ached triumphantly. Finally when she had thought she would collapse from the heady cocktail of pleasure and exhaustion someone had untied her and with strong arms guided her, still blindfolded away from the table.

She touched the back of her head, realising that she was still wearing the silken cloth. Slipping the thick fabric down over her eyes she discovered she was in a large bedroom, beautifully furnished with antiques. Beside the bed a small lamp glowed softly, bathing everything in a golden glow.

Across a key backed chair her clothes had been carefully arranged, with her sandals beside it. Closing her eyes she let sleep claim her again, her dreams full of the wild excited anonymous caresses that had set her body aflame.

Later she was woken again by a soft tapping somewhere close by. This time when she opened her eyes she knew exactly where she was. A maid peered around the door. 'Miss Hunt?'

Gathering the linen sheets up around her shoulders Rebecca sat up. 'Yes?'

The girl came in carrying a cream silk peignoir and matching night-gown, which she lay across the end of the bed. Rebecca recognised it instantly as the gown de Viton had asked her about in Berdys. 'Mrs de Viton would be most grateful if you would join her for breakfast.'

Rebecca blushed, 'Mrs de Viton?'

The girl nodded. 'I'll wait outside for you and show you to the breakfast room, Miss.' She turned and left Rebecca alone.

It was with considerable apprehension that a few minutes later, Rebecca, dressed in the thin robe followed the maid through the huge apartment. The breakfast room was an enormous glass veranda that gave a stunning view out over Central Park. The room was full of palms and rich green vines making it seem as if the park extended right into the house. As she walked into the room Rebecca didn't notice Isabella de Viton sitting amongst a profusion of ferns and fragrant climbers. Instead her eyes were drawn towards the dramatic skyline of early morning New York.

'Good morning.' Isabella's distinctive accented voice made Rebecca swing round. She began to apologise for not seeing her. Isabella smiled. 'Think nothing of it, the view from this room enchants everyone. Will you join me?' She indicated the chair beside her at the cast iron table.

Rebecca nodded, her sense of discomfort growing. Isabella looked at her appraisingly as she poured coffee. 'Did you sleep well? I hope you were comfortable.'

Rebecca nodded. 'Yes, thank you,' retreating behind good manners to hide her embarrassment.

Isabella smiled, her fingers caressing the cup. 'I do know all my husband's secrets,' she said, so quietly that Rebecca could barely catch the words. The girl felt her colour rising but Isabella continued, 'And he knows all mine. So there is nothing that need be hidden between us.'

Rebecca bit her lip, wanting to ask why Isabella tolerated her husband's vices but was afraid to voice the words. Isabella de Viton's eyes moved slowly across Rebecca's body. 'I can understand why he likes you,' she said softly. As she spoke she reached out and idly drew a finger across Rebecca's breasts. Rebecca was so astonished that she nearly dropped her cup. The woman's touch was unemotional and matter of fact. 'He told me to tell you that he would pick you up from your apartment tonight at eight.' Rebecca began to protest but Isabella's expression stopped her. 'He doesn't like to be refused. I have arranged for Sarah Leinneman to send you something suitable to wear.'

'Mrs Leinneman?'

Isabella nodded, her eyes narrowing. 'Surely you must have guessed that it was Sarah Leinneman who let Leo know you were working at Berdys? She has an eye for girls who will excite him.' Isabella paused, expression hardening. 'He will tire of you, of course. He always does.'

'Aren't you afraid that he might tire of you?' Rebecca said softly, without threat. 'If my husband . . .' she stopped, unable to find the words to convey what she meant without sounding hurtful.

Isabella de Viton smiled lazily. 'He doesn't tire of me because I take pains to fascinate him.' She paused. 'I still intrigue him and I indulge all his little fantasies. You are just the latest of many. In return for my indulgence I have everything I could possibly want and more.' Her fingers once again stroked idly across Rebecca's body. The woman's touch disturbed her and Rebecca quivered as she felt the sensitive peaks of her breasts harden beneath the older woman's finger tips. Isabella de Viton smiled and dipped her head, closing her red painted lips around Rebecca's nipple through the thin silk fabric.

Rebecca gasped, feeling the woman drawing the peak in between her lips. 'No, Isabella,' she stammered in protest, feeling a strange plume of excitement lift inside her belly.

Isabella de Viton pulled away, her face still betraying the hint of a kittenish smile. 'Oh, come now, don't be coy,' she said, her eyes flickering with cool amusement. 'Leo and I share everything. Don't ever forget that. Our chauffeur will take you home after breakfast. Don't forget to be ready by eight.'

'My God, where have you been? You look amazing.' Edith Hartman stood in the kitchen of her apartment, still wrapped in her dressing-gown, as Rebecca opened the front door. She had travelled home in the beautiful evening dress and looked wildly out of place amongst Edith's shabby furniture and peeling paint work of the flat.

Rebecca smiled, trying to look relaxed, and did a little twirl to show off her elegant outfit. 'A dinner date. How about you?'

Edith snorted. 'We didn't go anywhere. Arnie was in a foul mood when I got home from work yesterday. He's gone down to his uncle's warehouse this morning.' She paused. 'He was really worried about you, Becky.'

Rebecca turned away, thinking about Arnie; no doubt he had had other plans for the way they should be spending their Saturday evening. 'I'm just going to get changed,' she said evenly.

Edith nodded. 'I'm making a pot of tea, Oh, by the way a courier brought over a box for you.' She stepped across the galley kitchen and took a large cardboard box in Berdys distinctive livery from the kitchen table. She grinned. 'Callum chasing you with expensive presents too now, is he? Some girls have all the luck.'

'Callum?' Rebecca began as she took the box.

Edith nodded. 'You were going to give him a ring last night, I thought . . .' She stopped, realisation dawning. 'Oh my God. It's that other chap, isn't it?' she giggled. 'The one who sent you flowers at work? Rebecca you're a real dark horse. I want you to tell me all about it. Did you go somewhere special, I thought you said he was married—'

Rebecca felt her colour rising as Edith snatched the box back out of her hands and pulled it undone. Inside, wrapped in palest pink tissue was a silver cocktail dress and elegant silver mules. Edith gasped. 'Oh God, this is so beautiful.' She lifted it out and held it up against herself. 'Your friend's got very expensive tastes. What's he like?'

Rebecca gently took the dress away from her and let it fold down in amongst the tissue, 'I think he's probably dangerous,' she said softly, thinking about Leo de Viton's dark hypnotic eyes and his aura of power.

Edith laughed. 'And rich.'

Rebecca nodded, 'Yes and rich. Now are you going to make the tea?'

Edith snorted. 'Of course, but only if you tell me everything about your mystery admirer.'

Rebecca smiled; she would tell Edith about the dinner party, the beautiful food and the wine – but she wouldn't mention Leo de Viton's dominant sensuality, nor anything about his chauffeur's electric caresses, or Isabella. She turned away, tucking the silver dress back into its box and closed the lid. 'Let me just get changed first.'

When Arnie came back in the middle afternoon he was sullen and uncommunicative. There was an air of silent accusation as he made himself something to eat. He barely said a word to either of the two women. Edith tried to talk to him but was met with a stony silence. He refused to meet Rebecca's eyes and after a few minutes vanished upstairs into his studio much to her relief.

Edith slumped down in the armchair by the window. 'I do love Arnie,' she said softly. 'He's just going through a difficult patch.'

Rebecca nodded. 'It would be easier for you both if I weren't here. You'd have your privacy back—'

Edith sighed. 'I enjoy having you here,' she said softly, but there was no real protest in her voice.

Rebecca smiled and nodded. 'I know, but we both know it was only temporary, besides,' she grinned, 'I'm expecting you to help me find a new place. Why don't we go for a walk, I'll treat you to a coffee?'

Edith nodded, 'All right, if you insist. There's a great place down on Bleeker Street. Arnie used to take me there . . .'

Arnie hadn't re-appeared by the time they got back. When Edith took him a meal up in the late evening Rebecca began to get ready for her meeting with Leo de Viton. Sarah Leinneman's taste was immaculate. The silver sheath dress fitted her as if it were made for her. Edith, watching Rebecca put on her make-up and rolling her hair into a soft pleat, let out a low whistle. 'You look like a film star.' She paused thoughtfully. 'Don't forget you've got work tomorrow.'

Rebecca frowned. 'Sorry?'

'I just thought I'd remind you in case you'd planned to stay out all night again.'

Rebecca clipped on a pair of earrings. She had a feeling that whenever she decided to come home, it wouldn't affect her job. A sharp clear picture of Sarah Leinneman's distinctive face filled her mind. Rebecca was certain that whatever happened Sarah Leinneman would see to it that her position at Berdys was safe.

She went down to the hallway at five to eight, her new dress covered by a coat. Outside the back door of the apartment block the sleek lines of Leo de Viton's limousine looked incongruous and out of place in the narrow side street. Behind the wheel she could see the handsome intimidating features of Leo's chauffeur. She shivered and stepped out into the cool night air.

Chapter 4

'Where are we?' Rebecca leant forward and slid aside the glass panel that divided the rear passenger compartment from the chauffeur.

The man glanced up into the rear view mirror, catching her anxious expression. 'Mr de Viton told me to bring you here.'

Rebecca peered out of the tinted windows and shuddered. The apartment houses were packed tight, row after row of tenements and shabby, rubbish-strewn streets rolled slowly past the car. Steam rose from the gratings, street lights painted pools of jaundiced yellow light that didn't cut into the shadows beyond. Rebecca pressed her face closer to the panel. 'Please will you take me home?' she whispered.

Behind the wheel the chauffeur laughed dryly. 'I don't think so, lady. Mr de Viton is expecting you.'

Rebecca glanced down at the door handle. The car was moving slowly, but even if she did get out where would she go? Finally the limousine turned into a narrow alley, pulling up close to a door. 'Anyway, you're here now,' said the driver.

Rebecca bit her lip. 'Are you going to take me to Mr de Viton?'

From behind she saw the driver's shoulders shrug.

Outside a shadowy group of figures moved past the car towards the door. A hatchway opened briefly before the door flashed open and let the people inside. The chauffeur turned towards her. 'Get out,' he said softly. 'See if they'll let you in.'

Rebecca wondered why he was doing this. Was this what Leo de Viton had asked him to do? She struggled to maintain her composure, grateful that she had brought her own coat with her. It just about covered the rich lines of the silver cocktail dress, making her more anonymous. She took a deep breath and opened the car door.

Outside the night air was sharp, an exotic smell floating on the icy breeze. As she stepped out onto the kerb the car suddenly revved up and pulled away sharply – with the back door still open. She gasped and leapt aside, watching as the chauffeur turned the car swiftly. The door snapped shut as the tail lights vanished around the next corner. For a few seconds she stood watching the darkness, feeling afraid and desperately alone. She had no idea where she was. In the alleyway the door was lit with a single overhead light. At least there were people inside; the narrow street was deserted. Nervously she climbed the steps and knocked. A few seconds later the small hatch opened in the door and from inside a pair of dark eyes surveyed her with open curiosity. The watcher said nothing.

Rebecca swallowed hard before she spoke. 'I've come to see Mr de Viton.' Inside she heard a sharp barking laugh and then the sound of bolts being drawn.

'Best you get in here then, honey,' said a deep voice as the heavy door swung open. Inside was a narrow passageway lit by a series of bare bulbs leading down a steep flight of stairs. The doorman was a tall coloured man with sharp perceptive eyes. He was dressed in a strange combination of evening jacket, a sunshine yellow shirt and pyjama trousers; at another time Rebecca would have smiled, now the fear drove away the humour. Her strange companion looked her up and down. 'You his latest, honey?'

Rebecca tried to get a grip on her anxiety and nodded. He shrugged. 'Dunno how he does it. Mind you they tell me money has a real big mouth. Go down them stairs, he's at the table right by the stage. You can't miss him.' Before she had chance to move he caught hold of her arms, pulling her close. He smelt of tobacco and cheap liquor, mixed with an acidic bite of cheap cologne. She flinched. 'You're real pretty, lady. When he's all done with you maybe you'd like to come back? I'll let ya in anytime, for a kiss.' His heavy lips pressed against her face, tongue working on her cheek while his hands snaked up around her waist. She gasped and jerked herself away from his clutches, bolting down the steep stairs.

From below came the echo of music and the stale smell of beer and cigars. She glanced back over her shoulder wondering whether it might be better to go back and take her chances outside. Only the prospect of passing the doorman held her back. At the foot of the stairs a set of double doors led into a large bar. Cautiously Rebecca stepped inside. Smoke hung in the dim light above a strange assortment of people. The room was packed with small tables. Most of the patrons appeared to be men, some were dressed expensively in evening suits, others in working clothes, vests and shirt sleeves. The few women who were amongst the crowd stood close by the bar. They were heavily made-up; street women who stared at Rebecca with undisguised curiosity. The sense of fear and unease grew as she struggled to get her bearings.

In one corner of the room was a small stage, backed by curtains where a band picked out a soft soulful melody. Beside them, seated at a table she could make out the distinctive features of Leo de Viton. If he knew she was there he gave no indication, instead his eyes were firmly focused on the stage. Rebecca pressed uneasily between the tight-packed tables towards him. The men pawed at her with their eyes and brushed their bodies against her. She felt as if every nerve ending was alight and wary. Just as she reached Leo's table a beautiful coloured woman stepped out from behind the stage curtains and walked up to the microphone. The volume of the band subtly increased and instantly the busy room fell silent.

The woman cupped the microphone with long fingers and leant closer. Her voice lifted in a sleepy blue rendition of something tantalisingly familiar. A show tune rendered smoky and slow by the deep dark voice of an angel.

Rebecca was stunned that out of such a terrible place such a voice could soar. Leo glanced up at her and indicated a chair. Without speaking she sat down, her eyes firmly on the woman on the stage. One tune rolled slowly over into another. Every eye in the place was on the singer as she eased herself across the stage, rolling her hips in time with the melody. She was mesmerising.

As her set finished the drinkers broke out into rapturous applause and the woman, having taken a bow, turned to Leo's table and smiled provocatively before slipping back behind the curtains.

Leo turned to Rebecca and smiled. 'Take off your coat,' he purred, glancing over his shoulder at a man who had appeared with a tray to take his order. Rebecca let her coat slide down over the chair, aware that around them eyes moved surreptitiously in her direction. Leo leant a little closer. 'You look quite stunning. What did you think of Carina?' he nodded towards the stage.

Rebecca shook her head. 'Wonderful, I've never heard anything like it.'

Leo looked pleased and lifted his hands to encompass the smoky drab room. 'I began here, newly off the ship, straight from Ellis Island. Bussing tables. This is my home.'

Rebecca looked at him. 'Here?' she said in astonishment, 'But I thought . . .' her voice trailed away as she glanced around the seedy bar.

Leo let his fingers stroke down slowly over her bare shoulder, a soft proprietorial touch that spoke volumes. 'You thought I was a wealthy man? Well, now I am. But I've never forgotten where I began.' He grinned. 'You know, this used to be *the* place to be, years ago before the stock market crash. It was full every night with the beautiful people slumming it.' He paused while the waiter brought their drinks. 'I met my wife here when I was nineteen. Or rather she met me—' He looked in Rebecca's eyes, waiting for a reaction.

She smiled, wondering what would follow. 'We all have to begin somewhere,' she said guardedly.

Leo de Viton laughed with delight. 'What a find you are, Rebecca,' he snorted. 'You're so right, we all have to begin somewhere.'

From between the noisy crush of drinkers the singer who had captivated the audience moved towards them. The crowd parted like a wave in front of her until she was level with Leo's table.

'Carina,' he said, both as an introduction and greeting as he got to his feet, while the dark woman curled herself sensuously alongside him. She didn't resist as Leo pressed his lips to her fingertips.

Carina lifted an eyebrow in greeting towards Rebecca. 'I suppose,' she murmured in a voice as rich as pure caramel, 'that Leo is telling you about his past? This place brings out the sentiment in him.' She leant closer to Leo, rubbing herself against him like a cat. There was an element of teasing affection in her voice. Rebecca shivered; the woman exuded sexuality possibilities.

Leo stroked Carina's cheek. 'Of course,' he said softly and then looked back at Rebecca. 'My first wife was in her forties; a beautiful spoilt woman with an insatiable appetite for young flesh. She picked me up and turned my life around. Until I met her I was Leon Vitonavisch, bus boy and would-be-farmer.' He smiled lazily, his fingers stroking almost unconsciously over the ripe swell of Carina's heavy breasts.

Rebecca was fascinated, trying hard to ignore the dark flashing eyes of the singer. 'And she married you?' she said unsteadily, watching the lazy progress of Leo's fingers. Under the cream silk of Carina's low cut dress Rebecca could make out the puckered outlines of the dark woman's nipples as they hardened.

The singer moaned softly and ran a cat pink tongue around her lips, her eyes never leaving Rebecca's face. The way she looked at Rebecca made her flesh tingle. She could feel a tiny flicker of something she had never experienced before in her life. She had seen the expression of desire on a man's face before but never on a woman's. Carina wanted her. The electric pulse the understanding sent through her belly was unnerving. She could sense the pulse rising in her throat and quickly looked away.

Leo, apparently oblivious, sipped his cocktail. 'I was saying up enough money to head west,' he said evenly. 'She came in here one night with her entourage.' He paused, staring out into the smoky air. 'She was rich enough to do exactly what she wanted and old enough not to care what other people thought of her.'

Carina leant closer, dark eyes alight and full of fire. 'Then she took this little boy home to her uptown apartment and seduced him.' She stroked Leo's cheek playfully. 'Poor little baby.'

Leo spun round and took Carina by the elbows, his eyes as icy as hers were hot. He moved closer to her and whispered something that Rebecca couldn't quite hear. The dark woman laughed and glanced at Rebecca. 'Why don't we go upstairs to my dressing-room? It's much quieter there,' she suggested huskily. 'Leo's got business and he hates to mix it with pleasure. C'mon, honey, let me tell you some more of Leo's secrets.'

Rebecca glanced at Leo who waved her away. 'Go on, I'll be up in a little while. I won't be long.' Rebecca gathered up her coat and followed Carina without another word.

The corridor behind the stage seemed unnaturally quiet after the raucous noise and heat of the bar. Carina moved like liquid silk; looking strange amongst the debris of barrels and boxes stacked behind along the walls. She led Rebecca upstairs into a small vestibule and closed the door behind them, shutting out the last of the sounds of the bar below. In the shadowy half light she turned and caught hold of Rebecca's shoulders. Rebecca stiffened under her touch, afraid of the things she felt inside and at the same time strangely excited. Carina pressed her back gently against the wall and brushed her lips against Rebecca's cheek. Rebecca gasped, stunned by the sensations the singer's touch lit in her. 'I'm afraid,' she whispered softly over the sound of her heart's frantic beat.

The dark woman's reply was a throaty chuckle, 'Don't be afraid, honey. I'm not planning on hurting you. If you don't like it all you have to do is walk away. I'll call you the cab myself.' She moved closer, her hands lifting to Rebecca's face. 'Why don't we just take it real slow. I can show you so many things—'

Rebecca shuddered as Carina moved away. From around her neck the singer pulled a chain and key and unlocked another door. Rebecca gasped. Beyond the plain wooden doors was a glittering, elegant salon panelled in soft mellow wood. Above them the room was lit by a delicate crystal chandelier and from somewhere close by came the soft strains of a dance melody. Carina turned and grinned as she went towards the sideboard. 'Champagne?'

Rebecca stared around in astonishment. 'I don't understand,' she began, feeling as if she was walking into a dream.

Carina handed her a glass and took her coat and bag. 'Leo's wife bought him the club as a little wedding present. I live here at the moment.' She sipped her drink and pulled a face. 'Well, for the time being, until Leo decides it's time for me to move on.'

'You're his mistress?'

Carina laughed. 'Well yes, I suppose I am. One of the many. What about you?'

Rebecca flushed. 'I don't know . . . I . . .'

Carina had moved closer, brown eyes alight with the fire Rebecca had seen in the bar below. 'You know, you're real pretty. I can see why Leo thinks you might suit him.' Carina's fingers stroked down over Rebecca's bare shoulders in the same proprietorial fashion as Leo's. 'He brings me all his latest finds, you know,' she said softly. She dipped her finger into the top of the champagne flute and

trailed icy bubbling liquid over Rebecca's bare skin. The
girl shivered and stepped away. Carina smiled pleasantly.
'I told you, honey. Don't be scared, you've got nothing to
be afraid of with me.' Her voice dropped lower. 'I ain't
going to hurt you. Why don't you come to me and let me
show you all the good things I can give you—' She slid
closer, closing her arms around Rebecca.

Rebecca hesitated for a split second, feeling the heat of
the woman's body against her. The singer lifted a finger
beneath Rebecca's chin and tilted her head. Before
Rebecca could resist the singer kissed her. Her soft
enquiring mouth was a revelation, her tongue pressed
gently for entry. Rebecca felt powerless to resist; her body
responded instinctively and she felt a flurry of expectation
and excitement low in her belly. She moaned softly,
allowing the woman to slide her tongue into the recesses of
her mouth. Carina arched her tongue, teasing it along the
sensitive ridge in the roof of her mouth. She tasted of
champagne.

Rebecca felt dizzy – as if the world had shifted – never in
her wildest dreams had she imagined letting a woman kiss
her – and she knew that she wanted more than just a kiss.
The prospect both astonished and excited her. Carina's
fingers lifted to the silky fabric of her cocktail dress, tracing
the curve of her breasts. She knew her nipples were already
hard, aching to be touched. For a split second she imagined
Carina's hot wet mouth sucking them in. Between her legs
she could feel the slick beginnings of wetness clinging to the
sensitive folds of her sex. Shocked by the strength of her
own passion she pulled away, gasping. 'No, this is too
soon,' she spluttered, 'I don't think I can do this . . .' but
her protest sounded unconvincing.

Carina circled her; a sleek, wild cat who could show her

the way into her own darkest dreams. The singer's hands reached up to the halter neck of her own dress, while she hummed wordlessly along to the tune coming from the radio. The contrast of the cream silk was startling against her mahogany-coloured skin. Her eyes fixed on Rebecca as she slowly, slowly, peeled the fabric down over her body. Rebecca was astonished, unable to tear her eyes away from the heavy ripe curves of Carina's torso. The woman slithered the dress lower, down over her full hips and the tantalising dark triangle below.

The dark woman's eyes flashed with amusement and desire. 'Too fast for you, honey?' she purred. She moved like a snake, undulating, her body shimmering in the soft lights. In spite of her shock Rebecca could feel her excitement growing and swallowed hard.

Carina moved nearer, stepping out of the circle of fabric around her ankles. 'Here, baby,' she whispered, taking Rebecca's wrists. She lifted the girl's hands to her ripe breasts. Rebecca gasped; the woman's flesh was warm and silky smooth, unlike anything she had touched before. The sensation astounded her and almost before she knew what she was doing she stepped into Carina's waiting arms. The singer moaned softly. 'Oh yes, that's it, come to me,' she murmured. 'Just let me touch you.'

The other woman's hands slid over her spine and she didn't protest as Carina slid the zip of her dress open. She shivered as the woman pushed the thin straps back over her shoulders. She found herself surrendering to Carina's caresses, fighting the conflicting emotions that her conscious mind threw up. The singer kissed her again, driving away the fear, lighting bonfires of desire in its place. She shivered as the dark woman's fingers sought out her nipples, circling the tight peaks with a delicate whispering caress. Her mouth moved lower, pressing against Rebecca's skin in silky moist kisses, drawing her nipples into her mouth, her tongue working the tight peaked flesh. Rebecca moaned and surrendered.

Close by she heard the sound of a door opening and froze. Carina smiled lazily. 'Relax, baby, it's only Leo. There ain't no fear here, only pure, white-hot pleasure. Let me show you.' As she spoke she lapped again at Rebecca's breasts. Rebecca felt the tension ease and the pleasure drowning out the voice of reason.

A second later she felt another pair of hands circling her waist from behind and the rough brush of Leo's cheek against her naked back. The contrast to the silky smooth skin of the dark singer made her shiver. With Leo's wordless encouragement Carina slipped Rebecca's dress down over her hips. Beneath she was wearing a pair of silky cami-knickers. Leo's fingers locked in the fabric and slid them down hot on the heels of her dress. He moaned softly as his hands snaked across her firm rounded buttocks.

Carina stood back and admired Rebecca's body, her eyes focusing finally over Rebecca's shoulder on Leo. 'You sure know how to pick them, Leo,' she said huskily. Slowly she lifted her long fingers to her own nipples; dark puckered saucers that stood out proudly in the subdued lighting. She looked back at Rebecca. 'You're lovely, honey, sweet as they come.'

Rebecca blushed, aware of the touch of Leo's hands lifting to encompass her small breasts, while behind she could feel the threatening press of his erection.

Carina smiled and turned to pour herself another glass of champagne. She was as comfortable naked as she was dressed. Leo had seen to that. She watched the pale sylph-like form of the English girl; her eyes were alight with wordless desire and she recognised the hunger that glowed within them.

Rebecca's body moved back against Leo in an almost unconscious search for gratification – and they would find it. Carina sipped the cool champagne and then turned back towards them. She knew what Leo wanted now; she had fulfilled this fantasy a hundred times before. 'Let her go, Leo,' she said in a cool authoritative voice. She looked into Rebecca Hunt's anxious eyes. 'I want you to kiss me, honey.' As she spoke she let her fingers dip into the champagne glass and then snake low over her rounded belly. Her fingers opened the moist pink slit below. 'Here, I want you to kiss me here. I wanna feel your tongue deep inside me.'

The girl flushed crimson, her face contorted with fear and revulsion. Carina smiled lazily and lay back on a *chaise longue*, her long legs open, her finger working the dark hot bud between the sleek curls around her sex. She could sense the girl's hesitance, sense her mixed emotions 'Why don't you just come to me,' she purred, 'I need you, baby. I ain't going to hurt you—'

The girl shivered as Leo stepped away, allowing her to make the next step without any compulsion except the growing heat of for her own desire. Carina lazily lifted her other hand and tipped the champagne flute, letting a little of the icy cold liquid trickle over her heavy breasts. She closed her eyes and moaned, relishing the contrast of the icy chill against her hot sinuous body. Meanwhile her fingers worked the slick opening, dipping inside, stroking herself into arousal. She felt the girl moving closer, dropping to her knees in front of her, and smiled. Leo was right, the girl was a real find. She opened her legs wider, feeling the girl's fingers stroke nervously at her thighs; they were as cool as the iced champagne.

Rebecca was trembling, caught in the no-man's land between desire and reluctance. In front of her, Carina eased her body closer, a provocative dipping rolling action that revealed the delicate fragrant lips of her most secret places. She was so close that Rebecca could smell the rich oceanic scent of her body. Around the dark woman's fingers a glittering trail of excitement gathered. Rebecca groaned, knowing that behind her Leo de Viton was watching with interest. Knowing he was watching added to her confusion. Slowly she crept closer, letting her finger echo the enticing patterns of the singer's caresses.

The heat of the other woman's sex startled her. It seemed to pull her in like an intricate exotic orchid. She slid one finger down lower, allowing it to slide home into the deep recesses of Carina's body. She felt the woman's sex instinctively tighten around her and she knew she wouldn't be able to hold back. She imagined the same sensation between her own legs, imagined the way it would feel and whimpered softly. It seemed as if she were making love to herself. She remembered the way Callum had taken her to the edge of paradise with his tongue and suddenly she wanted more than anything else to take Carina to the same heady starlight plateau.

Pressing back the feelings of reluctance and fear she pressed her face closer, her lips seeking out the dark hooded ridge of the other woman's clitoris. Beneath her Carina mewled in delight and the taste of the singer's excitement flooded Rebecca's mouth; she was lost.

The tastes and smells were strange and at the same time hauntingly familiar, no more than a note away from the smell of her own body. Experimentally her tongue slid back and force, circling, sucking, flicking Carina's erect clitoris. The woman rewarded her with soft appreciative noises of encouragement and pleasure. Rebecca felt Leo moving towards her. She didn't miss a stroke as his hands travelled over her naked hips, his finger seeking out her sex. She could feel her slick juices trickling down onto her thighs. Leo grunted with satisfaction as he slid a finger inside her, another pressing forward to find the tight throbbing peak of her clitoris. It ached to be touched and she gasped with delight as his probing fingers found it. A split second later she felt his cock sliding home and her own body tighten deliciously around his shaft. The welter of sensations threatened to drive away all thoughts except for those of pleasure and the spiralling driving need to bring Carina and herself to the very edge of the precipice. She lowered her hips, encouraging Leo to fill her to the brim.

Under her tentative attentions, Carina opened wider, her fingers joining Rebecca's stroking teasing tongue – a magical wild bouquet of sensations. Rebecca gasped; it was impossible to work out where her body ended and those of her lovers began. It was as if every sensation was joined, drawn back and forth between them like a shared breath. Leo began to move frantically behind her, whilst Carina linked one hand in Rebecca's hair, encouraging her to come closer, to lap harder. Rebecca could feel the whole of the other woman's body humming, vibrating softly with growing pleasure as she drove her on and on.

Eagerly the dark woman lifted herself up, guiding Rebecca's fingers deeper. Rebecca was stunned as she felt the muscles deep inside Carina's sex begin to contract rhythmically, sucking on her fingers like a hot eager moth. She realised, as the singer began to buck and roll beneath her, that this was the compelling wash of her orgasm, flooding Rebecca's mouth with a rich sea taste that set every nerve ending alight. Leo, as if he could sense Carina's climax breaking, drove deeper into Rebecca. His fingers circled her clitoris again and again. Rebecca cried out, feeling the boiling waves of pleasure drawing her on and on until she thought she might pass out.

At the instant when the wild madness closed over her she felt Leo falter and then plunge recklessly into her, gasping and snorting against her naked back. Each tremor, each tight wild circle seemed to echo through them all, until at last, exhausted they collapsed down onto each other.

It was a few minutes before Carina rolled over on the chaise, stroking Rebecca's face with her fingers. 'I told you I could show you some good things, didn't I, honey?' she murmured sleepily. Rebecca, stunned by the intense gratification she felt, nodded dumbly, not resisting as the dark woman embraced her. Leo was the first to his feet, sliding his exhausted cock back into his trousers. He smiled at the two women and then refilled their glasses.

Rebecca sipped her drink, trying to get a grip on her shaking exhausted body. Leo nodded towards the door. 'We have to go now.'

Carina moaned miserably. 'Oh, Leo, so soon, why don't we have some supper? It's early yet.'

Leo shook his head, pressing his lips to the singer's forehead. 'Another night, Carina.'

Rebecca got dressed whilst Carina, still naked, rolled back onto the chaise. She watched Rebecca, smiling gently. 'Don't let it be too long before you make him bring you back to see me.' She paused, letting her tongue sweep around the delicate rim of the champagne glass. 'I'd really like to show you what I can do for you . . .'

Rebecca reddened, knowing that in spite of her embarrassment, she would relish the woman's attentions.

Leo laughed as he retrieved Rebecca's coat and bag from

a side table, 'Don't worry. We'll be back.' He lifted a hand in farewell, guiding Rebecca back out into the shadowy vestibule. He slipped his arm through hers, his hands moved slowly down over her dress. 'Slip off your underwear,' he said quietly. She looked at him in the dark and seeing the glittering highlights burning in his dark eyes, wordlessly complied. He nodded as she slipped her panties into her handbag.

When they walked back through the bar, Rebecca could feel the eyes of the customers following her and wondered if they had an inkling of what had taken place upstairs. On Leo's arm she passed the doorman without a second glance and stepped out into the cold night air. Under the street light Leo turned her towards him. 'Thank you for coming here,' he said softly, as the limousine drew up alongside the kerb. 'I would like to talk to you about your future.' The uniformed chauffeur opened the door for them.

'My future?' said Rebecca flatly, feeling the chauffeur's eyes on her body. Even if the clientele in the club had had no idea what had gone on in the upstairs room she was certain Leo's servant did. 'I don't understand what you mean.'

Leo guided her into the car's luxurious interior. 'Sarah Leinneman tells me you are staying with a friend and that you're looking for an apartment of your own.' He paused and lit a cigar. 'Perhaps I might be able to help you. I own several properties in Manhattan. It would be my pleasure—'

Rebecca looked at him coolly, 'I'm not sure I could afford the rent,' she said, watching his face. 'Carina is another of your tenants, isn't she?'

Leo laughed. 'My God, you're sharp. I would of course expect – what shall we call them? – visitation rights, but nothing, I'm sure, that wouldn't be to your tastes.' He stroked his fingers up over her thigh. 'And your tastes are growing all the time, aren't they?'

Rebecca blushed, 'Yes, I suppose they are,' she said.

Leo took a deep pull on his cigar. 'But there's no rush to decide, think about it. I can help you find somewhere suitable.'

Rebecca watched the shabby shadowy tenements roll past the car windows. 'Thank you.' She turned to look at him, thinking about Edith's cramped apartment and the dark intimidating presence of Arnie. 'I'm tempted, but what happens when you get tired of me?'

Leo lifted his hands in surrender. 'Nothing in life is forever, Rebecca. I can usually come to some arrangement with my tenants that is mutually beneficial.' His fingers lifted higher, pulling up the fabric of her dress. More and more of her thighs were revealed under the street lights. He slipped his fingers between her knees, teasing them apart. 'You know, you were magnificent tonight,' he whispered throatily. He moved closer closing his mouth over hers. His tongue worked along the rise of her lips; she knew he would be able to taste the subtle flavour of Carina and the thought rekindled the little flutter of desire in her belly. His fingers worked into the sopping pit of her sex and she moaned, sliding down in the seat to give him greater access.

For an instant she considered whether she should take him up on his offer. It was so tempting to be at his beck and call. If she accepted, she would be his entirely until he tired of her. But realistically she knew that she didn't want to live her whole life waiting for Leo de Viton's call, for Leo de Viton's word – however tempting his offer. Between her legs she could feel her desire mounting, in the meantime she would relish what he had to give her with no obligation on her part. She glanced up; in the rear view mirror she could see the cool steely eyes of Leo's chauffeur watching them. Knowing that he was watching added another dimension to her pleasure and she lifted herself higher, her skirt falling back to reveal the rise of her quim. If he wanted to look she would give him something to see. Leo moaned appreciatively as she slipped her hand into his crotch, beneath her fingers she could feel his hardness growing. She would show them both. Her fingers fought with his zip, trying to slide it down, quickly he grabbed her wrist, 'No,' he said gently. 'I've something else planned for you.'

Rebecca, caught up in the first waves of her excitement, looked at him and moaned softly. 'What?'

He folded her hands back into her lap and glanced out of the window. Outside the dark skyline was cut by cranes and derricks. The car was slowly making its way along a broad wharf littered with packing cases and netted cargo. She ran her tongue warily over her lips, 'Where are we? Why have you brought me here?'

Leo grinned, 'Will you do what I ask you?'

Rebecca swallowed hard, 'I don't know. What do you want me to do?'

Leo's formerly amicable expression hardened. 'Play my game.'

'I thought I had,' she said unsteadily, as the car slowed to walking pace. In the distance, in the shadow of a block of warehouses, a brazier burnt out a beacon of light. Even from so far away Rebecca could make out dark figures standing close to it for warmth. She turned to Leo. 'I don't understand. What do you want me to do?' she asked softly. Leo's fingers pressed firmly down on her clitoris, a jagged wave of pleasure juddered through her. She flinched, wishing that he didn't understand what her body craved.

Leo pointed through the windscreen, 'Sailors,' he said flatly. 'The girls come down here to pick them up. The authorities turn a blind eye to it. I'd like you to play too—' As they drew closer Rebecca could see the figures were a cluster of men in uniform swigging from bottles. Around them, entwined, prone, leaning against the warehouse doors were the predatory women of the streets. She shivered.

She turned to stare at Leo, feeling the anxiety rise in her belly. Inside she knew what Leo wanted from her. A glistening shard of fear and excitement made her stomach contract. The car drew to a halt in the shadows.

Outside on the dock a tall muscular man threw diftwood into the brazier sending a plume of sparks into the night sky. The chauffeur climbed from the car and crossed towards him. The tall man looked up warily at his approach and then waved a hand in greeting. Rebecca, oblivious to Leo now, pulled herself upright to peer out of the windows to see if she could catch what the two men were saying. As their mouths moved they both turned to look at the car and then slowly sidled up to it. The chauffeur opened the back door. Rebecca was suddenly aware of the cold and the way her skirt was rucked up to reveal most of her thighs. Beside her Leo de Viton was silent.

The man from the wharf eyed her thoughtfully, 'I'll need to see what she's got. Get out of the car, babe.' His accent was metallic and brusque.

She looked in appeal to Leo as the chauffeur helped her onto the wharf. His expression was unreadable as he said slowly, 'It's up to you. Why don't you show him, Rebecca?'

She could feel her face flushing scarlet. The cruel wind whipped at the thin cocktail dress, sucking away the warmth from the car. The tall man pulled a face. 'C'mon, I ain't got all night.' He looked back at the circle of light around the brazier. 'I've got clients waiting.'

Behind him monstrous shadows created by the fire were thrown up onto the warehouse walls. Figures linked and joined in lewd hellish poses. Tears pressed up in Rebecca's eyes. The chauffeur stepped a little closer but without threat; she knew the choice was hers; and the choice made her tremble. Slowly she lifted the hem of her dress, a little, a little, a little more, revealing her shapely thighs and between them the dark outline of her sex. The cold wind cut at her nakedness like a knife. The man nodded, looking back into the interior of the limousine. 'You wanna hang around and watch, mister? Only that'll be extra.'

Leo shrugged as he passed Rebecca's coat and bag out to the man. 'Watch? No, I don't think so. Just keep her warm. I don't want her coming back with a chill.'

The man leered obscenely. 'I don't think we'll have any problem there,' he said and caught hold of Rebecca's wrist. 'Come with me, babe, you're going to be the belle of the ball tonight.' Rebecca stumbled after him. To her horror she saw the chauffeur close the door of Leo's car and then slowly drive off across the quay.

She slowed down, watching the tail lights moving away. The man tugged her more firmly. 'Leo,' she whispered, suddenly terrified of what she had agreed to.

The man beside her laughed. 'That your boyfriend? Don't worry, babe, I'll get you back to him safe and sound when we're done here.' Around the fire her arrival had caused a stir. Men, crouched on balks of timber and barrels, looked up with dark feral eyes, whilst the painted women regarded her with open suspicion. The tall man propelled her closer to the roaring brazier so it was almost as if she were in a spotlight. 'Well,' he said slowly, picking up a bottle and taking a long pull on it. 'Let me see the colour of your money, boys. How much for tonight's special.'

He handed her the bottle and she took a long swallow, hoping the drink would dull her fear. The alcohol made her stomach scream out in complaint, its raw heat making her gasp. Around the fire the men looked her up and down like bidders at an auction. Rebecca closed her eyes, shutting out their unshaven rough faces. Leo's game suddenly seemed too dark, too frightening. She wondered if he would come back for her, but even as the thought crossed her mind, she knew he wouldn't. She flinched as a hand touched her shoulder. When she opened her eyes she was looking into the brutal face of a blonde man dressed in a heavy sweater and jeans. He unfolded a single note from his wallet and handed it to the tall man, 'Mine, I think,' he said in heavily-accented English.

The tall man grinned, 'All yours, maestro.'

The man's finger closed sharply around Rebecca's wrist and pulled her towards the shadows between the warehouses. The tall man lifted a finger to halt their progress and flipped something towards the sailor. Rebecca instantly recognised what it was, she had seen a similar packet when she had been with Callum O'Neill. 'American Army issue,' sang the tall man cheerfully, as the sailor tucked the condom in his back pocket. 'Enjoy.'

In the darkness away from the fire, the night wind was keener, the air heavy with the smell of diesel oil and fish and the sounds of the water lapping against the jetties. Rebecca shuddered, stumbling as her companion dragged her away to the relative privacy of the shadows. She had barely chance to catch her breath when he swung round and pushed her sharply up against the wall. The coldness made

her squeal. Instantly his lips were on hers. He smelt of
cheap liquor and the ripe aroma of male sweat. His hands
grabbed at her breasts, tearing the thin fabric of her dress
in his attempt to free them. She was terrified as he fumbled
with her dress, jerking it up to expose her swollen wet sex.
His fingers plunged into her without any prelude, invasive
and hungry. He snorted and whispered something in his
native tongue. She didn't understand the words but
recognised lust and desire in any language. He fumbled
with his flies, pinning her with one hand while he fought to
free his thick swollen cock. The meagre light showed its
aggressive arc, jutting towards her. He pressed the condom
into her frozen fingers. 'Here,' he grunted thickly. With
shaking hands she unrolled it, praying that she wouldn't
drop it amongst the debris and filth around their feet. He
moaned excitedly as she closed her fingers down over him,
rolling the rubber down. As she worked he forced his knee
between her thighs, forcing her legs open for his entry. As
soon as she let go of his cock he plunged inside her,
snorting and struggling to drive himself home.

His lips sought out her breasts, exposed and bitterly cold
amongst tatters of her cocktail dress. Then his teeth closed
on the sensitive peaks making her cry out with pain. Her
voice seemed to excite him more, he thrust up into her
again and again. Tears of fear and humiliation coursed
down her face as he fought his way, unheeding, towards his
climax.

'Leo,' she sobbed miserably, as his tongue lapped at her
swollen breasts. The man's breath was hot and foul on her
naked flesh. His fingers, tight around the base of his shaft
brushed against her as he pushed himself still deeper. To
her horror she realised she was excited. Her pleasure was
growing with each dark animal thrust. He slid a hand

roughly under her thigh, dragging it around his hips as he tried to press deeper still. She screamed out as the first wave of her climax hit her; stunned that the rough, cruel man could excite her so much.

He bucked again, impaling her, twisting himself closer and closer as if he were trying to get his whole body inside her. She slid her hands up under his sweat stained jumper, raking his back with her fingernails, biting down into the thick muscles of his shoulders, wanting him to feel her pain – instead her attentions drove him crazy with lust.

Out at the edge of the warehouses she didn't see the distinctive outline of Leo de Viton hidden amongst the dark unnerving shadows. He wanted a cigar but was afraid the glow would give him away. Instead he leant back against the rough walls watching his little protegee driving the foreign sailor out towards the edge of excitement. Her small features were white with fear and cold as the sailor pounded into her. Leo could make out the pale orbs of her small breasts, exposed to the man's brutal caresses. He glanced back towards the fire where the street girls were watching him. He could have anyone of them for the price of drink. Some of the men huddled by the brazier passed a bottle between them. The pimp told Leo they were waiting to try Rebecca's elegant English body for themselves. He smiled. Hidden in the shadows beside him he could sense the mounting excitement of his chauffeur. He touched the man gently on the shoulder. His servant moved closer, kneeling in the filth and mud. Leo de Viton sighed as the man opened his trousers and took out Leo's thick swollen phallus and slipped it between his lips. Leo leant back hard against the wall, his attention on the pale outlines of Rebecca as she thrust forward one more time.

* * *

It was the early hours of the morning before the tall man called a taxi for Rebecca to be taken home. She dragged her coat around her shoulders to cover the wreckage of her ruined cocktail dress. Her mouth was bruised from hot, animal kisses, her sex sore and throbbing. She closed her eyes imagining the anonymous wild faces of her lovers as they had fought their way to delight inside her. She was reluctant to go back to Edith's apartment. Edith would want to know what had happened to her – and Arnie might guess. She asked the driver to slow down under a street light and took her address book out of her bag. 'Can you stop at the next phone?' she asked the driver.

He looked at her in the rear view mirror. 'I don't want you turning no tricks in my car, lady,' he said, chewing a matchstick. 'Less'na course you're planning on giving me a freebie.'

Rebecca flushed scarlet. 'Just take me to a phone,' she whispered.

'Jesus,' said Callum O'Neill as he helped Rebecca upstairs into his apartment, 'what the hell happened to you?'

Rebecca winced. 'I was playing a game,' she said, lowering herself gingerly onto his sofa.

Callum lifted an eyebrow. 'And did you enjoy it?'

Rebecca eased off her filthy shoes, not meeting his gaze. Callum shrugged philosophically and went into the kitchen. 'I'll run you a bath and get some coffee. You look bloody terrible. Why don't you let me take your coat?'

Rebecca shook her head and grinned. 'You don't want to see what the rest of me looks like.'

Callum leant around the kitchen door. 'Are you okay though?'

Rebecca nodded. 'I'm fine, just tired and dirty and in need of a friend.'

Callum pulled a face. 'Well, in that case. I'm your man. Are you going to tell me who the referee of this game is?'

Rebecca shook her head. 'Not until after I've had a bath, I'm feeling a bit fragile.'

An hour later Rebecca was curled up in front of Callum's stove drinking hot bitter coffee and nibbling at the plate of sandwiches he had made her. She looked round the comfortable book-strewn apartment. Lamps were lit on almost every surface and under a large window a desk was covered with reams of paper.

'Did I get you up?'

Callum snorted and shook his head. 'I wish. I find it easier to work at night.' He looked at her over the rim of her cup. 'So, are you going to tell me about it?'

Rebecca pulled her borrowed dressing gown tighter around her shoulders. 'I'm not sure I'm ready to own up. Have you heard of man called Leo de Viton?'

Callum expelled a short burst of air. 'Jesus, who hasn't? He's a great big fish in a big muddy pool.' He looked steadily at her. 'And he's the new games master in your life?'

Rebecca nodded.

'Well, aren't you the lucky lady, aim high they always tell me. I thought he was married.'

Rebecca blushed crimson. 'He is.'

Callum laughed. 'My, my, Miss Hunt, you've certainly changed since we came across the Atlantic.' He sat down beside her and lay his hand on her shoulder. She winced. Callum looked at her questioningly. 'What's the matter?'

'I'm sore, that's all.'

Before she could protest Callum gently pulled the soft

cotton robe down off her shoulders. Her shoulders and breasts were reddened, bruised, livid teeth marks discolouring the delicate skin around her nipples, her back a mass of scratches. He hissed out a sound of disapproval. 'Jesus! You like this kind of thing?' he whispered in disbelief.

Rebecca looked down, reddening with embarrassment. 'No, not really,' she said softly. How could she explain to Callum it had been her submission to Leo's strange and wild desire that had been the thing that excited her. She looked up into his concerned face. He would understand. She began in a halting voice to explain, while Callum rubbed balm into her bruises. If he was shocked he didn't show it. He listened in silence while she explained about Arnie and Edith and Sarah Leinneman, how she needed to find a new apartment, and about Leo's offer of assistance.

When she'd done he made them more coffee. 'So, are you going to let him set you up in a little lovenest, playing slave to his master?'

Rebecca looked out into the yellowing light of the coming dawn and shook her head, 'No, I don't want to be trapped by him but I have to get away from Arnie. Leo gives me a feeling of sexual freedom, Arnie made me feel as if I'd been taken.'

Callum laughed. 'All in the mind, lady, if you ask me.' He glanced around the sitting-room. 'You can come and stay here for a while if you like. It's not much but it's home,' he said with humour. 'It's only twenty minutes in on the subway from Berdys and I'll can help you find somewhere else.' He held up his hands in surrender as she looked at him in astonishment. 'And no, I won't rent you out to a pack of sailors to make you pay your half of the rent.'

Rebecca reddened. 'It wasn't quite like that.'

Callum looked sceptical, 'No? I think he's using you, too much too fast – but the choice is yours.' He paused. 'No more lectures, what about taking me up on my offer?'

Rebecca considered for a few seconds. 'Would you mind me being here? Wouldn't it disturb you?'

Callum shrugged. 'Not for a while. I don't plan on it being a permanent arrangement.'

'Then yes,' she said with a yawn.

Callum picked up the coffee cups and headed for the kitchen, talking as he went. 'Okay. Then we'll go over to Edith's tomorrow and pick up your things. How about you get yourself off to bed? You look all in. I've put a night-shirt out for you in the spare room. If you like I'll ring Berdys and tell them you're sick—'

Callum looked back from the doorway and grinned. It was too late. Rebecca Hunt was already asleep.

Chapter 5

On Monday Rebecca slept most of the day, while Callum had made it his business to go over to Edith's apartment, before she left for work, to arrange to collect Rebecca's things. Edith had assumed Rebecca was moving in with Callum and he did nothing to persuade her otherwise.

It was first thing Tuesday morning before Rebecca went to Berdys. As Rebecca made her way out of the lift and across the sales floor it seemed a life-time since she had stood alongside Lily Reubens at the lingerie counter in her Berdys uniform. No one commented on her absence and she was soon absorbed into her work. The store was so busy that she had little time to think about anything else. At lunch time Sarah Leinneman sent down a messenger to say that she would like to see Rebecca after work. Reluctantly, as the store closed, Rebecca headed up to see Sarah who was waiting in her office. The older woman invited her to sit down and looked at her coolly. 'So how was your dinner with Mr de Viton?'

Rebecca's gaze didn't falter. 'I'd imagine it was much the same as yours,' she said evenly, watching Sarah Leinneman's face.

Sarah sighed, 'He is an addiction that it's hard to recover from.' From beside her desk she pulled out a bouquet of roses and white narcissus. 'These arrived for you this afternoon with his compliments.'

Rebecca took them, letting the fragrance embrace her. 'They're very beautiful, but why didn't they come yesterday?' She stared at Sarah Leinneman. 'I understand Mr de Viton's interest in me has a lot to do with you. Did you ring him to tell him I hadn't come in to work?' Rebecca fought to retain her composure, but inside she was trembling. Sarah Leinneman had picked her out for Leo like a dress from the rack.

The older woman shook her head. 'No, his secretary rang me.' She paused, watching the girl thoughtfully. 'Are you all right?'

Rebecca laughed sarcastically. 'I'm not really sure. Are you going to ask me out to dinner on his behalf again?'

'No,' said a low familiar voice from the doorway behind her. Rebecca swung round sharply and looked up into the eyes of Leo de Viton. 'I'm here to ask you myself.'

Rebecca shivered, feeling a little flutter of excitement in her belly. His eyes flashed as he continued, 'I've asked Sarah to pick you out a beautiful gown.'

Rebecca shook her head. 'I'm not sure whether I want to go with you or not. There isn't much left of the last dress she picked for me.'

Leo moved closer. 'Oh, Rebecca. Are you telling me it didn't excite you to be desired purely for your body?' He stroked her neck softly, his touch was electric. 'I've booked a table at Antonio's at eight, best seafood restaurant in the city. They serve wild sea bass in sage; it is perfection.'

Rebecca looked up at him. 'Mrs Leinneman says you are an addiction.'

Leo laughed with genuine amusement. 'Oh, I am.' He glanced at Mrs Leinneman. 'Sarah, will you bring Rebecca her gown? I'd like you to help her get ready.' Without a word Berdys senior personnel officer got to her feet. Leo de Viton extended a hand towards Rebecca. 'Come with me,' he said softly. 'We have so many more games to play, but tonight we'll eat and you can tell me about yourself.'

It was almost midnight when Leo de Viton's chauffeur delivered Rebecca back to Callum's apartment.

Upstairs Callum was frantic. 'I thought you'd been kidnapped by that bastard,' he snapped as she waltzed into the sitting room.

Her head was reeling from the wine and the heady atmosphere of Antonio's restaurant. Leo, true to his word had listened attentively and dazzled her with his bright mind and conversation. He had been a perfect companion. The evening had been a great success. She had felt the eyes of the other diners following them as they'd taken their seat and felt flattered by the attention. They had danced. Leo was a wonderful partner, with just the hint of something dark and more compelling beneath the surface of his charm.

'So where have you been?' Callum's voice sobered her up in an instant.

'You're not my keeper,' Rebecca snapped back at him.

Callum ran his fingers through his hair. 'I'm sorry, you're right, but I've been worried.' He grinned. 'I was about to start combing the docks for you.'

Rebecca felt a little tight knot of fury in her belly. 'How dare you? I told you because I thought you'd understand.'

Callum looked uncomfortable. 'I do,' he began and then stopped. 'No, I don't, if I was de Viton, I'd want you for myself. I wouldn't want to share you around.'

Rebecca paused mid-stride. 'Do you want me for yourself?' she said softly.

Callum sighed uneasily, 'No, yes, no . . . shit, I don't know. I'm just afraid that you're going to get hurt if you mix with de Viton.'

Rebecca sat down on the sofa. 'Do you mean physically or mentally?'

'I don't know, both, I suppose.' He stopped and glanced towards the spare room. 'I collected the rest of your things tonight and met Edith's boyfriend, Arnie.' He paused. 'I see what you mean about him.'

Rebecca shuddered. 'He frightens me.'

Callum laughed. 'And de Viton doesn't? Oh, by the way, Edith asked me to give you these—' He walked over to his desk and pulled a large marbled folder out from under a pile of papers, on top was a letter from England.

Rebecca sighed. 'Oliver,' she said, laying the envelope down beside her.

'And the folder?'

Rebecca pulled a face. 'No idea.' She opened it and smiled, instantly a welter of memories came flooding back. 'Oh, I'd forgotten all about these,' she said quietly. 'Edith must have brought them with her from England.'

Callum sat down beside her. 'What are they?'

'Sketches I did when we were stationed together.' She pulled out the tattered sheets of drawing paper and handed them to Callum, who stared at them in amazement. 'You did these?'

Rebecca poked him in the ribs. 'Don't sound so astonished. I was involved in map-making, drawing has always been one of my hobbies.'

Callum stood the first sketch on the table, propping it upright between a lamp and a vase. The drawing was of a strikingly handsome man, caught in profile against a bleak winter's landscape. 'This is great—'

Rebecca laughed. 'No, it's Oliver. I drew it from a photograph. Not very flattering. I'm afraid. Oh, here's one I do like.'

Callum took the picture out of her fingers. It was a stylised, mystical landscape bordered by trees. The effect was intriguing. Callum sat back. 'You know, you're wasted in Berdys. Have you ever thought of doing this for a living?'

Rebecca pulled a face. 'Hardly.'

Callum glanced at the phone. 'I know some guys down in the Village who know about art and illustration. Would you mind if I took these down to show them?'

Rebecca grinned, letting the remains of the champagne she had drunk with Leo carry her away. 'Not at all, do what you like with them. I'm going to bed.' She clambered unsteadily to her feet and headed towards the spare room.

'What about Oliver's letter?' Callum asked, holding it out towards her.

Rebecca snorted, perturbed by the little dart of pain his name have her. 'What about it?' For an instant she felt tears prickling up in her eyes. 'Look, I'm sorry, Callum, I really need to sleep,' she said flatly.

In the lamp-lit room Callum turned the sketches towards the light. Oliver's picture was drawn with great love and tenderness – what it lacked in technical merit was compensated fro by the gentle caring touch of the artist. Callum glanced at the unopened letter. Oliver Cresswell, wherever he was, was a fool.

'Did you write to her?'

Oliver Cresswell looked blankly at his godfather, feeling the warm glow of the scotch threading its treacherous path through his veins. Finally making sense of the words, but only after they were repeated, he nodded. 'Yes, I told her

I've had time to think and that we need time to talk.' He paused watching the logs burning low in the grate of his godfather's London study. 'I told her I need her more than everything else in my life and that I want her to come home as soon as possible.'

George Winterton snorted. 'Go after her, man. Good God, do you need it spelt out? You make it sound as if she has to come running back to you with her tail between her legs.' He stopped, seeing the hurt in Oliver's eyes. 'Confound it all, man, this isn't like you. What do you say we go down to Soho?' He grinned impishly, 'Or let me take you round to my dear friend Sophie's cat-house. One of those pretty little kittens she employs will take your mind off Rebecca for a while.'

Oliver laughed. 'I wish it were that easy. All the time I was away fighting I thought about coming home to Rebecca. I whored my way across Europe keeping tight hold of this vision of purity and loveliness that I would marry. She kept me strong. Knowing that she was waiting for me helped me to get through—'

George smiled indulgently. 'My dear boy, living with a vision of purity and loveliness would bore you rigid.'

Oliver flushed crimson. 'I know that. I had this magnificent fantasy of making love to her on our wedding night, taking her higher and higher, showing her all the pleasure we could share.' He stopped, the colour in his face intensifying. 'And then I couldn't bloody-well restrain myself. I acted like a total cad. I should have been stronger for us both.'

George laughed in spite of his godson's pain. 'Good God, man, why, for heavens sake? The girl loved you, what's more natural than that? She needed to show you.'

Oliver refilled his glass. 'I know that, but the damage was

done so quickly. When we made love – when it was over – I should have taken her in my arms and pledged my undying devotion. Instead I was so shocked that I'd given way I couldn't speak.' He looked up into the older man's eyes. 'It sound ridiculous, doesn't it? What makes it worse is that the reality was so much better than my carefully embroidered fantasy. But by the time we got home the damage was done – there was this dark unhappy silence that I couldn't find the words to fill. She thought I was rejecting her.' He paused. 'And now I keep going over and over it in my mind, ploughing the same damned furrow, trying to find some way to make it right. Then there was the farce with my mother's wedding dress.'

George groaned. 'Oh please, not again, Oliver. Don't do this to yourself. Go after her.'

Oliver shook his head. 'When mother suggested she wore that damned dress all I could see was my hot sweaty hands on Rebecca's breasts; pawing at her like some unleashed beast. It was pure lust, George, let loose on the woman I love.'

George topped up his own glass. 'And all the more terrible because she was quite obviously enjoying it?'

Oliver froze. 'No, no, not really—' he said stiffly, running his finger back through his dark hair. He was lying. Her compliance, her eagerness had shocked him and at the same time delighted him. She was every bit as eager as he had hoped for – except that the timing was all wrong. He had anticipated unlocking the passion in her when they were safely married, when it was *right* – how foolish that word sounded. It had cost him so much. He looked miserably at George. 'I don't suppose you fancy coming on a trip to New York with me, do you? I couldn't bear to be alone if she told me to clear off.'

George patted his godson's shoulder tenderly. 'Of course, old chap. Let me talk to my good lady and I'll see what we can arrange.' He paused. 'Actually we've got friends over there, I could arrange for us to pay them a visit. Do us good to blow some of the cobwebs out of out hair.' He stopped and glanced at Oliver. 'See what the post brings and then I'll contact my friends. Hope springs eternal and all that. Now, can I interest you in a spot of supper?'

Callum O'Neill tucked Rebecca's portfolio under his arm and headed up the stairs to his friend Geno's studio. The stairwell smelt of damp laundry with an overlay of turps and linseed oil. The top floor opened up into one huge room with enormous skylights which flooded the bare boards with daylight even on the darkest days. The great sheets of glass had one disadvantage; in summer the room was like an oven, while in winter they sucked every last ounce of heat from the studio so that it was like an ice flow.

Oliver pulled his coat tighter around his shoulders and called a greeting. From the far side of the room Geno Amerti looked up from his canvas and grinned. 'Callum O'Neill, what the hell brings you back? I thought you were still in England.' His New York drawl was overlaid with a hint of his native Italy which gave his voice a musical sing-song quality.

Callum smiled. 'I've brought something for you to have a look at. I wondered if you'd give me your opinion on these.' He held up Rebecca's folder.

Geno shrugged, blowing on his frozen fingers. 'Only if we can do it over a *cafe creme* in the patisserie. I'm chilled right through to the bone.'

Callum nodded. 'Why not?'

In the warmth of the cafe across the street, with his hands wrapped around a mug of steaming coffee, Geno nodded as Callum showed him Rebecca's sketches. 'You know they're good, you don't need me to tell you that. I often wonder why you didn't stay with art yourself.' Geno looked at Callum thoughtfully. 'You were a good artist, very talented . . .'

Callum grinned. 'Call me old-fashioned but I like to eat once in a while. These were done by a friend of mine who's staying over at my place.'

Geno tugged at his lip with paint stained fingers. 'There's not so much call for pencil sketches. The galleries want paintings. You know that. Does he paint too?'

Callum shrugged. 'I don't know – and it's a she, not a he.'

Geno laughed. 'So, you finally change your spots? I thought all your little protegees were boys, Callum? Handsome, muscle-bound young men straight up from the sticks.'

Callum reddened. 'Never exclusively.'

Geno snorted with delight. 'No, no, you're right. This girl has talent. These landscapes are almost illustrative – maybe she should try magazines as well as fine art. There is a good market there. Well paid too.' He looked at Callum thoughtfully. 'What's your interest in her?'

'She's my friend.' Callum sipped his coffee. 'And to be honest I suppose I'm trying to rescue her from something that I think she'd be better off out of.'

Geno raised his eyebrows. 'So, what is it that this girl doing that you disapprove of?'

'Working in Berdys during the day . . .' Callum began. He was about to bring up Leo de Viton when his friend cut him off with a burst of laughter.

121

'She needs rescuing from working in a department store? At least she's getting the money to eat regularly. Unless she's desperate to embrace poverty I'd tell her to stay where she is. Maybe paint in her spare time. She's certainly got the talent to make some extra money. I could give you a few names of people that might be interested enough to look at her work – if she paints.' He grinned at Callum. 'I'm assuming, as she's staying with you, that she isn't keen to embrace chastity either. How about obedience?'

Callum snorted. 'That's part of the problem. She's got herself tangled up with a guy who likes the idea of total control.'

Geno grinned. 'In the bedroom?' Callum's expression gave him the answer. 'Oh, come on, Callum, obedience was never so bad – You know it's just a pantomime. Play-acting. An exciting little game—'

Callum nodded. 'Yeh, but I'm not so sure . . . I just don't trust this guy. I thought maybe if I could find her something else to do. Get her away from Berdys and him – something that she enjoyed.'

Geno roared with laughter. 'You're trying to cure her by making her paint? This I would like to see. I should leave her where she is, Callum. Good money, perks and at least it's warm.'

Callum slid the pencil sketches back into the folder. 'I thought you might be able to help.'

'Don't look so hurt,' Geno said gently. 'You know how hard it is to make a living as an artist. If she needs studio space, then, yes, of course she can come up and work in my place.' He paused. 'For a small consideration, I'm not a charity. As for work, well, I can give you some names as I've said. I know a few people who'd be happy to pay for a decent life model, but they pay a pittance. Maybe she is better off where she is.' He drained his coffee cup and offered it to the passing waiter, who refilled it. 'Besides, you can't rescue someone who doesn't want rescuing and from the look on your face and the things you've said, I'd guess your friend is quite happy with what she's doing. It's you with the problem, old friend. Is this jealousy I ask myself?'

Callum shrugged. 'I'll tell her what you said. And if I pay for the coffees can I come back and get that list of contacts?'

Geno grinned. 'For that I'd want at least a breakfast.'

Callum snorted. 'You drive a hard bargain, Geno.'

His friend laughed and waved the waiter back.

Rebecca closed the door of Callum's apartment and eased off her shoes. 'I used to think the underground was bad until I tried the subway. I thought you said this place was only twenty minutes from Berdys? It's taken me nearly an hour to get home.' She stretched luxuriously and slipped off her coat. 'God, it's really cold out there. How's your day been?'

'Fine,' Callum looked up from his desk and grinned. 'What, no Mr de Viton tonight?'

Rebecca flushed. 'No, I thought he might ring Sarah Leinneman but he sent these instead.' She produced a great bouquet of creamy-coloured roses from the hallway.

'So you haven't been forgotten.'

'Apparently not.' She glanced round the sitting-room and laughed. 'So, what's all this about?' In one corner of the room, under a large lamp, Callum had set up an easel and draped a comfortable armchair with a bedspread.

'Something a friend of mine said today. He loved your sketches and asked me if you painted too.'

Rebecca lifted an eyebrow. 'I haven't painted for years. What were you planning? A crash course?'

Callum shook his head. 'No, I thought I'd paint you. I once fancied myself as a starving artist. Here.' He poured her a glass of wine. 'I've cooked us some supper and then I thought maybe we could get to work.'

'What about your novel?'

Callum grinned, 'You can't rush a masterpiece. C'mon let's eat. I'm starving.'

Rebecca rolled over slowly onto her belly. 'What about like this?'

Callum shook his head, watching the curve of her breasts move with liquid intensity as she posed for him. 'No, if you lay like that I'll be tempted to put down my pencil and come over there and screw the ass off you.'

Rebecca giggled and took another long pull on her wine glass. 'Maybe that's just what I want,' she purred. Her words were slightly slurred from the effects of the alcohol, her pale skin flushed with a hint of pink. Callum sighed; she looked almost edible. Her eyes flashed mischievously. 'Why don't we swap roles? You take your clothes off and let me paint you. I've never painted a naked man before.'

'Later. It's been years since I did any painting. Seeing Geno today made me realise how much I missed it.'

On the armchair Rebecca turned languorously onto her back, eyes closed, legs slightly apart so that the soft light from the lamp threw her slim body into golden relief. 'There,' hissed Callum. 'God, don't move, you look wonderful. Hang on.' He picked up the roses from Leo de Viton that Rebecca had abandoned on the sofa and started to pluck the petals.

As the first one touched Rebecca's belly she opened her eyes. 'What in godsname is that? Oh, my flowers. What are you doing to them?'

Callum pulled out another handful of petals. 'Just adding a little magic, now lay still. I want to try and get this down.' He stepped behind the easel and picked up a piece of charcoal. Rebecca looked like a wild angel. Her soft hair tumbled down onto the bedspread, her eyes were closed, her expression relaxed, with a lazy sensuality. Callum hesitated for an instant before he made the first mark on the virgin canvas. If he wasn't careful, he could very easily fall in love with Rebecca Hunt. As he lay the charcoal on the canvas and felt the first satisfying bite against the rough surface Rebecca moaned softly. He was tempted to lay the charcoal down and forget the whole idea. She was an erotic masterpiece and he doubted that he could do her justice with his painting – with his body it would be a different matter.

Leo de Viton had his chauffeur park the limousine in the side alley off West Fourth Street and then walked back to Callum O'Neill's apartment block. Sarah Leinneman had said Leo was an addiction, the man laughed to himself as he buttoned his heavy overcoat against the bitter night wind. What Sarah hadn't reckoned on was that Rebecca Hunt might be addictive too – he hadn't intended to see her but something compelled him to seek her out. He climbed the steps up to the apartment building. He would knock, hoping she would answer and then suggest they went for a walk, for a drive – almost anything – and then he would make love to her. She would tell him how it felt when the sailor had forced his way inside her. Leo shivered, thinking about her delicate body pressed hard back against the warehouse, legs spread.

Inside he climbed the stairs two at a time until he reached the top floor and then glanced at the piece of paper he had written her new address down on. The taxi driver who had brought her home had been most helpful. This was the place. He hesitated for a second before knocking; he was not used to doing the chasing, his women came to him as he ordered. Crawled on their hands and knees if he commanded it. As he lifted his fist to knock something stopped him, from inside the flat he heard a soft throaty moan of excitement. He hovered indecisively for a second or two before dropping to his knees and peering through the keyhole. Inside there was some light but he could see nothing clearly. Rebecca's voice taunted him again; a simple guttural cry that convinced him she was making love.

He got up and slowly turned the door handle; he didn't for one second presume it was unlocked, New Yorkers locked themselves in as a matter of course. To his surprise the door gave a little. With infinite patience he eased it open. Inside was a shadowy entrance hall, barely more than a door's width square which opened into a larger sitting-room. Pulling the door to he stepped inside and pressed himself against the wall, peering into the room beyond. The anticipation that he might be caught gave him an added thrill. What he saw in the room's softly-lit interior delighted him.

Under the window, to his right, Rebecca Hunt was laying, naked, in an armchair, her long legs hanging lazily over each arm. Between them a man knelt, his face buried in her sex. Leo hissed out a soft breath of pleasure as Rebecca lifted herself up towards her lover's tongue; her expression was ecstatic. Eyes tight closed she shivered and then moaned again, her delighted throaty noises a delicate counterpoint to the wet muffled sounds of her lover's attentions. Beside them, standing on the easel was a charcoal drawing of Rebecca stretched out for her lover's pleasure, legs open a little, a teasing, modest invitation, her breasts tilted up, her mouth open in anticipation. Leo shivered; he had to have the drawing.

Beside the easel Rebecca whimpered with delight and his attention was dragged back to the living erotic tableau. The man got up, arching over Rebecca and slid himself home into her waiting eager body. Leo glimpsed her open glittering sex for a split second before the man found his place. Leo's growing excitement made him less cautious. As the man plunged deep into Rebecca's compliant body she opened her eyes and Leo de Viton knew he had been seen. Her mouth opened in a silent gasp of shock and surprise. Her body tensed and her lover drew back a little. 'What is it?' he whispered huskily. 'I'm not hurting you, am I?'

Rebecca closed her arms around his torso, lifting her legs so that they circled his waist. 'No, it's all right,' she whispered, guiding his head down into the curve of her shoulder. She pressed herself eagerly against him, her eyes locked on Leo's in an expression of pure defiance. Leo smiled, not bothering to hide himself as Rebecca wildly drove the man and herself out beyond oblivion. White hot crystals of orgasm exploded over them both in heady shuddering waves. Gasping, Rebecca's lover collapsed down onto her, his muscular body slick with sweat – even then Rebecca did not let her gaze falter. Leo lifted a hand in silent salute.

Before they had a chance to recover Leo de Viton stepped silently out through the little hallway and closed the door behind him. He would ring Sarah Leinneman to arrange to meet Rebecca himself, but first he felt the need for relief. Carina's distinctive features flashed in front of his eyes but even as he thought it, his imagination added the captivating charms of Rebecca Hunt pressing her tongue deep in Carina's wild slick sex. He shivered and set off downstairs.

Next morning Rebecca hurried through the staff entrance at Berdys, cursing as the elevator doors closed almost in front of her nose. She glanced at her watch; damn Callum and his optimistic assumption that his apartment was twenty minutes from work. She snorted and then smiled as she remembered the night before; he had made her body sing, gently taking her again and again to the heights of passion. She could still feel his soft sweet kisses, the caress of his skilful fingers as he stroked the soft curves of her belly. It was as if he were trying to show her the antidote to Leo's dominance.

The darker memory of Leo de Viton's flashing predatory eyes replaced Callum's face as soon as she thought his name. What the hell had he been doing in the apartment? She pressed the call button on the lift, realising after making love and the effects of the wine, she had given Leo's presence barely any thought.

The elevator doors opened again and she stepped inside, still thinking about Leo de Viton and the expression on his face as he had watched her making love with Callum. When she reached the lingerie department she barely had time to step out of the lift when a girl in Berdys livery hurried across to her. 'Miss Hunt?'

She nodded, looking around the shop floor to see if she could see Lily Reubens or any of the other shop girls. 'Yes, what can I do to help you?' she said pleasantly. Inside she already knew who the message was from; she recognised the girl from Sarah Leinneman's office.

'Mrs Leinneman would like to see you before you start work.' Rebecca nodded and followed the girl silently back into the elevator.

Inside Sarah Leinneman's office there was no pre-amble, no polite good morning or warm welcome. Sarah looked up from her work. 'A car will be picking you up at ten from the staff entrance.'

Rebecca was furious. 'Don't I have a choice about this? What about my job? I need to earn a living.'

Sarah Leinneman looked at her coolly. 'Oh, you will, don't worry. Leo never lets his girls go without.'

Rebecca's mind raced. 'I'm not one of "his girls" ', she snapped. 'Do I have any say in any of this? He is making assumptions—' Her voice faded. Wasn't that part of the attraction? That he had taken her, ordered her like one of his delicate frothy purchases from the lingerie department and was using her because he could – and might – lose interest just as quickly? She trembled thinking about his strikingly handsome face, the thin undeniably cruel line of his lips—

Sarah Leinneman put her pen down. 'Of course you have a say,' she said flatly and picked up the phone. 'Would you like me to ring him? I can stop this now if that's what you really want.'

Rebecca bit her lip. She shook her head.

The older woman lay the phone back in its cradle. 'Your position with Berdys is safe while you want it, but I think you'd already worked that out. I've organised your clothes.'

Rebecca looked up. 'Packaged me for him, you mean?'

Sarah smiled. 'If that's how you prefer to think of it. Mr de Viton said that you may not be back until the weekend.'

'The weekend? But I can't . . .' Rebecca blustered, trying to imagine what Leo had planned for her; the possibilities were unlimited. Her mind filled with a collage of images; the chauffeur, the cool bite of the dining table against her back, the smell of the wharf, Carina's dark flashing eyes and Callum's face, alight with anger and concern as he had taken off her bathrobe when she'd come back from the docks. She steadied herself against the edge of Sarah's desk, trying to get a grip on her thoughts. 'I have to ring the person I'm sharing an apartment with,' she said steadily. 'They'll be worried if I don't come home tonight.'

'Edith Hartman is in today, would you like me to tell her for you?'

Rebecca shook her head. 'I've moved out.'

Sarah indicated the phone. 'Would you like to give them a call from here?'

Callum lifted the receiver at the second ring. 'Hi.'

'It's me. I've just rung to say that I may be away for a few days.'

She heard Callum take a deep breath. 'Are you going to tell me where?'

In the office Rebecca looked at Sarah Leinneman's face and shook her head. 'No, no I'm not sure at the moment and I'm not really in a position to talk right now.'

Even before he spoke again she could sense Callum's growing anger. 'Don't tell me, a little trip with your good friend Mr de Viton. What, is there a new ship in?'

Rebecca swallowed, feeling her colour rising. 'I really can't talk now, I'll be back in a few days.'

Callum's reply was an angry snort.

Rebecca moved closer to the windows of the limousine. The drive out to Long Island was nothing like she had imagined. Suburban sprawl gave way to acres of farmland – quite unlike anything else she'd seen in New York. The winding roads were dotted with white clapboard houses and stands of mature trees. Her mixed feelings about leaving New York city were quickly replaced by surprise and curiosity at the beauty of the rich autumn landscape. The car headed along the rural routes out towards the South Fork of Long Island, burning up the miles under its white wall tyres, through a string of seaside villages.

Even the intimidating outline of Leo's chauffeur at the wheel of the limousine couldn't rob Rebecca of the feeling of having escaped. In the afternoon they turned off the main road and stopped the car under the shelter of a small wood while Leo's driver served her a picnic lunch. His obsequious manner didn't quite disguise his interest in her. Although she could sense the uniformed man's desire she doubted that he would dare make a move unless he had been instructed to by Leo. He pulled a chair from the boot and indicated that she should take it. Rebecca pulled her coat around her shoulders and stepped out from the car, pleased to be able to stretch her legs. Although it was late in the year the wind was mild, bright sun kissing the landscape with mellow golden light.

When he thought she wasn't looking the chauffeur's eyes moved across her as he arranged the picnic table, lingering on her legs, moving up slowly over her breasts. Rebecca watched him, wondering what game he and Leo were playing.

As he took out a wicker hamper she caught his eye. 'Are you going to join me?' she said gently, indicating the table.

The man looked puzzled.

'For the picnic?' she pointed towards the basket he was carrying.

'You want me to?' he said thickly. 'I have food in the car.'

Rebecca shook her head. 'No, please, eat with me.' She looked up at his great muscular bulk and unnerving Slavic features and wondered what had brought him and Leo together. 'How long have you worked for Mr de Viton?' she said conversationally.

He shrugged. 'Not answer questions,' he said. 'My English is not so good. I drive.' He nodded towards the car. 'I'm a very good driver.'

As he spoke he watched Rebecca uncross her legs. She blushed, she hadn't intended to encourage him; she was just curious. He looked away quickly as if embarrassed at being caught looking. He meandered slowly back to the car to collect his own lunch. Watching him, she found it hard to reconcile his unease with the image of him crouched between her legs, nuzzling her sex like an eager puppy – a puppy keen to please his master.

She could almost feel Leo's strong arms around her waist, lifting her evening dress to expose her delicate secret places to his paid servant. She shuddered and turned her attention to the lunch that the man had unpacked for her. Perhaps it might be better if they didn't find a way to share their secrets.

It was late in the day when the car stopped again, turning slowly into a tree-lined avenue. In the distance Rebecca could just make out the lights of a house. She leant forward and opened the panel that divided her from the driver. 'Is Mr de Viton already here?' she asked, pointing towards the distant glow.

The man nodded. 'He drove himself down last night.'

With every passing mile, as the light faded, Rebecca had felt a growing sense of apprehension. Now that they had arrived she tried to quell the flutter of panic; had Leo decided to drive down after he had seen her with Callum?

She leant back in the comfortable leather seats, wondering what he had in store for her.

The chauffeur glanced over his shoulder and grinned. The effect on his brutal features was unnerving. Rebecca shivered, wondering what thoughts had amused him. Any feelings of having escaped from the city were rapidly disappearing as the car approached the dark silhouette of the house.

Close up the house was huge; a great colonial mansion flanked on either side by dark trees. The lights on the lower floor revealed wide, carefully tended lawns sweeping away into the darkness beyond. The car stopped, the only sound for a few second was the soft ticking of the hot engine. Rebecca swallowed nervously; they had arrived. There was no going back and no way out. The chauffeur climbed silently from the car and opened the door for her. Rebecca looked up at the dark lines of the huge house and felt a pulse of fear in her throat. Leo had called for her; she had obeyed. She didn't protest as the chauffeur helped her onto the gravel driveway.

Under an ornate portico the front doors swung open. Leo de Viton was waiting for her, framed by the door's heavy columns, his expression unreadable in the shadows.

'Good evening, Rebecca.' His voice was soft, almost tender. She walked towards him, while behind her the chauffeur removed the luggage from the boot. 'I'm so glad you could come,' Leo continued. She shivered; he made it sound as if she had been invited to a family party.

Inside, the hall reflected the same subdued luxury as his Manhattan apartment, a chandelier twinkled seductively above them, the walls were panelled from floor to ceiling in dark wood. From the centre of the hall a wide staircase curled up to a galleried landing above that surrounded all four walls. A liveried footman stepped forward to take Rebecca's coat, another to take the bags from the chauffeur.

Leo was dressed casually in cream linen trousers and a white shirt, a fair-isle sweater draped across his broad shoulders. He lifted a hand in invitation, oblivious to Rebecca's Berdys uniform. 'Perhaps you'd like to join me in the living room. I have arranged for my chef to prepare some supper. I hope you won't mind the informality.'

Rebecca followed him into an elegant but comfortable room and perched uneasily on the edge of a sofa near the fire. When they had gone to dinner together at Antonio's she had been struck by how gentlemanly Leo could seem. The social graces appeared to come naturally to him, but she knew from his reminiscences in the club where Carina sang that he must have learnt them; taught how to behave by an older woman grooming him for wealth and pleasure.

She noticed with a start that he was looking at her, as if expecting some kind of answer and realised with surprise that he had been speaking. 'I'm so sorry,' she said softly. 'I'm afraid I didn't hear what you were saying.'

He shrugged philosophically. 'Perhaps you were thinking about last night? Who was the handsome young man who was with you? Another lover?' He pulled a rueful face. 'Tut, tut, Rebecca, I would have thought you'd have realised that at the moment you are mine exclusively.'

Rebecca reddened. 'Exclusively?' she stuttered. 'What about the night down on the wharf? Or Carina?' She glanced back over her shoulder towards the open doors. 'Even your chauffeur and footman.'

Leo laughed. 'My choices though, my dear.' He stepped away from the hearth towards her, eyes darkening with sudden unnerving coldness. 'That's why I invited you here.

You're going to pay for your little misdemeanour.' She shivered. Noting her anxiety he smiled. 'But nothing too severe. I promise you it will just open another possibility in that growing repertoire of yours. Would you like me to tell you what I have in mind?'

'What?' The word was out before Rebecca had time to consider the implications.

Leo smiled, stroking his finger across her cheek. 'When I've had my supper you will follow me upstairs. I have a room there, a special room that I had designed to teach the girls who disobey me what it means, truly means, to be obedient.' He crouched down beside her on the sofa and took her wrist between his fingers. 'I will tie your pretty little body up. And you will let me do it, because you know you deserve to be punished.' He stopped and pressed her wrist to his lips, letting his tongue curl out a spiral of wet heat on the sensitive skin beneath her palm.

Rebecca felt dizzy; the heat of the room seemed oppressive. Between her legs she felt a tiny pulse of light; a white hot flash that told her that she would enjoy whatever it was Leo had to offer. The anticipation, the knowing, made her feel light-headed. She licked her lips. 'And then?'

Leo pushed himself back up to his feet. 'And then I will be able to do what I like with you.'

She looked away knowing her eyes betrayed the excitement she felt.

'I will ensure you are less eager to cheat on me again. Now tell me – who was your lover?'

Rebecca glanced at the fireplace, logs roared and crackled in the wide grate. For an instant the smell and the glow reminded her of England – and strangely enough of Oliver Cresswell. If it hadn't been for him she would never have come to New York, never have met Callum or Leo.

She glanced up at Leo who was waiting for his reply. 'Callum,' she said softly, 'Callum O'Neill. I met him on the voyage over here.'

While she spoke a servant arrived with a tray of food. Leo waved the man towards a small table behind the sofa and nodded at Rebecca. 'I want you to tell me about him. Is he the artist who drew the portrait of you?'

Rebecca nodded. 'He went to Greenwich Village with some of my art work and came back inspired himself. He thought I might be able to make a living by painting. I . . .' she stopped, wondering what else she wanted to say about Callum.

'Love him?' said Leo flatly. 'Is that your excuse?'

Rebecca shook her head, thinking about the uncomplicated friendship Callum had offered her, his kindness. 'No, he helped me when I was sailing over here. I was running away from a broken heart and he helped me to heal it.'

Leo snorted. 'I think I've heard enough. Take off your clothes.'

She looked up at him. 'But . . .' she protested. 'You said upstairs—'

His features hardened. 'Please don't disobey me, Rebecca. Stand up and take them off. Or perhaps you would prefer to leave now?' He glanced towards the open door.

She got up slowly and began to undo her blouse. Leo de Viton sat back in his chair and watched as she pushed it back off her shoulders, letting it fall to the floor. His eyes made her very self-conscious, he watched her coldly as if he had only a passing interest in what he was witnessing. She slid off her skirts, stockings, shoes – until finally she was naked amongst a heap of discarded clothes.

He nodded. 'Good, now pick those up and lay them on the stool and then you can bring me my supper.' She turned and went to the little side table to collect the tray, desperately aware of her nakedness.

'What do you want me to do?' she asked unsteadily.

Leo smiled thinly. 'Bring it here and be quiet. Silence is part of your punishment for the little tryst with your friend from New York.'

She swallowed nervously, but did as he said, kneeling close to the side of his chair.

'While you're here with me you will remain like this.' He ran his finger over her collarbone. 'And you'll be available for me – or anyone else – until I tell you otherwise. Do you understand?'

Rebecca nodded.

'Good.' He looked up again towards the doors of the room and smiled broadly. 'Ah, good evening, Isabella, my dear Judge Cranfield. I wondered where you'd got to. How was your walk?'

Rebecca flushed crimson and fought her first instincts to leap to her feet and run away. She glanced across the room; framed in the doorway Leo's wife stood arm in arm with a plump, red-faced man. Isabella de Viton caught Rebecca's eye and smiled icily. Quickly Rebecca looked away, her fingers tightening around the tray as Isabella and the judge stepped into the sitting room.

'Would you like me to pour you gentlemen a brandy to go with your supper?' said Isabella lightly. 'I know I'd like one, it's quite chilly out there tonight. How about you, Judge?'

Close behind her, Rebecca felt the judge take up his seat on the end of the sofa. He was so close she could smell the faint odour of cigars.

'Absolutely, need something to warm me up,' said the man heartily. His voice had a deep rich southern drawl. Rebecca stiffened as she felt his hands on her back, chilly hands, rough and invasive. She looked up at Leo in appeal and astonishment. He met her eyes fleetingly as the judge's hands slid round onto her breasts, cupping them and nipping at their peaks. Her nipples hardened instantly from the chill and from a subtle disturbing excitement of her wordless submission. Her hands trembled making the contents of the tray rattle. Leo took it from her, lay it on his own lap and began to eat, striking up a heated conversation with the judge about racehorses. Judge Cranfield seemed keen to talk, while his hands had free rein over Rebecca's breasts and torso.

Isabella came over towards the fire, carrying a tray of glasses and joined in the conversation as if Rebecca didn't exist. As the Judge spoke he ran his hands down slowly over Rebecca's body. Treating her like horseflesh, she thought as she fought to balance the strange mix of humiliation and elation. Her flesh tingled as he stroked her distractedly. She looked down at the floor afraid of what her face might betray to Leo.

It seemed an eternity before the conversation died and Leo lifted her chin. Rebecca realised with surprise that after a few minutes she'd stopped listening and hadn't heard a word of what they'd said. All her consciousness had been centred on the lazy stroking of her breasts by the judge. The wide circles had lulled her into a quiet sleepy trance. She looked up quickly.

'I've explained to my friend the judge that you require punishment,' Leo said.

Rebecca was about to protest when she remembered that Leo had forbidden her to speak. She nodded.

'Being a good friend he understands what's needed. Get up.' Stiffly Rebecca climbed to her feet. 'Now turn around, let my friend take a look at you. I'd value his opinion.'

Rebecca turned slowly, catching Isabella de Viton's interested expression out of the corner of her eye. The woman's undisguised desire made her flinch. By contrast the judge's expression was impassive, almost cold. He beckoned her closer to him and she dropped her gaze to the floor; he had looked at her with barely concealed boredom. He ran a hand up inside her thighs and slid a thick finger inside her sex; it was the finger of a man who couldn't care whether he touched her or not. He looked at Leo, addressing his comments not to her but to the man who commanded her; she might as well have been invisible.

'Nice and tight up there, maybe when you're done with her I can find her a place over at my place.' He looked Rebecca up and down, his finger still jammed tight up inside her. 'Nice little titties too.' He slipped his finger out and licked it. Rebecca blushed and then gasped as his fingers moved back further to the dark closure behind her sex. Coolly he pushed her legs apart, his mouth registering his disapproval at her reluctance to give him free access to her body. She shuddered as he stroked the forbidden puckering with detachment. 'Real tight,' he said unhappily. 'But it could change with a little tutoring, if you get my meaning.' He grinned lewdly at Leo. 'Surprised you ain't seen to that yourself.'

Leo lifted his hands. 'Well?'

Judge Cranfield sat back in his chair and looked her up and down. 'I prefer blondes, myself, Leo, but she ain't bad.'

Isabella got crossly to her feet. 'What is this, a horse sale? I thought you said you were going to punish her, Leo.'

Rebecca looked up at Isabella and was stunned to see the flash of delight in the other woman's eyes. 'You know how much I love to watch,' Isabella whispered creeping closer to Leo. Her face betrayed her lust. She dropped to her knees in front of him and lay her head in his lap. Casually he stroked his fingers back over her sleek dark hair and she rewarded him by running her tongue over her full lips, eyes dark and jewel bright. For an instant Rebecca glimpsed what it was that attracted Leo to her; Isabella was his equal. The two of them were a roaming pair of predators, relishing the extremes of human sexuality.

Judge Cranfield pushed himself to his feet. 'No, an' I ain't got all night either, Leo. Let's get on with this.'

Leo nodded and pushing Isabella aside got to his feet. He glanced at rebecca. 'Come with me,' he said, and without protest Rebecca fell into step behind him.

Chapter 6

The wooden floor was cold under her bare feet. Rebecca tried hard to control her breathing, concentrating on staying in control of her feelings. Leo and the judge had led her upstairs into an attic room bathed in moonlight. Isabella de Viton had followed close behind. Leo switched on the lights flooding the room with a subtle yellow glow. What Rebecca saw made her shiver. Leo held out his hands towards her. 'Come here,' he said in a voice barely above a whisper.

Before she could move Isabella snapped. 'No, Leo, let me do it.'

Judge Cranfield chuckled. 'I really wish I could find myself a good woman like you, Isabella. Here.' Rebecca watched as he handed Isabella two pairs of handcuffs.

The small dark woman snapped a single loop onto each of Rebecca's wrists and then lifted her eyes. They glowed coal-black, the pupils dilated with excitement. 'Do you know what they're going to do to you?' she purred.

Rebecca flinched, her mouth dry. The handcuffs twinkled in the lamp light, betraying the terror in her body. Leo took hold of her arm and guided her towards a huge metal circle set upright on the floor. Set in the circumference of the ring were metal loops. With practised hands Leo lifted her wrists above her head and snapped the

handcuffs into them. Rebecca let out a little mewl of terror.
Leo's expression momentarily softened and he pressed a
finger to her lips. At her feet the judge was applying ankle
restraints and locking them into the ring, pulling her legs
apart so that the small lengths of chain reached. Rebecca
whimpered; she was totally and utterly helpless.

Isabella stepped up into her line of sight, her features
alight and animated. She spoke to Leo. 'Now this—' she
said softly. From behind her Rebecca could hear Leo make
a small noise of approval and glanced down in terror at
what Isabella was holding. The woman laughed and moved
closer; between her fingers she held a leather harness. She
stroked a cool finger over Rebecca's throat, down onto the
curve of her breasts and moaned. 'I told you Leo and I had
no secrets between us,' she said. She cupped one of the
naked girl's breasts in her hands.

Rebecca cried out in fear as she felt something cold close
over her nipple and struggled to look down at the small
woman's fingers. Isabella was fitting a tiny clamp over the
delicate pink flesh. A second later Rebecca felt the cold
plate tightening sending red hot sparks of heat and pain
through her. She winced, horrified that beneath the pain
was a raw backwash of pleasure.

Isabella peered up into her eyes and smiled. 'We're not
so different you and I, except that I have Leo and intend to
keep him,' she whispered as she attached the second
clamp.

Rebecca bit her lips, tasting the coppery flavour of
blood. The two tiny clamps were joined by a fine chain to
the leather harness that fitted around her lower body. With
knowing fingers Isabella buckled the harness around
Rebecca's waist and this, her fingers stroking and exploring
as she did so.

Every time Rebecca twisted away from the dark woman's touch, the movement was echoed by a bittersweet tightening as the clamps closed over her nipples. She whimpered, tears filing her eyes. Finally Isabella stepped back to admire her handiwork. 'There,' she said triumphantly and looked past Rebecca to the two men.

Leo de Viton opened the cabinet by the door and removed a leather paddle on a wooden handle. It wouldn't break the skin but sting white-hot, driving the recipient wild with pain and pleasure. He glanced at the judge. Now that Rebecca could no longer see Cranfield's face the old man's impassiveness had vanished. His heavy features were flushed in anticipation of what was to follow. He slipped off his jacket and rolled up his shirt-sleeves, taking the paddle from Leo's hands. 'All mine?' he grunted thickly.

Leo nodded and stepped back while the red-necked judge weighed the paddle in his hands. Isabella circled Rebecca like a wild cat. Leo smiled and opened another cabinet to pour himself a scotch. His wife's skin glowed, her tongue running over her lips as she watched the girl fight helplessly against the restraints. He could sense the instant when the clamps bit, as he was sure Isabella could. When he had first met her he had made her made her wear them all the time to ensure she understood the meaning of obedience. He sipped his drink as the judge rolled back the head of the paddle and prepared himself for his first strike.

The girl hadn't anticipated the first blow, it bit hard into the full rise of her buttocks. She screamed out and bucked forward instinctively, exposing the soft inner folds of her sex, the clamps biting furiously at her flushed nipples. The judge looked at Leo and grinned, bringing the paddle down again. The crack of the leather against her naked skin was followed a second later by Rebecca's throaty shriek. A livid red flush lifted on her body as the paddle hit home again and again, making her call out, writhing deliciously against her restraints. After ten strokes the judge stopped, panting, his tongue hanging out. He looked at Leo, a question in his expression.

Leo drained his glass. 'Be my guest,' he murmured and the old man hurriedly shed his clothes. Isabella stepped up in front of Rebecca Hunt and dropped to her knees, catching hold of the thin leather harness. Leo moved closer to watch his wife's fingers splaying the girl's sex open and plunge her tongue inside. Behind, the judge stepped closer. Rebecca was panting, trying to find a comfortable position in the metal restraints and harness. A glittering bead of sweat dropped from her chin.

Rebecca, eyes tight closed, tried to grab hold of her mind and keep it from splintering under the barrage of sensations. She gasped as she felt the invasive press of a tongue in her sex, and sharp fingers spreading her wide. The muscles in her arms and legs trembled from the strain of hanging inside the circle. Her breath came in tight bubbling gasps, burning up through her lungs, while a great glowing raw-red arc spread out across her back and buttocks from the attention of the paddle.

The first blow had been like an explosion, threatening to drive away all reason. She had screamed out in fear, shock, pain and something else – something that drove her on like an electric and dark addiction that could not be denied. She felt a strange wild pleasure in her submission. Giving herself completely to Leo, his wife and the judge had given her a bizarre sense of elation. Chained she was free to enjoy whatever they showed her.

Rebecca opened her eyes a little, peering out under tear-stained lashes. The tongue of Isabella de Viton was amplifying the hot glittering sensations of pleasure glowing in her stomach. She felt the brush of something cool against her back and realised an instant later it was another person, the slightest hint of cigar smoke told her who it was. The judge caught hold of her waist, dragging her back towards him. Tiny starbursts of heat erupted in her mind as the nipple clamps bit into her flesh. Cranfield fought to find a way into her, fingers prising her open. His cold belly rubbed furiously against her glowing, red flesh as his cock pressed home. She shuddered, feeling her wetness closing around him in a tight excited grip.

Rebecca imagined Isabella de Viton's tongue finding him there, lapping at his thick phallus where their bodies met.

'Come to me, girl,' he muttered thickly as he plunged deeper, pulling her back again and again against his cool slick belly. Between her legs, Isabella de Viton's mouth closed over the ridges and folds of her quim, sucking her in, while her tongue moved lower, teasing at the junction where Rebecca's body met Cranfield's.

The image and sensations were too much; they rose like a sheet of white light inside Rebecca's mind. Almost before she realised what was happening she started to moan and buck, riding the great coursing plume of pleasure and pain that roared through her exhausted body.

The judge mewled in alarm as he felt the heat and the tightness drowning his self control and jerked her back hard. Deep inside Rebecca felt his cock pulsating as his own orgasm hit them and finally there was stillness. The only sound was the frantic panting breaths of the players.

Leo stepped up to Rebecca and unlocked her handcuffs, catching hold of her before she stumbled. He looked into her eyes and smiled. 'Your punishment,' he said flatly.

Rebecca shuddered, her body and mind still reeling from

the pleasure she felt. 'Yes,' she whispered breathlessly.

Leo de Viton grinned, stroking her face. 'I knew you would enjoy it,' and closed his lips over hers.

Rebecca let out a little shuddering gasp of delight and returned his kiss.

It was late when Leo de Viton's limousine drew up opposite Callum's apartment block. Callum O'Neill was sitting at his desk working and glanced out of the window. He saw Rebecca climb out and the man getting her bags from the boot. He bit his pencil furiously, unable to reconcile the anger and jealousy he felt.

A few minutes later he heard the key in the lock and hunched over his typewriter. He'd pretend he was so busy he hadn't heard her arrive home. He tapped frenziedly at the keys; the truth was that since Wednesday morning he'd done very little except think about Rebecca. He glanced guiltily at Oliver Cresswell's letter standing up against his in-tray. He had finally resorted to steaming it open – it seemed Oliver was madly in love with Rebecca too and, frankly, who could blame him?

'Callum?' Rebecca's voice reached across the room to him. He sat up slowly, stretching, pretending he had other things on his mind beside her return. 'Hi, how was your trip?' His heart fluttered as he turned towards her, she looked even more beautiful and more desirable than he remembered.

Rebecca stood her suitcase down on the floor. 'All right,' she said guardedly. 'Did you miss me?' His expression gave her all the answers she needed.

Her body still ached from the days spent in Leo's mansion. That first night in the attic she had learnt finally, that for her, passion, pleasure, pain and submission went hand in hand. She had staggered down from the metal hoop in the attic, feeling dizzy and exhausted. Leo had pushed her down onto the floor and made love to her, his wife watching whilst sipping a drink and talking to the judge as if they had been taking afternoon tea. And then Isabella had stood her glass down on the table and slipped off her dress. Slowly, with the grace of a ballet dancer, she had pushed Leo up on to his knees, lowering her creamy white body down onto Rebecca's face. Isabella's fingers had opened her own sex for Rebecca's tongue, while she had slipped her other hand through the links of the harness, tightening the clamps on Rebecca's nipples.

In the apartment Rebecca smiled unsteadily across at Callum, wondering if her eyes betrayed the satisfaction, the elation and the dark secrets her mind held. His eyes travelled up and down over her body. 'New dress?'

'Yes,' Rebecca smiled. 'Leo had Sarah Leinneman pack me a case.' She didn't mention this was the first time she had been anything other than naked since she had been driven to Leo's mansion.

Callum lifted his eyebrows. 'Oh, that was real kind of him.'

Rebecca couldn't bear the disapproval and hurt in Callum's voice. She glanced toward the kitchen. 'Would you like me to make us some coffee?'

Callum shrugged. 'All the same to me.' He picked up Oliver's letter from his desk. 'Oh, by the way. I wasn't going to own up but I steamed this open. Seems the man in your life – or should I say the other man in you life – thinks he made a great mistake and wants you back.' He turned the envelope over in his fingers. 'Says he loves you more than anything else on earth and begs you to reconsider going home to him.'

Rebecca stormed across the room and snatched the letter out of his hand. 'It's very rude to read other people's mail.'

Callum grabbed her, sliding his hands up inside her skirt, his fingers easing across the mound of her sex. 'Very rude to fuck other people's women too.'

Rebecca pulled herself away, reddening and not just at his coarseness. His fingers remained, sliding between her legs to explore her.

'What do you mean? I'm not your woman.'

Callum shrugged. 'Exactly, but I'm assuming Mr de Viton assumed you're his, or am I wrong? How does he feel about his new little slave girl playing house with a hack?'

Rebecca looked down at him, wondering how Callum would feel if he realised her trip to Long Island had been about just that. She shook her head, sliding herself away from his caresses. 'Do you want that coffee?'

Callum groaned softly. 'I want you more.' He stood up quickly and caught hold of her hips, turning her face down against the desk. The breath rushed out of her as he pushed her onto the paper strewn surface. 'Christ, I've been thinking about this ever since you left,' he grunted.

She tried to pull away, more through instinct than genuine fear. Her struggles seemed to excite him more. 'Callum, please, it doesn't have to be like this—' she squealed as he jerked up her skirt to expose the full curves of her backside.

'It's all right,' he said thickly. 'I won't hurt you. Or would you like it better if I did . . .'

The way he pinned her down excited her. Leo de Viton was responsible for these feelings, she thought wildly, as Callum forced her legs apart and he dragged her back towards him. She could feel the wetness and heat gathering between her legs and struggled against him. He had no intention of letting her get away and she knew that she had no intention of denying him what he wanted. He ripped her knickers aside, the fabric bit into her skin making her shriek and writhe under him.

No foreplay, no touching – he jerked down his trousers and plunged his raging angry erection inside her. Instinctively she arched up to meet him. Behind her he called out with a mixture of anger and delight, as her wetness engulfed him. Locking one hand tight in her hair he pulled her up into an erotic bow, while his other hand raked over her breasts. He snorted and bucked, taking her, using her – and she knew that she loved every second of it – the realisation stunned her, as deep inside she felt Callum's passion building. Leo de Viton had lit a dark fire in her body and Callum O'Neill was warming himself in its molten compulsive core.

When he had finished he rolled her over, his face still contorted with a mixture of anger, jealousy and wild passion. Roughly, he pushed her legs open and closed his mouth over her wet pulsating quim. 'There,' he said, looking up at her in the seconds before his tongue plunged into her again. 'This is what you've been missing.'

Rebecca gasped and then surrendered to him, letting him take her out towards oblivion.

It was much later when Callum finally got up to make them coffee. Rebecca lay on the sofa, her sex sore and bruised from Callum's desperate brutal lovemaking. He had taken her over and over again, his passion seemingly renewed rather then exhausted with every wild fight towards orgasm. She looked at him, picked out by the light from the kitchen. 'Why did you do that?' she said softly, pulling a blanket over herself.

He looked at her and grinned. 'You didn't like it?'

Rebecca groaned, her body still glowed from the pleasure. 'I didn't say that, did I?'

Callum leant against the door frame. 'The little green-eyed god perhaps. Maybe I wanted to claim you back from that bastard de Viton.'

Rebecca looked at him steadily. 'I like what he does to me.'

Callum groaned. 'Look, why don't you pack your job in at Berdys? Live here with me. Paint. If you want, I'll marry you. I want you.'

Rebecca pulled herself up onto her elbows. 'No, you don't, Callum. You want to stop Leo de Viton having me and that's different. Oh, and by the way, I've been sketching while I was there.'

Callum snorted. 'What, in between getting screwed by a row of able seamen? Come off it.'

Rebecca slid off the couch. 'Leo was there on business as well as pleasure.' Crouching on the floor she pulled her suitcase nearer. Inside on top of the clothes was a large sheet of card.

Callum, carrying the tray of coffee, crouched down beside her. 'Jesus, that's amazing.' He stood the coffee down and took the sketch into the light.

Set against a wild mystical landscape, was a tall man, his limbs and hair entwined and joined with ivy and vines, his muscular body not quite landscape not quite flesh. Callum let out a long low whistle. 'This is incredible.' He grinned, recognising his own features on the wild man's face. 'What did your friend think, you drawing the opposition?'

Rebecca closed her case, avoiding Callum's eyes. Leo had returned when she had been sitting in his study. She had been naked except for the harness, sitting in front of the fire, waiting for the words that would bring her to him for whatever pleasure he desired from her. He had taken the sheet from her fingers and smiled darkly. 'So this is how you see your lover, is it? A faun. A satyr.' He lifted his eyes to meet hers. 'You have it wrong, Rebecca, I'm the satyr not him. Get on your hands and knees.' She had crept towards him, eyes alight in an act of submission. 'Take me in your mouth,' he'd said. She had knelt up, undone his flies and taken him in front of the roaring fire. Sucked him dry while he held Callum's picture. When she was done he had lain the sketch down on the desk. 'My friend Judge Cranfield will be joining us for lunch, make sure you do whatever he asks. I need to ensure he is kept happy.'

Rebecca had nodded, the taste of Leo's excitement still on her lips.

Rebecca watched Callum O'Neill admiring the sketch; if only he knew the pleasure she had received in return for her submission.

Rebecca woke late on Sunday morning. She opened her eyes slowly, screwing them up against the bright sunlight. Her whole body ached. She looked around licking her lips. She had ended up in Callum's bed for one last round of passion. Groaning she pushed herself slowly to her feet as Callum appeared at the bedroom door holding an envelope. His expression was icy. 'Seems you have a little message from your friend de Viton, a messenger just delivered this.' He threw the letter onto the bed and hurried back out into the sitting-room.

Rebecca snorted and then called after him. 'What, did you decide not to steam this one open, then?'

Callum re-appeared as she was tearing it open. 'I don't

want to read anything de Viton might write but I was curious about Oliver. I think he is really in love with you—'

A key dropped out of the envelope amongst the crumpled sheets. Rebecca retrieved it and read the note. 'Leo's offering me the use of a studio and opened an account for me at Henleys the art store, "to encourage your talent", he says here.'

From the doorway Callum let out a sharp barking sound of disapproval. 'Jesus—'

Rebecca looked up at him. 'But I thought you wanted me to paint,' she said obliquely.

Callum leapt across the room and grabbed her shoulders. 'I wanted you to paint to be free of that man, not let him set you up in some cosy little artist's garret. You're being bought, Rebecca, and don't pretend you don't know that. You'll end up like Carina, de Viton's pet night-club singer, permanently at his beck and call.'

Rebecca disentangled herself from Callum's grasp and sat on the bed. 'Stop it. I haven't accepted, have I? I do know what Leo is doing.' She tucked the key back inside the envelope and lay it beside the bed. 'But I would like to paint again.'

'Well, then do it here, or let me take you down to Geno's studio. He said he'd let you rent a space at his place. You can tell de Viton to go to hell.'

Rebecca leant over, picked up one of Callum's shirts off the floor and pulled it on. 'I won't have the chance to say anything to him for at least a week. He's got to fly upstate for a business meeting.'

Callum smiled grimly. 'Good, I hope he decides not to come back. Maybe he'll find something else up there that takes his mind off you. If you're serious about wanting to paint again I can take you over to see Geno this afternoon.'

Rebecca frowned. 'What's wrong with this morning?'

Callum slid across the bed, fingers moving under her shirt. 'I've got other plans for this morning. God, you look wonderful.' He pulled her closer and she giggled.

Rebecca pushed her hands back through her hair and stood back to admire her work. The picture on the easel, created in water-colour, was a larger version of the sketch she had drawn at Leo's country mansion. Since Leo had gone upstate her days were simple and satisfying. She worked at Berdys during the day, taking the subway out to Geno Amerti's studio when she'd finished so she could paint in the evenings under the lights he'd set up to let him carry on when the natural light began to fade. It had been over a week since Leo had left on business – and as quickly as he had appeared in her life he seemed to have vanished and forgotten her. His absence left a rawness that she couldn't begin to describe. Callum came over to pick her up around eleven and they would walk, arm in arm, back to his apartment. A night owl by nature Callum would have supper ready and they would talk, share a bottle of wine and make long lazy love until Rebecca fell exhausted into his bed.

Geno, taking a break from his own canvas, came over to look at her work and nodded with approval. 'That's good, have you ever thought about using oils?'

Rebecca laughed. 'No, I've never really tried. Besides my work is too immediate – don't they take six months to dry?'

Geno nodded. 'A long time, it wouldn't be the first time I'd sent something out still tacky.' He stepped back and looked at Rebecca's painting again. 'Have you ever thought about illustration? I've got a friend over at Courts, the publishing company, who's always on the look-out for new illustrators.'

Rebecca shrugged. 'It's never been much more than a hobby, I'm hopelessly rusty. I just can't quite get it right yet, but it'll come.'

Geno grinned. 'Always chasing the perfect technique? I know how it feels, but don't be so hard on yourself, this is very good.' He paused. 'Could I let my friend see this?'

As he spoke the door to the studio opened and Callum came in, wrapped up against the chill of the night air. He peered at them over the top of his scarf. 'Hi, are you ready, Rebecca?'

She nodded and began to collect her things together. Geno pointed towards the easel. 'I was saying I'd like to take this over to Courts, if Rebecca will let me.'

Callum nodded. 'Good idea.' He looked at Rebecca, his usually warm eyes were steely.

She looked at him with surprise. 'What is it? Are you all right?'

Callum pulled an envelope out of his coat pocket with gloved fingers. 'It looks like your friend is back in town.'

As Rebecca stepped forward to take the envelope she saw the look that passed between Callum and Geno. She scanned the contents. 'He won't be back until the end of next week.' She looked at Callum. 'He'd like us both to join him for supper when he gets home.'

Geno snorted. 'Into the lion's den?'

'Will you accept?' said Rebecca, watching Callum's face.

Callum nodded. 'Of course,' he said bluffly. 'I want to see what it is you see in the man.' He caught hold of her round the waist, making her shriek with delight. 'And then I'll know exactly how to get the better of him.'

By the evening of their dinner date Callum's mood had hardened into a sullen thoughtful silence. As Rebecca slipped on one of the evening dresses that Sarah Leinneman had packed for her to go to Leo's Long Island retreat Callum prowled around miserably, fiddling with his dress tie. Rebecca turned round crossly; his bad mood was contagious. 'You don't have to come,' she snapped. 'I can always go on my own.'

Callum snorted. 'Yeh, well, of course, why not? God knows how long it will be before I see you again once you disappear into his clutches. Hasn't it been good between us without him around? He picks you up and drops you when it suits him. No, I'm going with you, but there's no law on earth that says I have to enjoy it.'

The doorbell rang. Rebecca looked up at the clock. 'He's early.'

Callum grimaced and stalked across to open the door. As the door swung open Geno Amerti sprung into the room, eyes alight and glittering. 'I've come straight over here from Courts, the publishers.' He grinned and leapt forward to embrace Rebecca. 'I took your painting up to the art director. He wants to buy it!' The words came out in a wild breathless jumble. 'He wants to see you, as soon as possible, bring anything else you've done. He's just commissioned a book and thinks your art-work would be perfect for it.' Geno whooped, almost as if it had been him that had had the success. Rebecca stood back in stunned silence. She had never assumed that Geno's enquiry would come to anything – nor really, that her art-work was that special – obviously she had been wrong.

Geno, still grinning madly, pulled a bottle of wine out of his coat pocket. 'We'll celebrate and I'll tell you everything he said.' Callum grinned and went in hunt of glasses and a cork screw. Rebecca glanced up at the clock – half an hour and Leo de Viton's car would be arriving to take them to dinner.

'So,' said Callum reappearing from the kitchen, 'how much? How many paintings? What's the book about?'

Geno held up his hands in protest. 'I don't know, it won't be a fortune but it's a great start. Get you a name.' He looked at Rebecca. 'You don't look pleased. What's the matter?'

'I'm shocked, I can't really take it in. It was my painting you took, wasn't it?'

Geno threw back his head and roared with laughter. 'So modest! Yes, it was most definitely yours, I'm so envious. I've been trying to get some of my work in with him for months.'

Callum grinned and uncorked the wine. 'Don't worry, I'll see you get a broker's fee, Geno. Here, have a glass of wine.'

Rebecca turned and went back into the bedroom. Callum called after her. 'Where are you going? Aren't you going to celebrate your success?'

Rebecca paused mid-stride. 'I am really pleased, thank you, Geno, but we've got a dinner date in half an hour, or have you forgotten, Callum?'

Callum's black mood returned, eyes clouding over. 'How could I forget,' he said bleakly. 'I thought we could have a glass of wine with Geno first.' He held her gaze steadily. 'Geno might be the one who helps me get you out from Leo de Viton's honeyed trap.'

Rebecca sighed. 'All right, let me just finish doing my hair. I won't be a minute.'

An hour later the limousine slowed to a halt outside Leo de Viton's apartment. Callum had been silent for the entire journey, eyes firmly fixed on the back of the chauffeur's head. Rebecca looked out of the windows wondering whether it had been madness to bring Callum with her. He and Geno had finished off the bottle of wine between them, Callum had already been brooding and miserable before he'd started to drink. In the street light his handsome features were set and angry, dark eyes flashing. She realised he was coming with the idea that somehow he could find a way to rescue her from Leo de Viton. How could she tell him that, far from being rescued, she wanted more of what Leo had to offer her, that his dark sexual dominance excited her beyond words.

Even though she had been more than content to live with Callum whilst Leo was away she was sharply aware that she was only waiting for his return. When Leo called she would come to him without question – the knowledge lit the tiny spark of desire insider her. She wanted Leo to command her.

The chauffeur opened the door and a footman came out to accompany them inside. Rebecca watched Callum appraising the interior with cool detachment. Inside the elevator she could see the tight throb of a pulse in Callum's throat as they glided noiselessly up to meet Leo de Viton.

'Ah, good evening,' Leo greeted them enthusiastically, as they stepped out into the hallway. He smiled at Callum, taking his hand and shaking it firmly. 'You must be Mr O'Neill, Rebecca has told me so much about you.' Callum was so surprised by Leo's cordial greeting that he could barely manage to return the compliment. Leo took hold of Rebecca's hands kissing her on each cheek, lingering just a second longer than was necessary. 'I've really missed you,' he said pleasantly. His expression made Rebecca's heart flutter.

From the double doors that led into the dining room Isabella de Viton walked towards them, smiling, and allowed herself to be introduced. Rebecca was impressed by their warmth; no-one looking at the introductions could possibly guess the tensions that bubbled just below the surface. Leo guided them into a small sitting room, where a uniformed man served them aperitifs and Leo embarked on a heated conversation with Callum about the freedom of the press.

The cocktails were large, the conversation stimulating and Rebecca realised after a little while that Callum had let his guard drop – he was actually enjoying the banter. Leo baited him mercilessly, asked him about his book, his column and Callum matched him blow for blow. Isabella de Viton caught Rebecca's eye and smiled, waving the servant to bring them all another drink.

It was nearly an hour later when they finally went into the dining room. The large table had been substituted by a smaller oval one, still as elaborately decked, but more intimate for a small dinner party. As the footmen cleared away the final course of a superb meal Leo looked up at Callum, who sitting opposite him. 'She is good, isn't she?' he said softly, lifting his glass in salute to Rebecca.

Callum, relaxed from good wine and the excellent food, flushed. 'I'm sorry, what did you say?'

Leo looked across at Rebecca who was staring down the table unable to believe what he had said. 'You know, Mr O'Neill, I've barely thought about anything else since I left New York. I assume you've been helping yourself to what is mine—' He paused. Rebecca glanced up and felt his cool eyes appraising her thoughtfully. 'Though I can understand the temptation,' Leo continued, refilling his wine glass. 'In your position I would have done the same thing.'

Callum folded his napkin back onto the table, his expression betraying his growing annoyance. 'Helping myself to what is yours?' he said coldly. 'I think you ought to know that Rebecca can make up her own mind.' He took a crumpled envelope from his pocket and threw it on the table. Rebecca recognised it as the one that had contained the key to the studio Leo had offered her. 'She doesn't need your help. Since you've been away she's found a place of her own to paint and been commissioned to illustrate a book.'

Leo smiled broadly. 'How wonderful, I'm delighted for you, Rebecca—' he glanced over his shoulder at the footman. 'Bring us some champagne – we must make this into a celebration. Well done, my dear.'

Rebecca looked up into Leo's eyes, his expression made her stomach contract – she could see the desire and the hunger within them. Leo turned to Callum. 'Did she tell you I'd had her beaten for sleeping with you?' His tone was light, almost conversational. Rebecca thought Callum was going to choke, as Leo continued. 'She enjoyed it, you would have liked to have seen it.' He closed his eyes as if conjuring up the memory. 'I had her chained, naked, the sweat glistening on her back. She writhes so deliciously, doesn't she? When I'd done she gave herself to me – and my wife – opening herself, begging me to take her. She was so wet . . .' He stared evenly at Callum as if encouraging him to say something .

Rebecca looked back desperately at Callum, praying he wouldn't leap up and attack Leo. To her astonishment she could see, mixed with the fury in his face, a flicker of lust – a bright spark of desire. He envied Leo de Viton's power over her. She shivered. Callum picked up his wine glass, bluffing his way forward. 'She is good,' he said, his voice betraying a flicker of emotion, knuckles white where they gripped the glass. 'I'll give you that.'

Leo smiled, leaning back in his chair, 'Perhaps we should share her? Would you like that, Mr O'Neill? How about now, on the table? She could take me in her mouth and you from behind.' Leo moaned appreciatively. 'What a tempting prospect. Her tight little body closing around us both, a delightful thought, wouldn't you say? How would you feel about that, Mr O'Neill, would that be to your taste?' Leo glanced briefly at Rebecca. 'All I would have to do is tell her, she does as I ask.' He lifted her hands. 'Stand up, Rebecca, let Mr O'Neill see what I mean.'

Without hesitation, her pulse racing, Rebecca stood up.

Leo de Viton nodded with approval. 'Good, good, I thought perhaps my absence might make you forget that I like to be obeyed. Now take off your dress.'

Across the table Callum swallowed hard, his eyes moving between Leo and Rebecca.

Rebecca lifted her fingers to the zip and let the frock fall to the floor, beneath she was naked except for a tiny pair of pants. She could see the look of need in both men's faces. Their mutual desire touched her like a warming summer breath. The candlelight on the table danced shadows across her breasts. Leo smiled. 'I've thought of her body all the time I've been away.' He glanced at Isabella. 'Clear the table for Mr O'Neill and myself. I assume he is prepared to accept my invitation.'

Callum said nothing, though Rebecca could see the pulse throbbing madly in his throat. Isabella slid the candelabra off the dining table plunging the diners into shadow. The tension hung in the air. Callum's eyes didn't drop. Leo looked at Rebecca. 'If you would like to take your place, my dear. Mr O'Neill and I are ready for you.'

Trembling Rebecca climbed onto the table, Isabella's flashing eyes caught hers as she knelt on all fours, facing

Leo. He stood up slowly while behind her she heard the crash of Callum's chair hitting the floor.

Leo, ignoring the noise, mounted the table. 'Now, my dear,' he said softly. She lifted her fingers to undo his flies. Her hands shook. Beside her, Isabella let out a soft throaty groan and stepped forward to help, her tiny fingers freeing the dark raging bulk of Leo de Viton's cock. Rebecca felt the soft brush of Callum's hands on her hips dragging aside the fabric of her knickers. A second later his fingers opened her and he pressed his cock into the warm confines of her sex. He moved slowly, as if relishing the progress of his body inside hers. His finger moved between her legs, searching out her pleasure bud. Groaning softly she leant forward. Cradling Leo's phallus in her hands she guided him into her mouth.

From the instant they began to move Rebecca was caught up in the wild unlikely passion. Callum pushed deeper, his hands holding her hips as if his life depended on it. His cock seemed to fill her to the brim, ripping and thrusting madly as if he could barely contain the desire he felt. Leo moved against Rebecca's tongue and lips, one hand locked in her hair whilst the other dropped to the back of her neck. Isabella watched them intently, her own eyes flashing with excitement.

Callum stared deep into de Viton's eyes, unable to believe what was happening – how had it come to this? Was it some mad scheme to prove he was as reckless and obsessed as his rival? Rebecca's sex gripped at him, driving away all reason, as his thighs pounded against her. Beneath him she moaned, the sound trickling out from around de Viton's cock. The image sent an electric thrill through him. She dipped her belly to allow him to slide deeper. The sensation left him totally centred on the hot tightness that engulfed him. He could feel the sweat lifting on his face and shoulders as he struggled to hold back the great waves of pleasure that fired through him. De Viton had thrown back his head, letting Rebecca service him with her mouth. De Viton was right in one thing; she was good, so very, very good that Callum was afraid he would lose her. He could feel her moving against his fingers, her wetness and the soft moaning betraying her growing excitement.

Beside the table Isabella watched the coupling with barely disguised pleasure. Callum swallowed hard as the woman turned her attentions to him, her eyes flashing wildly. She moved around him lazily. Callum, caught up in the intense wild dance toward his climax could sense her, see her, feel her moving around him with deliberate steps, every nerve ending alight, but couldn't turn to watch her progress.

Suddenly he felt a cool hand slide between his legs, cool fingers cupping his scrotum. The lightest pressure on the throbbing root of his cock was enough to pitch him over the edge. He was oblivious now to where Rebecca was on the spiral of pleasure – all there was was the hot intensity of his orgasm pulsing and roaring through his body. He let out a wild desperate scream as he pressed home into Rebecca's slick sex, Isabella's fingers trapped between his body and Rebecca's. One more ragged thrust and he felt Rebecca's sex contracting around him, sucking him dry, tearing away the vestiges of control.

Leo de Viton, as if he had felt the white hot pulse roll through the two of them, bayed wildly and crashed headlong towards his own release. Finally, exhausted, the two men collapsed down onto the object of their mutual desire, their breathing coming in raw feverish gasps.

Isabella de Viton slipped her hand out from between Callum's trembling thighs and got coffee, whilst the two men rearranged their clothes, only Rebecca remained on the table, shivering from the after-effects of their excitement. Callum looked at her, suddenly filled with an intense feeling of love and compassion. Rapidly recovering his composure, he looked at Leo de Viton. 'I want you to leave Rebecca alone,' he said slowly. 'I'm taking her home with me. You're using her. It's over—'

To his surprise Leo de Viton roared with laughter. 'Oh really, how astounding. Here we are, Mr O'Neill, both exhausted from taking our pleasure with her. Wouldn't you have said we are both using her? She's hardly some stupid ignorant savage, she knows what she wants and I can give it to her.' He let his fingers stroke along the crouching girl's naked spine. 'With me Rebecca will have everything she needs. I will provide her with everything she could possibly desire.' His eyes darkened. 'Every want, every desire for our mutual pleasure. I only invited you here out of curiosity and now that's satisfied I don't think there is any point in us meeting again. Now, would you care for some coffee before you leave?'

Callum was stunned and furious. 'I'm dismissed, am I? I'm not one of your goddamned lackeys, de Viton. Rebecca, get dressed you're coming with me.'

Rebecca didn't move.

Callum stood for a few seconds, the tension building in his gut.

Leo de Viton smiled lazily. 'I think you have your answer, Mr O'Neill.'

Callum clenched his fists, the tension spiralling into a white hot fury, he took a step towards Leo but before he could strike Rebecca caught his arm. 'It's all right,' she said sleepily, as if she were waking from a dream. 'Please, Callum. I'm all right, really.'

Helplessly Callum let his hands drop to his sides. What could he do if the woman he wanted to rescue refused to be freed? Geno Armeti had said as much in his studio. The bluster fell away to be replaced by feeling of confusion. He turned to look at Leo. 'I'm not staying here,' he snapped.

Leo de Viton lifted his hands. 'I'm not keeping you here, Mr O'Neill, nor am I keeping Rebecca.'

Callum looked at Rebecca, her eyes glittered with passion, her body still hot from their lovemaking. She didn't move, but her eyes met his in silent appeal. Callum turned and walked slowly from the room feeling as if his whole life had been ripped into tatters. 'You won't win,' he hissed at Leo, as he reached the door.

Leo de Viton smiled lazily. 'Oh, I think I already have, Mr O'Neill,' he said coldly.

Chapter 7

Leo de Viton turned towards Rebecca, who was still crouched on the dining table. He lifted her face towards him with a single finger. 'So, that's your friend, is it, Rebecca? Your Satyr? Your faun? Your wild man of the woods?'

Rebecca swallowed hard, she had been so certain she was doing the right thing but now with Callum gone, a sense of isolation and nervousness returned. She nodded dumbly, afraid that her voice might betray her fears.

Leo smiled thinly. 'And of course you slept with him whilst I was away? I can see the temptation.'

Rebecca bit her lip; it was pointless to deny it. Leo extended a hand towards her and helped her down off the table. 'You realise, of course I have to punish your misdemeanour. What a shame the judge isn't staying with us. You know, you fascinated him. He told me that he would be glad to make room for you on his ranch. He was very insistent.' Leo let his fingers move across her breasts, nipping at the peaks. 'He values obedience as highly as I do.' His expression hardened. 'Go to the cabinet beside the fireplace and bring me what you find inside.'

Rebecca felt a pulse of fear. 'But I've already said I'd stay with you—' she protested looking towards the closed dining-room doors. 'I could have gone with Callum.'

Leo nodded, 'But you didn't, and by staying you agreed to accept what I had planned for you. Now, don't make me tell you again.'

Swallowing hard, Rebecca opened the cabinet; inside was a long-handled whip with a soft tasselled end. It felt cold under her fingertips. She glanced nervously over her shoulder at Leo, beside him Isabella nodded. Leo made a noise of approval. 'Go and find my chauffeur. He will punish you for me.'

Rebecca reddened and began to protect. 'But, Leo, I can't.' An unnerving image of the man's brutal Slavonic features filled her mind.

Leo de Viton held up hand to silence her. 'Do it now, I want you to ask him to use the whip on you, then we will put the little matter of Mr O'Neill behind us.'

Rebecca padded slowly into the corridor outside the sitting-room and the dining room. Through the open doors she could sense Leo's eyes on her. She felt sick, her nakedness and vulnerability adding to her overwhelming sense of apprehension. The huge apartment was dark and silent. She glanced at the elevator; only a few minutes before she had sent away the one man who was prepared to rescue her.

At the far end of the corridor was a green baize door, she opened it cautiously. Beyond was a landing and stairs leading up and down to what she assumed must be the servants quarters. The cold air struck her, lifting goosebumps on her skin. Up or down? She stood for a few seconds wondering what to do. Finally she went down, fingers closed around the long handle of the whip. As she got to the landing below a distinctive shadow moved up the wall below her. She swallowed hard and fought the instinct to flee; this was part of Leo's game, a game that she had agreed to play. A little flare of excitement rose in her belly. She had chosen to obey him.

The chauffeur climbed the steps towards her slowly, shoulders slumped forward. She wondered if Leo had summoned him from wherever it was he lurked – he still had on his uniform trousers but above he was in shirt-sleeves, sleeves rolled back to reveal strong muscular arms. She shivered almost unable to speak, suddenly remembering the picnic on the way to Long Island and the chauffeur's self-conscious almost shy behaviour. He obeyed Leo de Viton too. He looked up when he sensed her there. She held out the whip towards him in both hands. Her fingers were trembling, making the split end of the whip quiver uncontrollable. 'Leo says I have to be punished,' she said in a tiny voice.

The man nodded and took the whip from her. 'Come with me,' he said thickly and turned. She followed him back down the stairs. The cold air and the anticipation made her shiver. The next landing opened up onto a wide storage area. Boxes and shelves lined every wall. The man turned towards her. 'You want me to do this?' he said, nodding towards the whip. Rebecca hesitated, she hadn't expected to be asked. The man ran his fingers along the fine leather and then looked at her. 'I have to know this is what you want.'

'Leo said . . .' she began.

The man shook his head. 'No, you have to tell me this is what you want, nothing to do with Leo de Viton.'

Rebecca nodded. 'Yes,' she said unsteadily, watching the light as it picked out the grooves and tooling of the whip. She wanted to feel it on her naked back, wanted to cry out as the man used it to punish her. She shivered, wondering where these desperate thoughts had hidden themselves before Leo de Viton had freed them.

As if he could read her mind the chauffeur ran his fingers across her face. 'You want to feel this on your body,' he said. His eyes flickered menacingly. 'And the things I will do to you when it is done?'

'Yes,' she hissed unsteadily and knew, in spite of her apprehension, that it was true.

He stepped forward and extended one great paw. 'Then give me your hands.' He pulled a rope from the top of one of the crates and tied her hands together at the wrists. She closed her eyes, feeling the bite of the rope against her tender skin. He pulled her towards the centre of the room; below the single bare bulb was a metal hook. She shuddered, remembering the night in Edith Hartman's flat when Arnie had taken her upstairs into his studio, then she had been a novice. Was it something in her face that betrayed the direction of her desires? Had Arnie seen something that told him she would be excited by his rough dominant passion? If so, then Sarah Leinneman and Leo had recognised the same thing.

Above her, her wrists chaffed, arms calling out in protest as they took her weight. The chauffeur moved around her slowly, lengthening the ropes a little so that the balls of her feet rested on the floor.

She had assumed Leo would want to witness her act of obedience, that he and Isabella would join them, but all she could hear in the dark store room was the snorting rasp of the chauffeur's breath and the wild thumping of her own heart. She closed her eyes, as the heat rose from low down in her stomach she heard the head of the whip cut through the still air.

The first cracking, stinging touch of the tasselled end made her scream. Unlike the kiss of the paddle the pain was concentrated, driving away everything but the line of fire across her buttocks. She flailed forward, red hot tears coursing down her face. 'Please, please,' she sobbed, not knowing whether she was begging the chauffeur to continue or stop. The next blow was higher, white lightening striking across her spine. She bucked away, twisting on the rope to try and avoid the next bite of the whip's head. Too late she realised by turning, the whip would hit her flank, lifting a livid weal across the delicate flesh around her hips. The strokes now came in a flurry, high and low, she screamed out again and again, every conscious thought centred on the hot insistent bite of the whip and more disturbingly the pleasure that glowed inside her.

The adrenaline coursing through her body lit great fires of desire, twisting and plaiting around her sense of fear and humiliation. After seven strokes, counted somewhere in the rational distant part of her mind, the man stopped. For an instant she couldn't believe it was over and held herself ready and taut for the next blow. He moved closer; she could smell him, warm and hot, the undisguised smell of his male body. His hands lifted to her breasts, great pawing strokes that tore at her skin. He bit into her shoulder, making her jerk back against him. He whispered something to her in his own tongue, while his fingers snaked low and over her belly, seeking out the pit of her sex. Her mind screamed out as his shirt rubbed against the livid weals on her back.

'I have you now,' he murmured. 'They can't see us down here. You're mine.'

Rebecca shivered, as the man's fingers pressed into her, dipping, smearing the wetness of her excitement and Callum's out onto her thighs. The slick juices cooled quickly in the night air. Against her shoulders the man mumbled noises of pleasure, dipping into her again and again. His lips and tongue worked across her back and neck. She knew she was sopping wet and could sense the chauffeur's growing excitement – soon he wouldn't be able to hold back, he would take her. She imagined feeling his cock pressed up inside her body, imagined his rough shirt pressing against the raw contours of her back and shuddered. His finger dipped lower, tracing a line across the delicate bridge of flesh that divided her moist fragrant sex from the darker forbidden opening behind. She froze as she felt one of his thick fingers stroke at the tight band of muscles. 'No,' she whispered on a fearful outward breath. His reply was a soft grunt as his other hand looped around her, rubbing a callused thumb over the sensitive hood of her clitoris.

She let off a soft wail of pleasure as he moved back and forth across it. Despite her fears she began to move with him still aware of the presence of his finger on the tight bud of her anus. She could feel her excitement building; the kiss of the whip, the sense of excitement that came from being tied and seeking out her punishment – the dark surrender kindled the fire inside her. She knew that the man's rough caress would bring her to orgasm while still behind, between her rounded glowing buttocks, the single finger worked sliding her juices back, seeking entry. She tried hard to resist him, tried hard to control the growing spiral of pleasure that would give him entry to whatever part of her body he desired. She could feel her body responding to his intimate caress inspite of the protest of her rational mind. The fingers of his other hand worked feverishly, bringing her so close to release that she thought she would faint. Just as the first white hot waves gathered under his thumb where it moved against her clitoris she felt her body opening to him; the dark closure drawing him in.

She gasped in horror as he moaned and pressed his finger home. The sensation startled her, the tight throbbing depths of her body closed eagerly around him. It was enough to drive away the last vestiges of reason. Suddenly her climax crashed over her in wild electric waves. Behind her the man grunted in satisfaction, pressing home his fingers into both orifices again and again. She sobbed, leaning back against him. Even amongst the waves of delight she was astounded that her rogue body could betray her with such bizarre dark pleasures.

She hung against the ropes as the last ripples of pleasure ebbed away, leaving her shaking and breathless. Slowly the chauffeur drew out his fingers, leaving her feeling raw and empty. Now, she thought, he would let her down and she would go back upstairs to Leo, the punishment complete.

She heard him moving away and opened her eyes. Between her legs her sex glowed, dripping with excitement and pleasure. She sighed and then a second later froze as she felt the chauffeur's hand slide between her legs, back to the dark rose bud of her anus, still glowing from his attentions. His touch was cool and slick, his fingers working something oily into the delicate puckering.

'I won't hurt you,' he purred in his thick accent. 'Don't fight me.'

She heard his zip sliding down and let out a dark unhappy cry as she sensed what was to follow. His breath roared red-hot against her shoulders and she felt the press of his cock against the tight opening behind her sex. 'No,' she whimpered again, but knew that her protest wouldn't be heard. Slowly her rogue body opened for him, his progress was almost imperceivably slow, at odds with his brutal appearance. She snapped her eyes tight shut, trying to close out the image of him filling her from behind. The oily lubricant trickled down her thighs to mingle with the juices of her pleasure. She called out as he finally pressed himself home inside her – shocked by the intense sensations his violation lit inside her. The tightness drove the breath out of her. 'Oh my God,' she snorted as he began to move, fingers snaking round her so they slid up to fill her sex. Deep inside she could feel her excitement rekindling and finally she relinquished all control and fear, letting her body lead her back into the red roaring bonfire of pleasure and pain.

When Rebecca finally climbed the stairs back to Leo de Viton's apartment she was trembling. Her whole body, every nerve ending, every fibre was raw and exhausted. In the dining room Leo watched her return with dark glittering eyes and took the whip from her shaking fingers. He turned her gently, looking at the livid weals on her back and the one which snaked low across her flank. She couldn't find any words and didn't protest when Isabella wrapped her in a bathrobe and guided her towards the fire. Leo handed her a brandy and sat opposite her.

After a few minutes she finally found her voice and stared into Leo's eyes. 'How can you be like this?' she said, her voice thick with emotion as she lifted the brandy balloon in his direction. 'One minute you send me to be – to be . . .' She paused, collecting the words together inside her mind. 'To be buggered and beaten by your chauffeur, the next you wrap me up like an invalid and comfort me with drink.'

Leo smiled lazily. 'It's a just game, Rebecca. Surely you know we are playing a game, you and I? A sensual electric game. There is no compulsion, no malice, only pleasure.'

He paused and glanced at Isabella, who was standing beside him. 'We are all explorers, searching out new frontiers of ecstasy. Don't tell me that what you've discovered doesn't excite you?'

Rebecca stared into the grate. 'I'm not sure, my body tells me it's pleasure, my mind isn't so sure.'

Leo nodded. 'We hurt no-one.' He paused. 'Will you let me find you an apartment? I would like to provide for you.' His voice was soft and compelling.

Rebecca laughed, and looked up into his eyes. 'You mean keep me close at hand like Carina down at the nightclub?' The singer had wanted them to stay; she spent all her time waiting for Leo's call. Leo shrugged wordlessly, Rebecca knew there was no way she could spend her life waiting, however tempting the reward. He constantly confronted her with a choice – now she was going to take it.

Leo shrugged. 'If that's how you see it.'

Rebecca got up slowly and picked her dress up from where some-one had folded it over the back of a chair. 'I'm not sure whether I like all the things I've discovered about myself, Leo. I think I'd like to leave now.'

Leo lifted his hands. 'You're free to go whenever you want, but reconsider my offer of help.' He paused. 'Will you go back to Callum's apartment?'

Rebecca shook her head. 'No, I don't think so, not tonight. Maybe not at all. I'll go to Edith's. I need time to think, perhaps Callum is right, perhaps it is time for all this to end.'

'I'll call my chauffeur to take you home.'

Rebecca shook her head again. 'No, I'll call a cab.' She dropped the bathrobe to the floor and slipped on the evening dress, oblivious of her nakedness.

Isabella stepped forward. 'Before you go, even if you won't let Leo help you, will you consider coming out to Long Island again with us? We are having a party next weekend. Think of it as one final wonderful expedition into pleasure – at least wait until it's over until you decide whether you truly want to turn down what Leo is offering you.'

Rebecca suddenly felt immeasurably tired. 'May I think about it?'

Isabella nodded. 'Of course. I'll go and arrange a taxi for you.'

Rebecca waited alone with Leo in the elegant apartment. He studied her face with gentle curiosity and then finally spoke. 'You are a remarkable woman, Rebecca, think carefully before you disentangle yourself from me. I could make you very happy.'

Rebecca smiled lazily. 'I know, Leo, that's the most awful thing about it. It would be so easy to just lay back and accept the tempting things that come with your promises – but I would never be free, would I? I would always be yours to command, to control, to drop if I bored or displeased you. I'm not sure, for all the excitement you can offer, that I want to be that vulnerable. I came to New York to begin again; to be free of another man's expectations of me—'

Leo shrugged. 'All right, but think about Isabella's invitation. It will be a masked ball for our friends. In fact we have guests coming over this week from England. Isabella's parties are becoming world famous,' he laughed. 'She is planning a living exhibition for our guests to view and used by those we invite.' He moved closer to her, stroking her lips. 'Imagine that, my dearest, chained up for someone else's pleasure. It would be so good . . .'

Rebecca shivered and moved away. 'Let me think about

it,' she repeated softly, grateful when Isabella came back into the room to say the cab was on its way.

Rebecca rang Edith Hartman at the first phone booth she came to and was relieved when her friend said she could stay overnight without asking any questions.

Less than an hour later the taxi drew up in front of the familiar apartment block in Greenwich Village. Upstairs on the second floor a light burnt in the window of Edith's flat. Climbing the steps Rebecca remembered her arrival just a few weeks before; it seemed as if that was a lifetime ago now and as if she had been a different person.

Edith opened the door in her dressing-gown, her face betraying her concern. 'Hello, are you all right?'

Rebecca nodded. 'Yes.'

Edith looked her up and down and shook her head. 'I'll put the kettle on. Arnie's got a driving job over the weekend, so I'm here all on my own.' She struck a match. 'Have you had a tiff with Callum? I didn't like to ask over the phone. He seems such a nice chap.'

Rebecca sat down in the one comfortable armchair and stared out at the night and the lights of the city. 'You could say that,' she said softly, thinking about the way she had turned him down. It might have been better if she had gone with him.

Edith pulled up a chair from the kitchen table. 'You can stay here as long as you like. You know, Arnie really missed you. Things haven't been the same between us since you left.'

Rebecca sighed. By coming back to Edith's she had jumped out of one frying pan into another. She smiled at her friend. 'That's really kind but if I could just stay tonight.'

Edith nodded. 'Whatever you like. Oh, by the way, I

meant to bring this over to you. It arrived a couple of days ago.' She got to her feet and took a letter from the mantelpiece. Rebecca's heart sank; it was an airmail envelope with English stamps, it had to be from Oliver. She turned it over in her fingers for a few seconds before ripping it open. It would save Callum the trouble of steaming it open, she thought wickedly, as she read the contents. The first few words made her freeze. She looked up at Edith. 'What's the date today?'

'Friday, the seventeenth, why?'

'Oliver is on his way to New York. He says he's going to arrive on Monday the twentieth. He wants to see me face to face. Oh, my God.' She paused, her mind racing. 'I've got to get away from New York.'

Edith looked puzzled. 'But why? Surely you can just tell him it's over – once and for all.'

Rebecca bit her lip. In her mind she could see Oliver Cresswell's handsome features, his broad shoulders as he made his way through the crowd from the troopship towards her. She still loved him; the realisation hit her like a body blow. The man she had run away from was the man she truly wanted, but how could she face him now? Her mind ran through the possibilities, there was only one solution. She looked at Edith. 'May I use your phone?'

Edith nodded. 'Of course, you know where it is.'

With trembling hands Rebecca lifted the receiver and rang Leo de Viton's number. When it was answered on the second ring she said quietly. 'This is Rebecca, I've considered your invitation to the party on Long Island next weekend.' Her statement was greeted by silence, she bit her lip and continued unsteadily. 'I wondered if I could go down there tomorrow. I really have to get out of New York.'

Leo de Viton's cool electric voice answered, 'Of course, my dear. I'll send my chauffeur around for you first thing tomorrow morning.'

Early the following afternoon Callum O'Neill was in his apartment trying to work on his novel. Notes and sheets of paper lay in disarray across his desk. He looked at the words he had typed fighting with his imagination to keep the image of Rebecca Hunt at bay. When he had arrived home the night before he'd blotted out the confusion and the pain with whisky. The after-effects still lingered inside his head; a dull miserable headache that did nothing to improve his mood. He glanced down into the street below, half expecting to see the sleek lines of Leo de Viton's limousine pull up outside.

'This is bloody ridiculous,' he snapped aloud. 'Jesus, she decided to stay with him. Her choice, free choice.'

The words did nothing to relieve the sense of fury and confusion he felt. He couldn't believe he'd agreed to make love to Rebecca with Leo de Viton and his wife in attendance, even so the memory was a compelling and erotic image burnt on his mind. He looked around; the apartment was littered with reminders of Rebecca's presence. Finally he picked up the phone; he would ring her, reassure himself that everything was all right and then ask her if she wanted him to take her things over to Leo's. He had to face the fact that it was over. He pulled a face as he looked for the number; it was a feeble excuse but it was the best he had.

It took him five minutes to find the number and twenty seconds to be informed that Rebecca wasn't there. He picked up his coat and headed over to Edith Hartman's' apartment – apparently, the cool voice at the end of the phone had informed him – she had gone to Edith's the night before.

Edith sighed as she let Callum in. 'Rebecca's not here. She left first thing this morning,' she said flatly, glancing over her shoulder into the empty apartment. 'Have you two had a row?'

Callum held up his hands in desperation. 'Not exactly. Have you got any idea where she might have gone?'

Edith invited him inside with a wave of her hand. 'When she got here last night she seemed, all right, well, a bit upset – I thought she might tell me why she'd rung, but she didn't say very much. Then I gave her the letter I had here from Oliver Cresswell. He was her fiancé, you know.' Edith paused, 'He's on his way to New York, he's arriving on Monday.'

Callum paused, wondering what Oliver's arrival had to do with Rebecca running away, but then again she had come to New York to escape Oliver in the first place. He nodded encouragingly. 'And then what did she do?'

Edith pointed towards the phone, 'She rang someone, I'm not sure who it was, something to do with a party on Long Island next weekend. She asked if she could go and stay down there for the week.'

Callum nodded; the only person Rebecca knew with a house on Long Island was Leo de Viton. He thanked Edith, and then went off to the offices of the *New York Argus* who published his weekly column. He had no doubt that someone at the *Argus* would be able to tell him whereabouts on Long Island Leo de Viton had his mansion.

Rebecca ate her supper in front of a roaring fire in the elegant study of Leo de Viton's mansion. The house was

silent though she knew that somewhere in its depths a bevy
of servants were preparing for Leo's arrival later in the
week. One of the footmen had already shown her to a
beautiful bedroom over looking the extensive gardens. In
the closet a collection of outfits hung ready for her use.
Rebecca hadn't asked where they had come from, she knew
she wasn't the first woman to spend time under Leo's roof.

Alone, she felt calm and free – able to get some distance
on the events of the last few weeks. Looking around the
beautiful room she wondered if it would be so easy to walk
away from Leo. He could offer her so much, though an
inner voice told her he would also demand a great deal in
return.

She needed time to think about Oliver Cresswell; she
certainly wasn't ready to see him until she'd decided what
to say. How could she begin to tell him what had happened
since she'd arrived in New York? And if she didn't tell him,
and he wanted back her as badly as his letter suggested,
could she live with the deceit? Would it be possible to walk
away from what she'd learnt under Leo's eager tutelage and
become another man's wife? A wife, she suspected, that
Oliver wanted to be as untouched and unsullied as the
driven snow. She shivered inspite of the roaring fire. She
could never be that woman again, if he truly wanted her he
would have to accept her as she was. She would stay at
Leo's for the week and then after Isabella's party go back
to New York and have it out, once and for all, with Oliver.

Finally there was Callum. Callum who wanted to rescue
her for himself but at the same time had been drawn
willingly into Leo de Viton's erotic web of pleasure. She
could still imagine him straining to fill her whilst Leo had
pressed his cock between her waiting lips. The feeling of
having the two men inside her had lit an indescribable

feeling in her belly. How had life become so complicated?

A liveried servant brought in a tray of coffee and liqueurs. Rebecca thanked him and then sat by the hearth, watching the fire until the flames faded and died – her mind full of the images of the men in her life and the complications and delights they brought with them.

On the dark road that led to Leo de Viton's mansion, Callum O'Neill was at the wheel of his friend, Geno Amerti's, ancient and eccentric pick-up truck watching the autumn landscape roll past. On the passenger seat he had a road map and the address of the mansion, kindly found for him by a girl on the back desk at the *Argus*. The one thought that kept him going was the fact that he was convinced Rebecca was running away from Oliver Cresswell and not into the arms of Leo de Viton – if that had been the case she would have stayed in New York. He would find her.

He grinned to himself as he wrestled with the huge steering wheel; Geno's truck wasn't exactly the white charger he had in mind but then again, any port in a storm. Away to his right was the road that would take him down to the coast and the select environs of the Hamptons; the area where everyone who was anyone had a summer home.

Checking his mirror he turned the car, wondering if he might be better to sleep a little and make the last stretch of the journey in the cold light of morning. He shrugged; maybe in the morning the trip wouldn't make so much sense. He hit the gas – it wasn't that far now.

Chapter 8

Rebecca hadn't realised Leo's house was so close to the sea. Out beyond the boundary walls, through a stand of wind-blown pines, was a great sweep of golden sand. It was mid-morning. Dressed casually in slacks and a jacket she'd found in the closet, Rebecca headed towards the out-of-season surf, watching the stiff breeze lick the breakers into plumes of foam.

'Morning, how'ya doing?' A familiar voice followed her on the wind.

She jumped with surprise and then swung round. 'Callum? How did you know where to find me? What on earth are you doing here?'

Callum O'Neill grinned and stepped out from under the shelter of the pines. He hadn't shaved and his clothes looked as if he'd slept in them. He bent sharply in a sweeping mockery of a bow. 'I'm beginning to ask myself the same question. I suppose I'd got some strange notion that if I turned up here you'd beg to be rescued, let me take you away from all this.' He extended his arms in a broad sweep to encompass the beautiful scenery and the majestic lines of Leo's distant mansion.

Rebecca giggled. 'I'm really flattered but you needn't have worried. I've already decided that I have to break off the relationship with Leo. Leo de Viton isn't the reason I came to Long Island.'

Callum nodded. 'I heard. Edith told me that Oliver is due in tomorrow. What are you doing here? Running away or taking the time to work up a strategy to see him off once and for all?'

Rebecca laughed. 'I only wish to God I knew, maybe a bit of both.'

Callum took hold of her hand. 'Why don't you just come back to New York with me? I'd fight off all the bad guys, Leo, Oliver, just point me in the right direction. I'm deadly serious.'

Rebecca let him pull her closer, his arms encircling her waist. Their lips were just a fraction of a moment apart when she moaned softly and pulled back. 'No, Callum, please. Stop it. I really need to think. I've told Leo I'd stay down here and go to their party on Friday night.'

'And then?'

Rebecca shrugged, falling into step beside him. 'Back to New York to talk things through with Oliver.' Her voice faltered over the words.

Callum looked at her. 'Why do you sound so unsure? I thought all that was cut and dried.'

She nodded miserably, stuffing her hands into her jacket pockets. 'So did I, but I've been thinking.'

Callum stopped to pick up a pebble and flicked it out across the waves. 'Bad move, thinking only ever makes things worse.'

He was right, thought Rebecca, watching as he skimmed another across the surf. It sank with a resounding plop.

There was nothing she could do to unravel things that had happened since she'd sailed for New York. And besides, a furious little voice snapped inside her head, why should she? She had no doubt Oliver had . . . she stopped, what had Oliver done? He had understood what her body needed when they'd made love on the train, though that now seemed like a distant memory. The way he had touched her, she knew it hadn't been his first time and she hadn't really considered for an instant that it might be. She had assumed he would be more experienced. It made his reaction even more infuriating, except . . . she had seen the pain in his eyes and the love, almost drowned out by his stunned surprise. If only they could have talked then. If only she had waited – a string of 'if onlys' filled her mind and a tight unhappy knot of grief formed in her throat. Tears pressed up in her eyes. There was no way to undo what had been done.

Beside her Callum was whistling. He looked up and grinned. 'I'd marry you,' he said conversationally as another stone skipped and hopped across the water.

She laughed, pushing back the sense of pain. 'Thanks, but no thanks, I'm on the run from one proposal. I don't think I could handle another one right now. If this publisher is keen to take my pictures, then maybe I'll set up on my own. Work at Berdys until I've got a little bit of cash behind me—'

Callum lifted an eyebrow. 'Stay within easy reach of Leo de Viton.'

Rebecca shook her head. 'No, this party really is the last of it. He wants too much from his women.'

Callum looked her up and down. 'So you've conceded that you'd just be another veil in his harem?'

'I've just said I'm not going to stay with him. Do you need it in writing?' She stared out over the grey sea. Her voice sounded firm and resolute but in her heart she suspected that Leo might prove to be too much of a temptation to abandon completely. She turned back to Callum. 'I can't expect you to stay around until I've made up my mind what I'm going to do.'

Callum turned round so that he was facing her, walking with his back to the wind, 'Who me? Well, actually I've been thinking about taking a holiday.' He gazed around the windswept beach. 'There's no way I could afford to visit a place like this in the summer on my wages. I think I'll just find myself a place to stay – at least for this week. I could do with a break.'

Rebecca tutted him wryly. 'Until after Friday?'

Callum grinned. 'Yeh, why not? Maybe you'd like a lift back to the city once the party is over. I used to spend a lot of time up here when I was a kid, my dad's got a place over on the far side of the bay.' He pointed into the distance around the far sweep of the coastline.

Rebecca smiled. 'Oh, of course. I'd forgotten your daddy has a shipping line, so maybe you won't be in a hotel but tucked up in a cosy mansion.'

Callum snorted and looked down at his dishevelled appearance. 'The way I look they'd never let me in. Anyway his place will shut up for the season.' Suddenly he spun round and grabbed hold of her shoulders, his expression deadly serious. 'Why don't you come back with me, for real, today, now – I think I'm falling in love with you.'

Rebecca backed away. 'Please, Callum, don't do this to me. I don't think I can cope with it.'

Callum flinched. 'Do this to you? What about me? But, if that's the way you really feel—' he said quickly. He turned away to hide his expression, Rebecca wished she could see what was in his eyes. 'I'll be back down here on the beach, same time tomorrow,' he said over his shoulder, the wind carrying his voice to her. 'I'll see you then, okay?'

Before she could call her reply he jogged back in amongst the pines and she couldn't bring herself to run after him.

* * *

At the dockside in New York, George Winterton peered along the quay while Oliver Cresswell found a porter. He glanced down at his pocket watch. 'Said they'd sent a car,' he announced flatly, as Oliver re-appeared followed by a uniformed man.

'We could get a cab.'

George shook his head. 'No need, old chap. I'm sure the car will be here, never known Leo to let me down before.'

As he spoke a tall Slavic man in a lovat-green uniform made his way towards them. He tipped his cap as he approached. 'Mr Winterton?'

George nodded. 'Absolutely.'

The man bowed slightly from the waist. 'If you'd like to come this way, Mr de Viton's car is waiting for you.'

'So what's this friend of yours like?' said Oliver once they were comfortably installed in the back seat of Leo de Viton's limousine.

George sucked his lips thoughtfully, 'Odd ball really. Very influential, owns a lot of property, very shrewd business man, came up the hard way, though you'd never guess it when you meet him.' He snorted, undoing the buttons of his overcoat. 'He married well, back in the twenties to a society heiress. Old money with an eye for a bit of rough. She was a funny stick, his first wife. Got through the depression because she didn't trust banks, everything she owned had been turned into objects, things; gold, diamonds, property, cars, real estate, farms. Her last investment was in Leo and it paid dividends. She married him when she was in her forties and he wasn't much out of his teens. Dead now of course, shame really, they broke the mould when they made her. Met him in London years ago at Sophie's'.

Oliver looked confused. 'The whorehouse in London?'

George chuckled. 'Don't look so shocked, Oliver. She was a woman of diverse tastes. She liked to watch her trained stud at work – I think she realised she couldn't quell Leo's taste for flesh of his own generation so she encouraged it, but only on her terms. Leo's second wife's a corker too.' He grinned and rubbed his hands together. 'He bought her in a street market from her pimp and turned the tables, gave her what his first wife gave him. Money, position. Whatever your tastes Leo de Viton can fulfil them.'

Oliver reddened. 'I've come to New York to find Rebecca,' he said hastily.

George grinned. 'Well, of course, my boy, but there's no need to miss out on *all* the local delicacies. We've been invited to one of Isabella's infamous parties on Friday night.'

'Isabella?'

'Leo's second wife, she's a real stunner. And while I'm here I'm going to take a visit to Leo's place down on Long Island. Bought it for a song apparently and done it up.' He glanced across at Oliver who looked decidedly uncomfortable. 'But there's no need for you to come with me, old chap. You stay and sort out this nonsense with Rebecca, I'm quite capable of amusing myself.'

Oliver nodded. 'Maybe if we do talk this thing through I could take Rebecca to Isabella's party?'

George threw back his head and laughed. 'I wouldn't if I were you, old chap. Not that sort of do, if you get my drift.' He tapped his nose conspiratorially. 'Not that sort of do at all.'

In Leo's Long Island mansion Rebecca sat in the study and

watched the clock tick past the minutes; Oliver's ship would have docked by now. Her stomach was turning over and over – Oliver Cresswell was now in New York. She had rung Edith Hartman the night before and begged her to tell Oliver nothing. Edith had agreed, although she had protested that she knew very little anyway. Rebecca had asked her to tell Oliver to meet him at Edith's the following Monday. By then she hoped to have sorted out the confusion that threatened to engulf her. Meanwhile the clock tick, tick, ticked away the time since Oliver's ship had docked.

'Excuse me, miss.' A uniformed servant appeared in the doorway. 'There is a gentleman to see you.'

Rebecca felt her colour drain, surely Oliver hadn't arrived early. How had he found her so quickly? Before she could take it in she heard Callum O'Neill's familiar voice in the hallway and sighed with relief. Callum stalked into the study turning his hat between his fingers. 'I thought you and I had a date to meet on the beach this morning? I've been hanging around for nearly an hour,' he said crossly.

Rebecca uncurled herself from the *chaise*. 'I'm so sorry, I was thinking about something else and I'd completely forgotten—'

Callum looked wounded and grabbed theatrically at his chest. 'Oh my God,' he moaned, grinning. 'Instantly forgettable, I don't think I'll ever live it down.'

Rebecca laughed. 'Pull yourself together and let's have some tea. We can go for a walk afterwards.' She smiled at the footman who viewed Callum's dishevelled appearance with evident distaste. 'May we have a tray of tea?'

The man pulled his face into a moué of displeasure, but nodded and vanished back into the house. Callum sidled closer, eyes alight. 'God, you look so gorgeous. I've been thinking about you all night. I'd imagined us rolling naked in the surf together, breakers crashing over us—'

Rebecca laughed again and gazed out of the window at the stormy grey sky. 'We'd die of exposure, you fool. Get closer to the fire, you look frozen.'

Callum obediently dropped to his haunches in front of the hearth and stretched out his fingers towards the roaring log fire. He smiled. 'You know you look so right in this place, I'd like to paint you here.'

'In Leo's study?' she said incredulously.

Callum nodded. 'That's right. Against all the dark wood panelling, naked, laid across his cherry leather *chaise*.' He paused. 'You would look beautiful. I can see it now. Will you let me do it?'

Rebecca couldn't disguise her astonishment. 'What? Are you totally mad? This is someone else's house, you're not invited. I've got no idea what Leo will say if he finds out you've been here, let alone paint me in the nude—'

Callum lifted his hands in mock surrender. 'Does it matter? He'd probably be over the moon, all the more reason to punish you.' He crept closer, nuzzling against her thighs. 'Did he really beat you?'

Rebecca nodded. Callum's eyes flashed with something she couldn't put a name to; the confusing cocktail of shock and excitement that she felt herself. His fingers lifted, parting her thighs, sliding ever closer to her sex. She shivered, torn between telling him to stop and the desire to feel him touch her again. 'And did you like it?' he purred mischievously.

She nodded, afraid of the words. She glanced toward the door as Callum's finger slid dangerously over the outside of her panties, one finger stroking the delicate division of the outer lips. 'Stop it,' she said without conviction. 'The tea will be here in a minute,' she added quickly, thinking about the expression of distaste on the servant's face.

Callum groaned softly, lifting her skirt and pressing his face to her belly. She could feel the heat of his breath through the thin fabric, heating and cooling by turns. Her pulse began to throb – his desire electrified her. She moaned softly. 'Please, Callum,' she whispered, 'Leo's footman will be back in a minute . . .'

Callum's voice echoed against her belly, lazy and absorbed. 'You really think he'd notice?' he said softly, his lips brushing the sensitive flesh. 'I'd imagine our friend de Viton pays them damned well for their silence. Ummm, you smell delicious, wouldn't you like me to just slip my fingers up into you, let my tongue glide across those beautiful wet places—'

Rebecca shivered, the soft glow of desire flickering and dancing in her belly. His fingers slid under the fabric as she heard the footsteps of the servant bringing the tea. She jerked away, her face flushed and glowing.

Callum grinned up at her as the man crossed the room and lay a tea tray on one of the side tables. If the man had seen anything his face didn't betray it. He glanced in her direction, 'Will there be anything else, miss?' he said softly. Rebecca shook her head but couldn't help noticing a slight edge to his tone.

As soon as the servant had left Callum sprang to his feet and went over to the desk that dominated the centre of the room.

'What are you doing?' snapped Rebecca incredulously as he began to try the drawers.

'He must have pencils and some paper here, somewhere. I thought I'd draw you now.' He looked back at her. 'Why don't you take off your clothes while I take a look?'

Rebecca rolled her eyes heavenwards. 'For goodness sake, Callum, you can't be serious – you're crazy. Leave the desk alone.'

Callum pulled a face. 'It's locked anyway.' He stepped towards her. 'But I don't really care. I'll come back tomorrow morning and draw you then and I won't take no for an answer.' His eyes were darkening rapidly and she sensed that his thoughts had turned from fun to something more enticing. 'Now I just want you—' he whispered huskily.

She stepped away from him, feeling a tiny thrill of expectancy. She shook her head but they both knew it was a lie. He touched the pearl buttons on the front of her dress, fingers sliding under them, teasing them open. She stiffened, aware of the open door to the hallway and how foolish this was. The only sound in the room was their breathing and the soft hiss of the fire as his lips pressed to hers.

'I'm going to have you here,' Callum said in an undertone, 'across Leo de Viton's desk. Right in the heart of his damned kingdom.' His other hand snaked down over her thigh, pulling up the material to reveal her stocking-tops. His touch seemed to burn into her skin. 'And that uniformed lackey is going to come running to see what the fuss is about; I'm going to make you yell out so loud . . .'

Rebecca felt like a hunted rabbit; she had never seen Callum look so fierce, so intent. He pushed her back towards the desk, spreading her legs with his feet as he forced her down. Now his hands were rough, ripping at her dress, a tiny peal button pearl button exploded away from its stitching and ricocheted across the room. 'You like it rough, don't you?' he hissed, sliding his hands up over her chest inside the top of her dress, 'Well, in that case I'm your man.' His hands tore apart the thin material of her bra.

She let out a little squeal and stared up at him. 'Callum, this is complete madness,' she said breathlessly, trying to regain some sense of control. He snorted, his familiar features hardened, as if the desperate desire had changed him in the course of a few seconds into a total stranger.

She whimpered knowing it was pointless to resist and as she did the fire in her stomach roared with a white-hot flame. She felt him ripping away her pants, exposing her. He hunched across her body like a wild animal, his hands seemed to be everywhere, his mouth a split second behind them. He sucked at her breasts, teeth nipping at the swollen dark peaks, opening her legs wider with his hands.

His wild, raw desire was electric, she could feel the pulse of it throbbing in her own body – a stunning, reckless compulsion. She reached up and jerked his jacket back off his shoulders, suddenly alight and as needy as him, her lips meeting his in a frenzy of hot aggressive kisses. She dragged at him, rolling back and forth under his weight, ripping at his shirt buttons, wrapping her fingers into his hair. He moaned and closed his lips around her nipple, sucking it into his mouth, milking her, drinking her dry. Between her legs his fingers ripped at her dress, frenzied, desperate caresses that threatened to shred the fabric.

'I'm going to make you beg me for more,' he roared suddenly. 'I'm going to make you think you're dying.' His fingers plunged into her, fighting the wreckage of her underwear as he sought entry. She rolled away from him; she wouldn't be denied his body and fought to undress him, wriggling away from his rough caresses. The insanity of what they were doing was lost as she felt a great wave of excitement filling her. Her body trembled with anticipation as he momentarily let go to throw off his jacket and his shirt, fingers dropping to undo his flies. For an instant they were both still and he looked down at her. She could almost see through his eyes as he drank in the details of her body. She was laying back across the leather top of the desk, dress torn open at the bodice to reveal the curve of her breasts, the hem dragged up around her waist exposing her open waiting wet body.

He shuddered, eyes half closed. 'My God,' he hissed and slipped his cock from his trousers. It leapt towards her like a wild animal. His eyes had narrowed to pin-pricks. She swallowed hard, feeling the sweat trickling down between her breasts, her heart hammering out a wild tattoo in her chest. He stepped closer, his finger closed around the base of his shaft. 'Is this what you want?' he whispered thickly.

She nodded, afraid to speak.

Callum shook his head. 'Not good enough. Last time you chose him, now I want you to tell me that you're choosing me.'

She felt the lightest brush of his cock against her thighs, its damp kiss made her shiver, a plume of pleasure coursed up through her. She nodded again.

'I need you to tell me,' he said coldly. The head of his phallus slid to lay between the outer lips of her sex, a heady forerunner of the delight that she knew would follow. She felt her whole body reaching out towards him as if her sex could drag him in.

'Tell me—'

She looked up into his eyes, her own desire and need reflected in their darkness. 'I want you,' she whispered huskily between dry lips. 'I really truly want you—'

He slammed his cock into her, opening her deepest contours in his path. She screamed out with the pleasure and suddenness of his entry. His thrust seemed to knock the breath out of her.

'Again,' he snorted, pressing still deeper.

'I want you,' she screamed and lifted her hips to meet his stroke.

'Again.'

'I want you,' she sobbed, feeling the wild dark spiral of passion rolling out from the wet junction of their bodies. 'I want you.' And with the first ripples she surrendered herself entirely to her want, riding his body far out beyond the stars, letting the sensations engulf her whole being.

The de Vitons received Oliver Cresswell and George Winterton in the sitting room of their Manhattan home. When the formal introductions were over Leo showed them into the beautiful glass breakfast room for coffee.

'So,' said Leo, 'what brings you to New York, Mr Cresswell? Or are you like George here, a committed explorer?'

Oliver took the coffee that Isabella de Viton offered him and flushed slightly. Leo de Viton was an intimidating host; beautifully dressed, with striking features. He seemed to take in every detail of his newly arrived guests in an instant. If anything his wife was more stunning, as she handed him the cup her eyes lingered on his face, her eyes alight and glittering. 'Please, Mr de Viton, do call me Oliver . . .' he began uncomfortably.

George Winterton interrupted him. 'Oliver, here, is on a matter of the heart. L'amour.'

Leo looked heavenwards, smiling slightly. 'What pain we put ourselves through for women,' as he spoke he glanced at Isabella. 'I thought perhaps we could take in some of the sights while you were staying with us.'

George nodded. 'Actually, I'd rather hoped I might go out and take a look at your place on Long Island, I once

spent a summer there at Tiger Ward's place – haven't been
out there for years.'

Leo nodded, 'Well, of course. But how about you, Oliver?'

Oliver Cresswell glanced at the de Vitons, there was
something unnerving about them both; they had the eyes
of resting predators. He felt as if they were curled and ready
for the hunt. He glanced around the room, trying to marshal
his thoughts. 'I hoped to spend some time looking for my
fianceé.' He paused wondering how much he should tell
them.

The glittering light in Isabella de Viton's eye's
intensified. 'You're engaged to an American, Oliver?'

Oliver reddened under her undisguised curiosity. 'No,
my fiancee came over here a few weeks ago. Er . . .' he looked
at George for assistance but saw none. 'She and I had a tiff,
you know how these things can be,' he said lamely.

Leo nodded sympathetically. 'Of course. Well, in that
case, if George would like to spend some time in the
country I can arrange for him to be driven down there, and
perhaps my wife will be able to help you? What is your
fiancé's name – presumably you know where she is
staying?'

'Yes, she's staying with an old friend who she met in the
WAAF. Her name is Rebecca, Rebecca Hunt.'

As he said Rebecca's name he saw something flash in
Leo de Viton's eyes, it was so quick that he wondered if he
had imagined it. It was a look of recognition and surprise.
Oliver leant forward. 'Do you know her?'

Isabella de Viton laughed, the sound of her voice
breaking the eye contact between Leo and Oliver.
'Goodness, Oliver, New York is a huge place. People are
arriving all the time – the land of plenty and all that.' She
began to talk about the immigrants, the docks, the beautiful

places to visit, whilst Leo began to talk about business to George. It wasn't until later that Oliver realised that the de Vitons hadn't actually answered his question.

Later that day George Winterton stood by the window watching the sunlight slowly fading, whilst Leo de Viton poured them both a brandy. 'So, Isabella has taken Oliver out to view the town?' said George, as Leo handed him a glass. 'I had no idea I was so damned tired. Hope you weren't offended by my dropping off after lunch.'

Leo shook his head. 'Not at all. Isabella is planning on taking Oliver out to dinner and then on to a show. He can begin his search for Miss Hunt, his lost fiancee, tomorrow.'

George looked at his host quizzically. 'Is there something you aren't telling me, Leo? We've known each other a good many years. Shared a woman now and then—'

Leo smiled, revealing his perfect white teeth. 'You're not going to believe this, but I know Rebecca Hunt.'

George's jaw dropped. 'What? You're joking? Well, that's absolutely marvellous. What an incredible coincidence. I must tell Oliver—' his voice faded quickly. 'Why didn't you tell him when he mentioned her earlier?' Even as he spoke, George felt a flicker of comprehension dawning. 'My God, she isn't one of yours, is she, Leo?'

Leo de Viton shrugged. 'Sadly, no, not really. She is, however, fascinating. Have you met her?'

George shook his head. 'No, I'd assumed Oliver would bring her to meet me at some stage before they got married. I'm his godfather, you know.'

'A great pity that you haven't seen her, she is magnificent. A friend of mine brought her to my attention, thinking she might be to my taste.'

'And is she?' George asked with barely concealed curiosity.

Leo took a long pull on his brandy. 'Oh yes, very much so. I'm astounded that your godson let her go. My God, she is a real find.' He sat down in one of the leather armchairs and closed his eyes for a few seconds. George had no doubt he was re-running some past erotic glory with Oliver's fiancee. His only one true regret was that he wasn't privy to it – Leo de Viton's tastes were very similar to his own. He watched Leo light a cigar. Though Leo was a few years younger than George they had shared several favourites at Sophie's cat-house in London. He remembered a particularly agile Eurasian whore who . . . Leo de Viton's cultured voice snapped him back from a particularly vivid recollection of a heady menage à trois.

'Sorry, old chap, I didn't quite catch what you said,' George said, aware of the not unpleasant ache in his groin.

Leo smiled. 'She's staying at my house on Long Island.'

'Rebecca Hunt?'

Leo nodded. 'The very same.'

George let out his breath in a long slow hiss. 'Good Lord, what are you going to tell young Oliver?'

'Nothing for the time being. I'm sure her room mate knows where she's gone and the newspaper reporter she's been seeing. If Oliver finds her then I'll tell him I was acting on Rebecca's instructions. She seemed very keen to have time away from New York to work out what she was going to say to your godson.' Leo de Viton grinned. 'Quite a remarkable coincidence though, isn't it? The boy was a total and utter fool to let her go in the first place. Rebecca Hunt is a banquet.'

George rolled his brandy balloon around thoughtfully between his fingers. 'Still all right if I go down to your country place?'

Leo nodded. 'Yes, of course, then you can judge her for yourself.'

'And what about Oliver? I'm very fond of him, I can hardly keep this from him. He's been beside himself.'

Leo looked pained. 'Oh, come on, George, of course they'll find each other, but in the meantime why not enjoy the sport? Plead ignorance, say nothing.'

George laughed. 'Why not? But you will ensure they meet up, won't you? I couldn't bear to see the boy go home empty-handed.'

Leo gazed into the grate. 'Oh, I'll make sure they meet,' he said evenly, eyes alight and glowing in the subdued light. 'You can be sure of that.'

It was late the following evening when George Winterton arrived at Leo's Long Island mansion and he met Rebecca Hunt for the first time. He was immediately entranced by her handsome face and lithe slim body.

Rebecca got to her feet and extended a hand as he was shown into Leo's luxurious sitting room. 'Delighted to meet you,' she said in a low sensual voice.

George beamed. 'Charmed, I'm sure. Are you Leo's house-guest too?'

Rebecca nodded. 'Yes. I'm a friend of his. One of the servants has gone to get you a supper tray. I'm sure you could do with something to eat. May I get you a drink?'

George eased himself close to the fire, watching the girl glide effortlessly across the room towards the sideboard. Leo was right; Oliver Cresswell was a complete fool.

She laughed suddenly. 'I do apologise, you must think me terribly rude, we haven't been introduced. Leo rang this afternoon to say someone was coming to stay, but didn't mention your name. I'm Rebecca, Rebecca Hunt.'

George nodded. 'Delighted to meet you, Rebecca.' He paused, wondering how much she knew about Oliver's connections and family. It might not do to give her his surname in case he gave the game away. 'You wouldn't think me too under-handed if I only told you my first name, would you?'

Rebecca looked at him. It was obvious she understood something of Leo's private life and shook her head. 'Of course not. What would you like me to call you?'

'George,' he said, taking the glass she offered him. 'I'd be pleased if you would call me George.'

They chatted for a while about England and the voyage over, the drive down to Leo's house. If she noticed that he was a little guarded in what he revealed about himself she didn't show it. Instead she laughed at his jokes, folding herself comfortable into one of the armchairs that flanked the hearth and chatted away merrily. Later when she excused herself for bed George sat and watched the fire until it died in the grate.

Rebecca Hunt was stunning, in the glowing embers he conjured up an image of her – sylph-like, pert breasts touched by fire's flickering glow, while in his mind's eye he watched Leo taking her again and again. In his imagination he could sense the glowing ache across her back and buttocks. He had seen Leo in action with his broad leather paddle before, George shivered. It was going to be an interesting few days.

Back in New York, Oliver Cresswell, having received Rebecca's message via Edith at her apartment was beside himself.

'Monday,' he snapped unhappily at Isabella de Viton. 'I sail the damned Atlantic to come and find Rebecca and

198

when I get here she refuses to see me until Monday.' His frustration made the pulse rise in his throat.

Isabella watched him with interest. 'Perhaps we will find her before that,' she purred.

Oliver looked at her sharply, detecting a hint of amusement in her rich European accent. 'What do you mean?' he said, watching her face.

Her expression was impassive as she indicated he should sit down beside her. 'Stranger things have happened, Oliver. Why don't we go out to supper? Leo is busy with some business clients and won't be back until later. You and I could go dancing at the Cat Club, you'd love it there.'

Oliver sighed. 'Why not,' he said flatly. 'I've nothing else to do until Monday.'

Isabella pulled her beautiful face into a little moue of displeasure. 'How very tactless, Oliver. I'm quite hurt. Why not enjoy yourself? At least you will be able to come to my party on Friday. You will come, won't you?' Her eyes darkened mischievously.

Oliver licked his lips. 'I'm so sorry. I didn't mean to imply you were a poor second choice,' he said unsteadily.

'Apology accepted.' She got up and smoothed her cocktail dress down over her breasts and hips. Oliver couldn't resist the temptation to watch as her tiny hands slid slowly over her ripe curves. She looked up at him and he felt his colour rise sharply. Isabella laughed as he mumbled an apology. 'Oh please, don't apologise, Oliver, I'm extremely flattered. But I shall insist you come with us to Long Island now, after all, as you say, you have nothing to do until Monday.'

Oliver nodded, unable to quite ignore the way Isabella's nipples hardened against the soft silky fabric of her dress.

* * *

When Rebecca Hunt came downstairs the following morning for breakfast George Winterton was already awake and making himself at home in the little dining room that over-looked the terrace at the rear of Leo's mansion. He smiled and got to his feet as she came in. 'Good morning, my dear.'

Rebecca smiled. George had the bearing of an ex-military man. Whatever his secrets – and Rebecca was sure he had them – his manners were impeccable.

'Did you sleep well?' she enquired conversationally as she unfolded her napkin over her lap.

George nodded. 'I certainly did, I've been exploring the house this morning. Wonderful situation Leo has here.' Rebecca poured herself some tea as he continued, 'I assume the sketches in the study are of you?'

She blushed crimson. Callum, true to his word, had arrived back with a pad and pencils the morning before George had arrived. She glanced up at her breakfast companion, fighting to maintain her composure. Although the drawings hadn't been hidden it hadn't occurred to her that George might discover them. 'A friend did them,' she said softly, concentrating on her tea cup. 'He's on holiday down here.'

George lifted an eyebrow. 'And he came to draw you here?'

Rebecca nodded. 'It's his hobby.' She lifted her eyes to meet his, steeling her resolve not to show her embarrassment. 'I'm sure if you are a friend of Leo's you must have a hobby too?' She pointedly emphasised the word 'hobby'.

George chuckled. 'Touché, my dear. Does Leo know your friend is visiting you here?'

Rebecca kept firm hold of her emotions and her

expression, 'No,' she said firmly, not dropping her gaze, 'but I am aware of the consequences.'

'Good,' said George Winterton. 'The sketches, by the way, are quite impressive.' He smiled knowingly. 'I take great pleasure in observing things of beauty. Might I ask if you are planning a repeat performance?'

Inspite of her resolution Rebecca felt her colour rising again. 'What are you suggesting?' she said, the words out before she had thought about the result.

George lifted his hands. 'Merely that as an observer of the sublime I'm very interested in – what shall we call it?'

'I think voyeurism is the word you're looking for, George,' said Rebecca badly.

George Winterton threw back his head and laughed. 'My God, I can see why Leo likes you. Yes, my dear, voyeurism it most certainly is.' He leant closer. 'And if you know its name I shall be just as direct with my next question. Would you permit me to watch you posing for your artist friend?'

Rebecca hesitated. She felt a little thrill; she remembered how she'd felt when Leo had stepped unnoticed into Callum's apartment. Knowing he was there had added another dimension – a secret excitement that had set her body alight. She looked at George Winterton with cool detachment, praying her eyes would not betray her. 'Yes,' she said very quietly and got to her feet. 'If you will excuse me I think I'll go for a walk before my friend arrives.'

George smiled. 'Of course, my dear. Am I to take it that this little exercise takes place in the study?'

Rebecca nodded again. 'I'm expecting my friend to arrive around ten,' she said, closing her fingers tightly inside her palms so that George wouldn't be able to detect the tremor in them.

George Winterton nodded. 'I shall be ready,' he said, returning his attention to his breakfast, 'Enjoy your walk.'

'Where do you want me this morning?'

Callum O'Neill grinned at Rebecca. She was dressed in a soft pastel robe that covered her demurely from throat to ankle but he knew that beneath it she was naked. A huge fire roared on the grate in the study making the room deliciously warm.

'Don't tempt me, at least not until I've done some work,' he murmured, unfolding his easel.

Rebecca laughed and poured them a cup of tea. 'I thought you might have been thinking about me all night again.'

Callum looked across at her; there was something different his morning. She seemed to exude a sexual, sensual otherness – a brazen confidence that hadn't been there before. She moved with the grace of a dancer and he wondered if it was her or his artist's eye that saw every movement as an erotic pose. Firelight glowed through the thin fabric of her wrap, picking out the contours of her body in silhouette.

He took the cup she offered him, aware of her subtle perfume and beneath it the more hypnotic compelling scent of her body. She folded herself up near the hearth, close to his feet. Callum looked down at her and suddenly understood saw what Leo de Viton saw – a beautiful compliant woman whose excitement came from submission. He shivered, feeling a familiar stirring in his groin. He stroked her hair as if she were a sleek cat, she responded instantly by brushing her face against his fingers and making a soft purring sound in her throat.

'So what do you want me to do?' she said in a whisper.

Callum touched her shoulder and in the same low voice said. 'Take off your robe.'

She complied wordlessly. Her body was stunning. On the previous days she had been reluctant, afraid in case they were caught – but today something had changed. She stood up, letting the fire's light play along her slim lines.

'I'll be punished for this,' she said, her eyes dark with desire.

Callum swallowed furiously, he was strangely excited by the idea of taking a whip to her delicate pale skin. 'And you'll enjoy it . . .' he said flatly.

She nodded, running her fingers slowly down over her breasts and waist, letting them stroke the firm flesh of her thighs. 'Oh yes,' she said. 'Yes, I will.'

Callum could feel the unbelieveable heat in his groin and knew she would do anything he asked of her. He could sense her submission and her excitement hovering beneath the surface. He could feel her desire for him to dominate her; she was giving herself to him and the idea electrified him. For a few seconds he couldn't move. The prospect of her submission was too heady to contemplate.

He licked his lips. 'I think,' he said unsteadily, 'that I should punish you for choosing Leo instead of me.' As he spoke he felt beads of sweat breaking on his top lip.

She dropped her eyes to the floor, dipping her head so that he couldn't see her face, but he could see the slight flush on her cheeks and the way her skin seemed to glow with an inner light. He knew what he would do now, something that had excited him for years, 'Come here,' he said softly. 'And lay across my knees.'

She slowly folded her body over his. He could feel her breasts brushing against him. The heat of her body pressing down into his groin was almost too much; he slowly drew

back his hand in a wide arc. As he brought it down with a
resounding crack across her buttocks she cried out, flexing
against him. He felt the heady press of his growing
excitement in his groin and swung his hand again. The
second blow cracked on her pale pink skin, raising a red
hand mark. She bucked under it, exposing the moist pink
folds of her sex. He shivered and smacked her again, feeling
the pulse roar through him as she wiggled and squealed
under his attentions. The fourth stroke was harder still,
making her snort with pain. His palm stung but instead of
taking his hand back, he let it linger, teasing open the slick
wet entry to her quim. She moaned, dropping her belly to
give him entry. Before she had time to think, he lifted his
hands and smacked her again. She yelped and he relaxed
his knees and let her roll in a crumpled heap onto the floor.
As she turned over he could see the flush on her face and
the way her nipples had hardened; she was wildly excited.
Glimmering in the dark, diamonds of wetness clung
invitingly to a hair around her sex. Callum could feel his
control ebbing, he slid his fingers into the hard swell of his
groin and undid his flies. 'Come here,' he said huskily. She
lifted herself up onto all fours, eyes chastely averted as she
crawled towards him. She rested her face on his thighs. He
felt her breath on his throbbing cock and gasped with
pleasure as he felt her mouth engulfing him. Closing his
eyes he grabbed hold of her hair and relinquished his
control.

Across the study, hidden inside the closet, George
Winterton took a deep breath as the girl's lips and fingers
started to work on her lover's raging angry cock. He could
see the curve of her breasts, the soft arc of her belly and the
enticing picture of her fingers sliding between her legs,

fondling her own sex. By God, she was good. He had to ensure that Oliver discovered what he was missing – with a wife like Rebecca no man need ever go hungry or unsatisfied again. Leo de Viton had been right; Rebecca Hunt was a banquet.

Chapter 9

Early on Thursday morning the quiet of Leo de Viton's Long Island mansion was shattered by the arrival of a convoy of trucks bearing all kinds of luxuries. Rebecca stood at the foot of the stairs and watched in astonishment as the great entrance hall was decked with fairy lights, candles, a champagne fountain – under the sweep of the stairs a stage was set up complete with spotlights and microphone.

George Winterton came to see what all the noise was about and smiled when he saw Rebecca was already there. Since their rendezvous in the study the previous morning George had retired behind a discreet façade of good manners. They both headed for the study, narrowly avoiding two burly work men carrying a huge carved plinth.

Rebecca ordered them a tray of tea whilst George installed himself beside the fire. 'Have you ever been to one of Isabella's parties?' he asked. Even with the doors closed it was impossible not to hear the comings and goings outside.

Rebecca shook her head. 'No, I only met Leo a few weeks ago.'

George nodded sagely. 'Before the war he and his first wife hired a country house for the weekend whenever they visited England. They were amazing events I can assure you. Something that one never forgets.' He looked at her, eyes moving slowly across her body. 'Mind you, there are many things one experiences courtesy of Leo de Viton that stand out in the memory.'

Rebecca glanced at the clock above the mantel piece, pointedly avoiding George's eyes. 'I have to go out soon,' she said evenly.

George sighed. 'Your young artist friend? I thought perhaps you might be planning a repeat performance this morning.'

Rebecca glanced at him and smiled. 'Oh really? I draw the line at performing with a house full of strangers. I'm not sure I'm ready to be discovered naked on the hearth rug by the workmen.'

George smiled thinly. 'Pity, it might add a certain *frisson* to the proceedings. By the way, I've taken your young man's sketches for my own amusement. I shall just have to wait until tomorrow night for another viewing.' He paused, watching her face. 'Though I'm sure it will be worth my patience.'

The door of the study opened and the uniformed footman who had seen to Rebecca's needs since she had arrived stepped into the room.

'Miss Hunt?' Rebecca nodded and the man turned and walked back into the hall, indicating she should follow. 'Mr de Viton has instructed me to move you out of the main house until the party is over,' he said once they were out of earshot of George Winterton.

Rebecca felt a little flurry of annoyance. 'I see, have you any idea why?'

The man looked at her levelly. She had no doubt, from his expression, that he had seen many girls come and go at Leo's instruction. For an instant he couldn't quite hide the look of superiority and disdain in his face. 'Mr de Viton has invited several of his most influential friends for the weekend,' he said slowly, as if she might be unable to follow what he was saying. There was something disturbing about his manner. Rebecca nodded; the implication was that she wasn't quite good enough to mix with Leo de Viton's social elite. 'He asked me to take your things over to one of the guest bungalows.' He paused, the superior look still lingering on his face as he handed her a key on a leather fob. 'There will be several other friends of the de Vitons staying there, so you won't be alone. And perhaps you would so good as to remain there until the de Vitons arrive. I do hope you won't mind?'

It was most definitely a rhetorical question. Rebecca felt a plume of anger. She was not a commodity that could be pushed around. She looked at the man coldly. 'Of course,' she said, 'if that is what Mr de Viton wants.'

Inside she was quietly furious as she fell into step behind the footman, who led her out through the maze of corridors into a wide avenue of trees. Hidden from the house, but barely more than a stone's throw away, was a cluster of small bungalows arranged around a central courtyard. As Rebecca stepped under the entrance archway a familiar figure greeted her. 'Carina?' she said in disbelief. The sultry night-club singer was climbing out of a sleek silver coupe. Her maid followed carrying the luggage.

The singer turned and smiled. Her fluid movements lit something in Rebecca's subconscious, a little unfulfilled ache of desire that surprised her. Carina turned at the sound of Rebecca's greeting and smiled broadly. 'So, honey, we meet again. How's it going?' she purred in her distinctive low voice. 'I kinda hoped Leo was going to bring you back to the Club.' She hurried across the flagstones and embraced Rebecca, pressing herself so close that Rebecca could feel her heart beat. 'Part of Leo's menagerie too now?'

Rebecca flushed. 'What do you mean?'

Carina pulled away and grinned. 'We're all part of his collection of curios, honey.' She took a set of keys from the footman, waving him away, before leading Rebecca into one of the bungalows. It was obvious that it wasn't the first time Carina had spent time as a guest there.

The singer glanced over her shoulder as the maid set the bags down on the floor. 'Hasn't the Italian vixen given you your instructions yet?'

Rebecca shook her head. 'Isabella, you mean? No, I haven't seen her. I've been staying in the house since the weekend.'

Carina grinned, dropping her fur stole over one of the elegant leather chairs that graced the main living area. 'You ought to think yourself privileged. Usually the cattle are kept out here in the sheds.'

Rebecca felt the colour leaving her face, 'I don't understand.'

'You soon will, babe. Over the next twenty-four hours this place will fill up with senators, movie moguls, big-big business men and until the party they wanna keep us outta sight.' She grinned. 'But not outta mind. Tonight the guys will play cards and drink heavy. Maybe if you're lucky, as you're flavour of the month, Leo will send for you. Then tomorrow night the fun really begins.'

Rebecca sat down heavily. 'I still don't know what's going on, Leo invited me to his party . . .'

'Yeh,' said Carina, opening the cocktail cabinet, 'but not as a guest, baby, or they wouldn't have shipped you over here. You're on the menu.'

Leo's words suddenly came back to her from the night she had spent with Callum at the de Vitons apartment. 'It will be a masked ball for our friends. In fact we have guests coming over this week from England. Isabella's parties are becoming world famous,' Leo had laughed. 'She is planning a living exhibition for our guests to view and used by those we invite.' He'd stepped closer to her, stroking her lips. 'Imagine that, my dearest, chained up for someone else's pleasure. It would be so good . . .'

Isabella had stepped forward. 'One final wonderful expedition into pleasure – at least wait until it's over before you decide whether you truly want to turn down what Leo is offering you.'

Rebecca stared at Carina. 'We are the exhibits?' she muttered in astonishment.

Carina nodded and handed her a martini, her fingers lingering a second too long on Rebecca's. 'Well, we ain't the waitresses, girl.'

As Rebecca took a long pull on her glass there was a knock on the door. When she looked up Callum O'Neill was looking in through the glass.

Carina saw the look that passed between them. 'You know this guy?'

Rebecca nodded. 'He's my knight in shining armour.'

Carina grinned lazily. 'I'd better let him in then, his armour might rust out there.'

Callum stepped inside and nodded a hello to Carina. 'What's going on? That footman guy over at the house said you were staying down here now?'

Carina lifted an eyebrow in Rebecca's direction and fixed Callum a drink. Rebecca sighed. 'Party arrangements,' she said slowly.

Carina threw back her head and laughed. 'My God,

you're good at understatement and how come you've got him hanging around?' She jerked her thumb towards Callum. 'Leo usually frightens off the opposition real early on.'

Callum stared at the beautiful coloured woman with barely concealed annoyance. Rebecca touched his arm to calm him and moved along the settee so that he could sit down beside her. 'This is the last time I'm going to see Leo,' she said slowly. 'After the party that's it, I've decided I'm going back to New York.'

Carina looked at her thoughtfully. 'With him?' She pointed to Callum. 'He is real pretty.'

Rebecca sighed. 'Perhaps.'

Callum, his voice still tight with confusion and annoyance looked between the two of them. 'Would either of you like to tell me what's going on here?'

Rebecca shook her head. 'Not really. Just calm down and don't take it out on Carina.'

Carina giggled and pulled a pack of cards from her handbag, 'How about we have a game to pass the time until tomorrow?'

Callum looked stunned. 'You mean you're waiting here for the party too?'

Carina fanned the deck with the practised hands of a card sharp and eyed him thoughtfully with her conker-brown pupils. 'Sure honey, we're the main attraction. Now, why don't you pull up that little table and settle yourself down? It's gonna be a long long day. My maid'll take care of things.' She glanced at Rebecca. 'You got a key too? I'll get her to sort out your clothes out as well.'

Without another word Rebecca handed Carina the key fob that the footman had given her. It seemed pointless to do otherwise.

* * *

Oliver Cresswell stretched luxuriously in the back of Leo de Viton's limousine, watching the scenery roll past the windows. Beside him, Isabella de Viton was reading from a leather bound notebook that she had produced from a handbag. Her beautifully painted sensual lips silently mouthed the words as her finger moved down an unseen list.

Oliver tried hard to keep his mind off her. The elegant wife of his host had an unsettling effect on him. Several times when he glanced up she seemed to be watching him. Isabella looked up, catching his gaze and smiled broadly, lips drawn back over her perfect white teeth. 'Bored?' she purred, closing the notebook with a flick of her wrist.

Oliver coughed to clear his throat, 'No, no, not at all,' he said uncomfortably. 'I was just watching the countryside. I've never been to Long Island before. George was here several years ago . . .'

Isabella dropped her hands onto her thighs whilst her eyes still held his. 'Oh, I think you're lying,' she said in an undertone. Slowly, oh so slowly, she slid up the expensive fabric of her travelling outfit, revealing more and more of her shapely legs.

Oliver swallowed uncomfortably, trying hard not to let his eyes drop to the cunning, smooth actions of his hostess's fingers.

'Wouldn't you like to touch me?' she murmured, running her tongue over her lips.

Oliver coughed. 'Yes, yes of course I would,' he said unsteadily. 'No man could find you anything other than irresistible.'

Isabella laughed and then eased herself back into the leather upholstery, the hem of her skirt just an inch or so from the cleft of her sex. 'Then why are you trying to resist me? Why don't you just let go—' Her eyes darkened and she ran her fingers higher still, her nail varnish a stunning contrast to her delicate, pale olive flesh. 'Haven't you thought about what it would be like to slide inside me? I'm so hot, so very wet inside—'

Oliver moaned. 'Your husband . . .' he spluttered.

His companion tipped back her head, and ran her fingers through her sleek, raven-black hair; the effect was electrifying. 'He won't be following us until later this evening and even then he'll be fully occupied. Why don't you come closer and touch me? I've noticed the look in your eyes the moment you saw me in Manhattan. I know you want to fuck me, why fight it?'

'Please, Isabella. You're another man's wife . . .' Oliver began to protest.

Isabella took one of his hands in hers, guiding it into the shadowy folds beneath her skirt. 'Oh yes,' she said, 'that is true, but before I married Leo I worked the streets. Don't tell me your friend George didn't tell you. I know what men like and Leo understands that too. Do you know why he loves me? Because I'm dangerous, other women come and go in his life but I'm for keeps. We like the same things, he and I.'

Oliver shuddered as his fingers slid between the silky soft skin of her thighs, above he could feel the heat of her sex, the damp exciting scent filling his mind as he moved closer.

'I want you to take me,' Isabella purred, sliding down so that she was laying across the seat. Her pelvis lifted under his caress, her glorious body opening to him. As his finger moved higher he felt the soft brush of silky hair and he realised with astonishment that she wasn't wearing underwear. The lightest caress of the dark outer folds made her moan invitingly. It sounded like a growl. He shuddered with pleasure, feeling his cock hardening rapidly. It was as if he was powerless to resist her. She smiled up at him with the eyes of a hunting tigress. Knitting her fingers in his thick hair she guided his face down towards her sex.

'Kiss me,' she murmured, 'I want to feel your tongue deep inside me. Remember I'm only a whore after all. You can do whatever it is you want to whores, Oliver.' As she spoke she opened her legs. Rose pink petals of flesh peeped provocatively from a matt of dark glittering hair. She wriggled lower, pulling him closer and he knew then he was lost. His resistance crumbled – overcome by the compelling animal scent of her eager body and the desire he had tried to suppress since they had met.

However foolish and dangerous this liaison was, he knew he was unable to hold back. He planted a tentative kiss on the mound of her quim, breathing in her odour. She let out a soft shuddering hiss of delight. 'Oh yes,' she breathed. 'Yes, Oliver,' she murmured, 'this is what I want . . .'

He moaned miserably, knowing what he was doing was madness, while his tongue lapped at her, his fingers seeking entry into the slick carnivorous depths of her body. The taste of her readiness flooded his senses, making him moan again – this time with pleasure. She lifted herself up, rubbing her quim onto his tongue and fingers as if her life depended on it.

He kissed and sucked and nibbled at the hood of her clitoris making her gasp with delight, while between his legs the throbbing press of his cock seemed almost unbearable. Isabella rubbed herself against him more firmly, linking her hands behind his head, dragging him closer and closer until he thought she might choke the life out of him. Just as he believed he might drown in the heady depths of her juices

215

she pulled away and rolled out from under him, her eyes glittering malevolently

Instantly he sat up. Blushing, he tried to say something; an apology, a sound of frustrated desire, anything to try and undo what he had done – until he realised what she was doing. Kneeling in the footwell, facing towards the rear of the car she bent over the seat, lifting her skirt up to expose the ripe curves of her buttocks.

She glanced across at him, face flushed and excited. 'There,' she whispered, 'Isn't that what you really want? Fuck me, Oliver,' she said unsteadily, her eyes glowing with a dark inner fire. 'I want to feel you buried to the hilt.' Her rich accent added a bizarre erotic twist, taking him back in his mind to the whorehouses in Europe he'd visited during the war. Any reticence or fear was lost in his pure, white-hot lust for her body.

He crouched behind her and did not protest as she guided him between her thighs until the crown of his cock rested just inside the hot engorged lips of her quim. Slowly, slowly, she eased herself backwards into the pit of his stomach and in doing so drew him into the tight, wet tunnel. He gasped as she flexed the muscles deep inside around his shaft, drawing him in further still. 'There,' she murmured, 'doesn't that feel good?'

Just when he thought there could be nothing else but the mad ride out to ecstasy she slid her hand back between their legs and cupped his scrotum, fingers working expertly at the very root of his cock.

'My God,' he hissed, as she started to thrust back against him, letting out a little grunt of pleasure. Her fingers and body set a compelling counter-point to each other 'My God—' He closed his eyes, burying his face in her perfumed hair and let himself be dragged into the wild unstoppable rhythm that would take him to the point of release. Beneath him Isabella bucked and writhed, moaning with delight as he impaled her again and again.

When it was over, Oliver self-consciously pulled himself out from her exquisite dangerous body, pressing his lips into the soft curve of her neck. He struggled to find something to say; thanks, an apology, an explanation. His sated mind fought to find something to convey the mixed emotions he felt.

Beneath him Isabella de Viton turned over, her expression triumphant. 'Well, Oliver,' she sighed on an outward breath, looking up into his eyes. 'How do I compare to your fiancee, Miss Hunt?'

Oliver was so stunned by her words that he just stared down at her.

Isabella laughed and slid back up into the seat, smoothing her skirt, picking up her notebook. Oliver slumped into the seat next to her.

She grinned. 'Perhaps you'll tell me later,' she purred and began to re-read her list. Oliver stared out of the window, unable to get a grip on the confusion raging inside.

He had to see Rebecca soon and clear the air – he had made a terrible mistake making love to Isabella de Viton. Rebecca certainly wasn't a natural predator like his companion for the drive to Long Island. He wondered desperately if Rebecca could ever find it in her heart to forgive him for being such a total fool.

In Carina's bungalow at the de Viton Mansion, Rebecca giggled and lay her cards down amongst the pile of matchsticks. 'There we are, I win again, I think.'

Carina laughed and Callum groaned as Rebecca scooped the pot towards her across the little side table.

Callum took another swig from his martini glass. 'For a girl who says she never plays cards you've sure got one helluva lucky streak.'

Carina giggled, leaning closer to stroke a long thin finger over Callum's rough cheek. 'Don't you fret, Mr knight in shinin' armour, we'll thrash the bitch on the next hand.' She glanced over her shoulder towards her maid who had laid the little dining table near the French windows. 'How long, Marcie, till we eat?'

The girl looked up, bright eyes flashing in coal-black skin and snorted. 'It's all ready but seems to me like you won't wanna be eating, the amount you been drinkin.'

Carina laughed uproariously. 'Quit griping, girl, why don't you come over here and sit in for a hand or two. We need to thrash this limey card-sharp.'

The maid laughed indulgently. 'Gimme a minute to turn off the chicken and I'll be with you.'

Carina tapped her nose drunkenly at Callum and winked. 'We'll get her this time round, Marcie's a natural.'

Rebecca watched the exchange with pleasure. Callum, once his fear had subsided, had really taken to Carina and they had been playing cards, talking, joking and drinking on and off all day since Rebecca had been so unceremoniously dumped in Leo's 'guest' bungalows.

Across the table, in the soft lamp-light, Carina leant forward towards Callum, her eyes alight and gently pressed her lips to his. 'Lucky kiss,' she said.

Rebecca could detect the little ripple of desire in the two other card players as she handed the deck to Callum. She been watching Callum's face all day and sensed his interest in Carina since they'd been introduced. 'Don't I get one?' she said unsteadily, gazing back at Carina.

The singer smiled lazily. 'Why, sure, honey,' and slid a

finger under Rebecca's chin, tipping it so that their lips met in the most delicate of kisses. Rebecca breathed it in, tasting the bitter liquor on Carina's lips and the lingering perfume of tobacco smoke.

'Ummm, you kiss real good,' said Carina as she pulled back, her eyes soft and unfocused with pleasure.

Rebecca glanced at Callum and could almost read his mind. He picked up the cards and shuffled them clumsily, eyes darting back and forth between the two women. 'How did you two meet?' he said with affected casualness.

Carina stroked a finger along her full moist lips. 'Oh, you think you're so smooth, boy, but I can see right through you. Leo, but you must of guessed that. He brought Rebecca out to the club to hear me sing.'

Callum nodded. 'Right—' passing the cards from hand to hand in a poor approximation of a shuffle.

Rebecca laughed, her face flushing red as she took another deep pull on her glass. 'Among other things.'

Marcie, the maid, moved across the room carrying a pile of plates. 'Carina is sure good at them other things,' she said mischievously and set the crockery down on the table. 'Now are you gonna eat or shall I just clear away these things so that you folks can get down to what's buzzing around between the three of you?'

Callum stared first at Marcie and then at Rebecca and Carina. 'You mean,' he blustered, 'you two . . .'

His voice faded as Carina ran her tongue provocatively around the rim of her cocktail glass. 'We sure did, honey, and let me tell you, cards ain't the only thing this girl is good at.' She giggled as Callum let the playing cards slide back onto the table. She waved to Marcie. 'Why don't you come and freshen up Mr O'Neill's drink, he looks as if he's gonna choke, and then we'll eat. What do you say, Rebecca?'

Rebecca looked drowsily at the two of them, both watched her face like hawks. She grinned, feeling the mischievous kick of the martini coursing her blood. She nodded. 'Wonderful idea,' and glanced at Callum, feeling the mischief combining with the little tingle of excitement that Carina's kiss had lit in her. She looked across at the singer. 'Didn't you promise me that next time we met, you'd really like to show me what you can do for *me* . . .'

Carina, eyes glittering, lay back in the armchair, blowing a plume of silver smoke into the lamp light. 'I think I remember sayin' something along those lines. You want that we should eat first?'

Rebecca giggled, nothing could have prepared her for what she had experienced since she arrived in America. She knew the drink was lowering her inhibitions; her mind replayed the erotic ballet in Carina's apartment in the night club. Between her legs she felt the soft flurry of desire growing. Callum looked so handsome in the soft light in the bungalow, Carina as beautiful as one woman should ever be. Outside the night was darkening rapidly and she could almost see the expectation hanging in the air between the three of them. She glanced at Carina who was waiting for a reply. 'Yes, all right. maybe it'll sober me up.'

Carina lifted an eyebrow. 'You wanna be sober?'

Rebecca nodded. 'Oh yes,' she said softly. If she was going to experience making love with Callum and Carina she wanted to be sober enough to relish every second of their combined caresses.

Callum stood up unsteadily. 'How's the dinner coming along, Marcie?'

The maid grinned. 'All ready if you wanna get up the table.'

While they ate the air between them slowly changed

from a hint of possibilities to an electric erotic hum. Marcie seemed to fade into the background as they watched each other, eyes twinkling, until finally the meal was done and cleared away and Marcie left.

Carina was the first to leave the table. She stood up slowly with the grace of a wild cat. She glanced first at Callum and then Rebecca, her hands snaking up slowly over her generous hips, up over her ribs, cradling her ample breasts. Callum's eyes glittered with desire. One of her long fingers lazily drew a circle around the outside of her blouse, her nipples hardening instantly and pressing through the material. She arched her neck back, moaning softly.

Rebecca watched as Callum pushed away his chair. He seemed to be beside Carina in seconds, kissing her throat, his fingers joining hers. 'You're so lovely,' he murmured throatily, encircling her with his arms, pulling her close into a long slow kiss. Carina slipped her arms around him, her body seeming to melt into his. Rebecca watched entranced as Callum began to undo her blouse, his lips tracing a path of kisses down her neck, across her shoulders. For an instant she was so entranced with their excitement that she didn't move, though the effects of their caresses lit a roaring blaze inside her.

Carina slowly disentangled herself from Callum's arms, her lips wet and full. She looked at Rebecca and extended a hand. 'Why don't you join us, honey? Why let him have the lion's share of all this good stuff?'

As she spoke Callum turned towards her too. His face was flushed, eyes dark pits of pleasure. She stood up slowly and walked towards them as Carina turned and led them into the bedroom.

It was Carina who turned round first to embrace Rebecca, her lips closing on Rebecca's mouth in a gentle sensuous invitation, while the singer's hands lifted to undo the front of her dress. Rebecca could see Callum behind Carina, his fingers working the coloured woman's breasts, undoing the buttons revealing more and more of her exotic exciting curves. In the half light they moved slowly, drinking in every sensation; a kiss here, a gentle stroking touch here, a soft throaty noise of pleasure, slowly peeling off their clothes until it seemed as if they had undressed seamlessly, like leaves falling to the ground.

Callum's excitement was obvious, his beautiful meaty cock arced forwards, begging for attention. Carina smiled and planted a single dry kiss on its engorged head before turning her attention to Rebecca, guiding her back into the broad bed. She lay her down gently, opening her legs with soft encouraging words and tingling caresses. Rebecca was stunned by the other woman's softness, her body felt like spun silk, her kisses as gentle as gossamer against her desperate eager flesh. Standing behind Carina, Callum watched, his face suffused with pleasure as Carina's kisses worked a scintillating spiral.

Callum couldn't believe what was happening in front of him, Carina had lain Rebecca back on the bed. As she bent forward, standing between Rebecca's legs, the two women's lips met in a long slow kiss. He shivered as he saw their breasts brushing, touching, nipple to nipple, the contrast of Carina's dark flesh stunning against Rebecca's cool pale skin. Between Carina's legs he could see the open moist folds of her slit, flushing from palest pink to crimson as her excitement grew, a glistening trickle of moisture nestling between the shiny dark hair.

He groaned, longing to feel his cock slide inside her, inside both of them – but another part of him hung back, he wanted to watch the two women together. Rebecca's eyes closed slowly as if she were drifting into sleep while Carina's mouth worked down over her chest, her fingers cupping the English girl's breasts, teasing at the already tight peaks. Carina's lips closed eagerly over the swollen buds, sucking them in, lapping. Rebecca let out a long low gasp of pleasure.

He could barely contain himself, unable to resist the invitation of Carina's exposed body he ran his fingers over her full shapely breasts and rounded hips, revelling in her delicate skin. His fingers worked lower, as if with a mind of their own, seeking the delicate oceanic contours of the scarlet flower that blossomed amongst the dark hair. Inside, the heat and the wetness took his breath away; this was paradise. Beneath him the dark woman was working her magical kisses lower and lower. He saw Rebecca buck and writhe with delight as Carina's tongue found the root of her pleasure.

He heard their moans, soft, throaty sobs of excitement and knew he couldn't hold back any longer. He felt as if every fibre, every tiny nerve of his body was on fire – aware, pulsing, eager to draw in the pleasure between the three of them. Slowly he guided his cock into Carina's body. The brush of her cool heavy buttocks against his belly sent a tidal wave of pleasure through him, followed an instant later by another as her tightness enfolded him, drawing him deep inside, cradling him within her throbbing wet walls.

He turned his attentions to Carina's breasts, teasing at the nipples, cupping, and stroking. The singer let out a low growl and pressed herself into his body, while beneath them he could sense Rebecca's glittering passion growing with every touch and stroke of the singer's tongue and lips.

His fingertips brushed Rebecca's hot writhing body and instantly imagined what Carina was tasting; the rich silvery liquid silk of love, the warm deep sea tastes of pleasure. He pushed deeper, letting Carina set the rhythm as he rode her on and on.

When he felt the first unstoppable tremors of his climax he was astonished to sense the same wild circles in Carina's body and, below her, in Rebecca's. It was almost as if they were sharing one mind, their bodies mirroring each others passion, intensifying and building each wave of pleasure until he thought he would go crazy in their mutual chase towards release. When the white-hot lights suddenly exploded inside his mind and body he knew the two women were there with him, irrevocably linked, spinning wildly out towards the stars.

Chapter 10

Dinner at the de Viton mansion that night was a formal affair. Oliver Cresswell, dressed in his dinner jacket had barely had time to talk to George Winterton since he had arrived. The house itself was astounding – a huge turn-of-the-century mansion, set back from the road in its own extensive grounds, beautifully furnished and already in the throes of being decorated for the next day's party. Leo de Viton arrived very soon after Isabella and Oliver, and George immediately whisked him away to his study for some sort of business conference. Isabella had vanished too leaving Oliver feeling ill at ease and still disturbed from his liaison with her in the limousine.

In his study Leo de Viton poured George Winterton a drink. 'Well, what do you think of Miss Hunt?'

George smiled. 'As you said, Leo, absolutely astounding. Splendid creature.' He paused. 'Your man took her away this morning.'

Leo nodded and lit a cigar. 'That was Isabella's idea, she didn't want Oliver running in to Rebecca before the party.' Leo took a long thoughtful puff on his cigar. 'Did Rebecca mention anything about leaving after the party?'

George shrugged. 'Not a word. I get the impression she is biding her time until she's spoken with Oliver.'

Leo nodded, staring into the grate. 'She's compelling. If

your godson hadn't been here I'd have put her through her paces for you. I suppose I have to admit defeat, she has already told me that this is the last time she'll be at my beck and call. A great shame—' his voice faded.

George smiled, detecting a genuine hint of regret in his old friend's demeanour. And who could blame him? He didn't intend to let Leo know that he had seen Rebecca in action with her American lover. Leo de Viton wasn't the only one capable of playing games.

The door of the study opened to reveal Isabella, she looked glorious in a low cut crepe de chine evening gown that clung to every curve. She kissed George gently on the cheek and then stood beside Leo. 'Everyone is almost ready for dinner, Leo, shall we go though?'

Leo nodded. 'Have you been over to see Rebecca?' he asked casually as he drained his glass.

'No, I haven't really had time yet,' said Isabella, slipping her arm though his.

As George turned to follow them he caught the briefest glimpse of something flickering in Isabella's eyes. He suspected she was jealous of Leo's obsession with the English girl, he was almost certain of it. The sooner Oliver and Rebecca got together, the better, for everyone's sake.

During pre-dinner cocktails Isabella and Leo re-appeared to introduce their guests to each other. Oliver Cresswell was struck by the fact that many of those present were household names – even in England – and that there seemed to be a dearth of ladies in stark contrast to the large number of prosperous and very well-connected men. Dinner was superb, though Oliver still couldn't shake the feeling of being the odd one out. Everyone else seemed to have been to at least one of the de Vitons' parties before and knew what to expect – by contrast, Oliver was playing it by ear. Finally, over cigars and brandy, George, red-faced and a little worse for wine, came over to talk to him. 'Well, how's it going?' he said heartily.

Oliver swirled his brandy balloon. 'Fine, George, just fine.'

His godfather peered at him. 'Doesn't sound it, why don't you relax and enjoy yourself? Tonight we chaps can let our hair down – ready for the revels tomorrow. Can't start until all the guests are here, a lot more will be arriving tomorrow.'

Oliver sighed. 'I think it may have been a mistake coming here at all,' he said, glancing up at Isabella de Viton, who was deep in conversation with a man Oliver recognised as part of the US Senate.

George followed his glance and grinned. 'Little cat seduced you, did she?'

Oliver reddened. 'My God, is it that obvious?'

George patted him on the shoulder. 'Anyone could see she had the hots for you, lad. Just one of those things.'

Oliver snorted. 'I only hope her husband is as understanding.'

George smiled and took a puff on his cigar. 'I wouldn't imagine Leo would turn a hair. Now let me show you to the gambling den. Leo said he's had a casino set up somewhere, why don't we take a spin on the tables?'

Oliver nodded, carefully avoiding Isabella's gaze as he followed his godfather out of the smoking room.

The following morning Rebecca was woken by a loud banging. She sat up too quickly and instantly regretted it – feeling the effects of the previous night's intake of martini. Beside her in the double bed Callum lay one side, while

Carina lay curled on the other. Recollections of the long delectable night spent in their arms made her smile. They began to stir as she clambered from the bed and pulled on one of Carina's robes. Glancing at the clock on the hall table she was astonished to discover it was almost lunch time. In the hallway Rebecca met Carina's maid, Marcie, who lifted an eyebrow in greeting.

'I heard knocking,' she said sleepily.

Marcie nodded. 'We got company. I'll go and get them up.' She paused. 'I s'ppose your knight in shining armour decided to sleep over too?'

Rebecca nodded and blushed. The maid grinned. 'Thought as much. By the way, your visitor is none other than the Italian vixen herself.'

Rebecca froze. 'Isabella? She's here?'

The maid nodded and disappeared through the door into Carina's bedroom.

Cautiously, tidying her hair, Rebecca opened the sitting-room door. Isabella de Viton stood in the centre of the room immaculately dressed, coiffured and made-up, a mink wrap thrown casually over her narrow shoulders. Beside her was the uniformed servant who had shown Rebecca to the bungalow the day before. He was carrying two large, pastel-coloured boxes.

Isabella looked up as Rebecca stepped into the room and smiled. 'Good morning,' she said in an undertone. 'I see you've made Carina's acquaintance. I do hope I wasn't interrupting anything too important.' Rebecca felt her colour rising as Isabella continued, 'I've brought your costumes over for this evening.' She paused, taking in the details of Rebecca's undress and gazed thoughtfully at the girl's body. The footman laid the boxes on a chair. Isabella turned as if to leave and then hesitated, 'Take off your robe.'

Rebecca looked up at her in astonishment. 'Pardon?'

Isabella stared at her darkly. 'You heard what I said. 'She nodded towards the boxes, 'I'd like to see you in your costume before I go.'

'I'll go try it on—' Rebecca began, glancing back towards the hall door. She couldn't help noticing the way the footman's eyes lingered on her body, she shivered involuntarily. She remembered the look of contempt on his face as he had given her Leo's instructions and the key to the bungalow. Isabella shook her head and sat down in one of the arm chairs. 'No, I want you to do it here. Now—' She nodded towards the servant, 'Get Miss Hunt her dress.'

The man stepped forward and opened up the top box; his eyes had narrowed to sharp splinters. Slowly he pulled out a long dress. Rebecca stared at the outfit in amazement and then at Isabella who met her eyes levelly.

'Now, take off your robe and put the costume on.' Her voice was cool and commanding. 'I haven't got all day.' Rebecca felt a little tremor of unease. Isabella nodded towards the servant. 'He will help you.'

Rebecca swallowed hard and let her robe fall to the floor, the servant held out her costume toward her, his eyes lingering hungrily on the uptilted curve of her breast before dropping lower to drink in the details of her sex. She shuddered as he stepped closer. The dress he held was like something out of a bizarre historical drama. The long-sleeved, emerald-green bodice was boned from waist to breast, with lacing up the back. From the waist, the skirt and a white, lace-edged petticoat beneath were cut in broad ribbons that reached the floor. Aware of their eyes on her Rebecca quickly slipped the dress on, not resisting as the servant moved behind her and began to fasten the laces.

His fingers fumbled, lingering too long on her naked back and neck while he threaded the laces and began to tighten them. He was so close that Rebecca could feel his breath on her skin.

Isabella watched them impassively until the strange dress was in place. The tight boning thrust Rebecca's breasts forward, the white lace trim on the bodice barely covering her nipples, whilst the split skirt opened with the slightest movement revealing her naked body beneath. The servant went back to the box and brought out an ornate mask made of gold fabric which covered Rebecca's face from her hairline to her mouth. When it was in place Isabella got up and circled Rebecca thoughtfully. Pulling her handbag open she removed a lipstick. 'The finishing touch, I think.'

Rebecca assumed that she was going to paint her lips, instead to her surprise, Isabella rolled down the edging of lace on the bodice and cupped one of her breasts between her fingers. The Italian woman was so quick that Rebecca didn't have time to stop her. Rebecca gasped as the woman leant forward, brushing the scarlet stick over her nipples. To her horror she felt them harden under the slick press of blood-red lipstick.

Isabella drew her lips back over her perfect teeth as the delicate buds stiffened. Rebecca stood motionless until the other woman had done and then shivered as Isabella stepped back to admire her handiwork.

The servant watched intently, unable to disguise his excitement. Isabella smiled. 'There,' she said and glanced at the man. 'Perhaps you'd like to put the lace back up?' He stepped forward, the mask for his mistress vanishing as he stared into Rebecca's eyes. 'Of course, Mrs de Viton, 'he said, as he fumbled with the front of Rebecca's costume.

His fingers rubbed at the reddened peaks, his face contorted with lust. Glancing down Rebecca could see the bulge in the front of his uniform trousers and felt a flurry of fear. Isabella's voice broke the intense look that passed between them.

'See that Carina gets her costume too. I'd like you to be at the house by six. I want to arrange the exhibition myself before out guests arrive. I'll see you later.' As Isabella swept imperiously from the room the servant looked at Rebecca and grinned lasciviously. 'I'll see you later,' he mimicked, and then followed in Isabella's wake.

Before Rebecca had time to take the costume off Carina came in, bleary-eyed and dressed in the clothes she had worn the previous day. She looked Rebecca up and down and grinned. 'You look like a Christmas tree, what did the vixen bring for me?'

Rebecca shook her head, her mind still on the dark hungry look on the servant's face. 'I don't know. I thought we might see Leo this morning.'

Carina was already opening the second box and giggled furiously. 'Looks like they've got us down as a matched pair, honey.' She spun round holding a dress almost identical to Rebecca's up against herself. The only difference was that Carina's dress was made of rich scarlet satin. 'Leo won't come here without her while we're on Long Island.' Carina grinned, 'That bitch hates me and if Leo's hooked on you, she'll hate you too. With her here we won't get a minute alone with him. She ain't as sure of him as she makes out—' Without a second's hesitation, Carina sloughed off her hastily donned day-clothes and pulled the costume on. 'The only way Isabella keeps him is by letting him do what he wants, she's got too much to lose to do anything else. You're gonna have to lace me into this—'

Carina said, wriggling the sleeves up over her arms. 'Looks like it's whores and highwaymen.'

Rebecca burst out laughing. 'What?'

Carina turned round so Rebecca could lace her up. 'The de Viton's always have a theme for their parties. We've had senators and slaves, vamps and tramps.' She winced as Rebecca pulled the laces tight. 'Whoa there, gimme some space to breath.'

Rebecca slackened off the laces. 'Sorry.'

'Jesus, what the hell are those—' Callum spoke from across the room. Both women swung round as he made his way unsteadily towards them cradling his head. He peered at them with a mixture of pain and barely disguised interest. 'You two look amazing.'

Carina did a slow twirl, the skirt opened to reveal her long shapely legs and amongst the white and scarlet the dark triangle of her sex. Callum sat down grinning. Carina's breasts rested amongst the broad band of intricate lace like an exotic confection. He looked at Rebecca who followed suit, letting the broad ribbons arc out from her lithe body. He glanced up into her eyes. 'Are you sure you really want to do this?' he said slowly. 'I mean you look fantastic but . . .' his voice trailed off. 'You'll have to beat the men off with a stick.'

Carina grinned. 'That's the general idea, shame you aren't coming. I've got this thing about knights in shining armour.'

Rebecca stroked his face. 'One last wild fling, Callum and then it's all over.'

Callum sighed. 'Then you'll come back to New York with me?'

Carina tutted, 'Lighten up, Mr White Knight, and get me my mask out of that box. I'll get Marcie to make us some coffee and then I think you'd better hit the road. Leo ain't going to be too pleased if he finds you tucked up with us two.'

Callum looked back and forth between their faces. Rebecca nodded, 'I think Carina's right, Callum, you really ought to go.' She could see the tenderness and the concern in his face and also the flicker of desire that the two of them aroused in him. She reached out and took him in her arms. 'Please, Callum. Just for tonight.'

He moved closer, pulling her to him, closing his fingers around her narrow corseted waist. 'God, you are so lovely,' he whispered. 'Why don't you just come away with me now? You and Carina.'

Rebecca shook her head. 'No, I've said I'll stay for tonight and that's what I'm going to do.'

He looked into her eyes. 'And what about tomorrow?'

She kissed him lightly, relishing the familiar feel of his lips and the subtle smell of his body. 'Tomorrow everything begins again,' she said softly. He returned her kiss, pressing her close to him, hands lifting to stroke and tease along her spine. She felt a ripple of excitement and moaned softly. Pulling away she smiled, 'Don't make this any more difficult, Callum. I've already said I'm going to stay.'

He nodded. 'Okay, I'll have that coffee and then get out of here. But I'll be back for you first thing tomorrow.'

She nodded.

It was mid-afternoon when Callum finally left, without him the bungalow seemed empty and the atmosphere flat. Carina lay across the sofa in a robe, eyes closed, her costume discarded beside her on the floor. Marcie cleared away while Carina hummed quietly to herself. After a few seconds she opened one eye. 'I think maybe that boy loves you, girl.'

Rebecca felt a little plume of sadness in her stomach. 'I know,' she said thickly.

Carina pulled herself upright. 'So are you going to go back to New York with him?'

Rebecca shrugged. 'First of all I've got to sort things out with Oliver.'

'Your fiancé?'

Rebecca nodded miserably. 'I've said I'll meet him on Monday to discuss our future.'

Carina snorted, ' "Our future"? I thought it was all over an' done with him?'

Tears bubbled up in Rebecca's eyes. 'I wish it was that simple. I loved Oliver for years.' She hesitated, 'I think even after everything that's happened part of me still loves him.'

Carina pulled a face. 'And what about Callum?'

Rebecca shook her head slowly. 'I don't know. I . . . I . . .'

Carina waved a hand to silence her. 'Don't get so blue, baby. It'll sort itself out.' She grinned. 'And if neither of them hit the spot there's always Leo.'

Rebecca groaned. 'Don't,' she said unhappily. 'I think I'm going to go and have a shower.'

The singer eased herself back onto the sofa, uncurling like a sleek panther, her robe clinging to every sensual exotic curve. 'Sounds like a fine idea. Would you like me to come and give you a hand?'

Rebecca laughed. 'Why not.'

It was almost dark when Carina and Rebecca made their way, arm in arm, across to the mansion. Around them, wrapped up against the cool night air, a masked crowd hurried alongside them. In the dark Rebecca caught momentary flashes of brilliant colour peeking out from under an assortment of dark overcoats. The atmosphere was strange; jovial and noisy but with a peculiar air of expectancy. Rebecca kept close to Carina who strode towards the house with a confidence that Rebecca didn't feel.

Inside the mansion they were directed into a large room where uniformed footmen stood waiting to take their coats and hand out glasses of champagne. Rebecca was astonished as she stepped inside; the room was filled with people of every kind, colour, shape and size. Everyone was masked, costumes glittering brilliantly in the light of the chandeliers. Beside her a voluptuous woman with titian hair and exquisite creamy skin was dressed in a scarlet corset which accentuated the breathtaking curves of her large body. Beside her a tall black man was dressed in a white shirt, open to the waist, with tight leggings which revealed every scintillating curve of his exotic muscular frame.

Carina handed Rebecca a glass of champagne. 'We are the pick of the crop, honey,' she purred, sipping from her glass. 'There's someone in this room to cater to every taste. And believe me, some of Leo's friends have some pretty strange tastes—'

Rebecca turned so that she couldn't be overheard by the laughing, talking crowd of people around her. 'Why does he do this?'

'Who, Leo?' said Carina, taking a hefty swig from her glass.

Rebecca nodded. 'It must cost him a small fortune.'

Carina grinned. 'And makes him one too. Powerful men have powerful passions. Leo de Viton supplies them – at a price.'

Rebecca froze, comprehension dawning. 'He blackmails them?' she said unsteadily.

Carina smiled, lifting her glass in salute to astounding blonde twins who waved a greeting in her direction. 'I don't think it ever comes to that,' she said from the corner of her mouth. 'He'd never need to go that far, there's just an understanding between him and the people he invites here, if you follow me.'

In a normal voice she introduced Rebecca to the two stunning girls. They were dressed in white, like peasant milk-maids, flowers plaited into their tussled, tumbling blonde locks. A footman circled between the groups handing out more champagne, Carina took another glass and handed it to Rebecca. When she began to protest Carina pressed it into her hand. 'Take it, honey, It's going to be a long hard night, this'll help you relax.'

It was almost an hour before Isabella de Viton appeared through the double doors at the end of the room. Silence fell in seconds. Rebecca was standing near the wall, letting the champagne bubble delightfully through her veins when Isabella lifted her hands for order.

Their hostess smiled warmly. 'Good evening, may I say you all look wonderful,' she said softly, glancing around the crowded room. 'Our guests are still eating at the moment so I'd like you all to be quiet when we go into the main house.' Rebecca turned to concentrate on what she was saying and felt a strange ripple of emotion. Isabella was flanked by the footman Rebecca had encountered earlier and Leo's chauffeur. She was glad that the mask hid most her face – she could feel her colour rising.

Isabella was explaining that the men should follow the chauffeur, women dressed in white should follow the footman and those in scarlet or green were to come with her. Carina who had been talking to the twins looked at Rebecca and grinned. 'Sounds like us, honey,' she said in a low whisper. For the first time Rebecca felt nervous. This was the moment when she surrendered to whatever it was the de Vitons had in mind for them. She tightened her fingers around her champagne glass to stop them from trembling.

As the groups began to separate, Rebecca fell into step behind Carina. The house where she had spent the last few days suddenly seemed alien. She barely recognised the main hall decked with candles and great swags of greenery. At the centre of the room was a huge four-poster bed, swathed in great folds of white lace, the covers folded back in invitation. On the stage under the stairs a group of masked troubadours played folk tunes. She looked towards Carina for reassurance but the singer was watching Isabella ahead of them as the Italian woman climbed the stairs.

On the first landing was a plinth, manacles set into each of the four corners. A footman guided the Junoesque bulk of the red-headed woman onto it. She crouched on all fours, her heavy breasts swaying slightly as the man secured her ankles. Rebecca swallowed hard, looking away as she saw the gleam of expectation in the woman's eyes. Isabella waved them on. Rebecca glanced back, the red-headed woman was secure now, the heavy folds of her full buttocks opening to reveal the delicate pink shell of her sex, surrounded by coppery curls.

Rebecca's apprehension grew with each step and alongside it the dark throbbing heat of anticipation. At each turn and alcove along the length of the corridors one or two of the group were left behind, to be attended to by the footmen. Finally there was just Carina and Rebecca. Isabella glanced over her shoulder at them and smiled narrowly. 'I thought you two might like the chance to be together as you seem such firm friends.' There was an edge to her voice and it struck Rebecca that of all of the exhibits in the mansion it was perhaps Carina and Rebecca that Isabella had most to fear from. She turned round to face them both, from the shadows the footman appeared carrying another box. Rebecca winced as he grinned at her from behind his mistress's shoulder. 'I think,' Isabella said quietly, 'that we'll dispense with the costumes you have on. These will suit you much better.'

Rebecca looked at Carina in desperation but Carina's eyes were firmly on Isabella's. 'What have you got in mind?' she said in her rich, caramel-brown voice.

Isabella smiled. 'Show the ladies,' she said to her footman, without letting her eyes flicker for an instant.

The man grinned and undid the box, inside were two shiny leather basques, with straps at the back. The bodice was cut low so that their breasts would be pressed forward and from the neckline were thin leather thongs from which hung a studded leather collar. Isabella smiled. 'Would you help the ladies out of their dresses?' she said coolly. Rebecca started to tremble as the footman walked around her and began to untie the laces of her long dress. Carina smiled pleasantly. 'Maybe you'd like to help me with mine, Isabella?' she said teasingly.

The other woman lifted an eyebrow. 'I don't think so. Rebecca, help her.'

With shaking fingers, Rebecca untied the laces of Carina's bodice while behind her she could feel the invasive prying fingers of the footman. He pushed her dress down over her shoulders, his rough fingers brushing her nipples. She shuddered as he turned to hand her the black leather basque.

The basque was skin-tight, the soft leather biting into her flesh. It finished at the top of her hips in a soft roll, shaped down in a triangle towards her sex. Carina helped her to fasten the straps, seemingly oblivious of the footman behind her fastening hers. Rebecca could feel the light electric hum of sensuality beneath her fingertips, glowing under Carina's skin. Carina eased back against her, purring softly. 'Ummm,' she whispered in an undertone, 'you feel so good.' Her ripe buttocks brushed Rebecca's belly and to her astonishment she felt a tight ripple of excitement deep inside her.

From the box, the man then produced short, high-heeled leather boots and black leather masks which he handed wordlessly to each of the women before gathering up the discarded remains of the long dresses.

Rebecca stared at Carina as she turned around slowly, she looked stunning; the black leather basque accentuated every subtle plain and curve, her breasts with their large dark nipples jutted forward, nipples that were already erect and swollen. Carina grinned and mouthed her a kiss. From the corner of her eye Rebecca saw Isabella grimace, as she stooped to slip on the boots. The boots had a small ring set into the stitching on the ankles. When they had put on the masks, Isabella smiled. 'Good, now follow me.' She glanced at her watch, 'Dinner will be over soon and I would like you two to be in place.'

Along the corridor was a circular open area where four corridors met. In the centre was a large padded plinth, subtly lit from above. Rebecca gasped as she saw the chains set into the base. Isabella smiled as she saw Rebecca's expression and held out her hand in invitation. Carina climbed onto the block first, crouching on all fours.

Isabella shook her head. 'Oh no, I'd like you on the bottom, lay down and let my man chain you in place.' Rebecca watched; Carina lay on her back, legs hanging

either side of the plinth while the footman secured her
ankles to the base. He slipped gauntlets round her wrists
securing her arms above her head. The tiny locks snapped
shut with a distinctive sound. Carina eased her hips down
until they were comfortable. Rebecca swallowed hard; her
companion looked astounding, an erotic masterpiece
waiting, open and ready for the attentions of a passing
lover. Rebecca could feel the little ripple growing inside
her, feel the heat between her legs. Isabella turned towards
Rebecca. 'Now you,' she said darkly. 'On all fours above
your friend. Isn't that how you like it?' she paused. 'Does
she taste good?'

Rebecca flushed and walked hesitantly up to the block.
Above them on one of the walls she could see a key hanging
– the key to their shackles. Dumbly, she mounted the
plinth, her sex a few inches away from Carina's face. She
closed her eyes as she felt the man snapping the chains into
her boots and didn't resist as he slipped the gauntlets over
her narrow wrists.

The sound of Isabella's voice made her shiver. 'You look
good enough to eat,' she purred. Rebecca stiffened as she
felt an exploratory hand run over her thighs. 'A final touch
I think.'

Cool fingers seized her breasts and she felt the slick kiss
of Isabella's lipstick outlining her nipples. She bit her lip,
feeling them harden under the other woman's attentions
and was relieved when Isabella finished. Below her she
heard Carina moan and knew that her breasts were getting
the same treatment.

'There,' said Isabella on an outward breath. 'I think
we're ready. I'll see you both later. Our guests will be with
you soon. I'm sure you will be very popular—'

From behind closed eyes Rebecca heard the soft

padding footsteps of Isabella retreating along the corridor. She let out a sigh of relief and opened her eyes, astonished to find she was staring into the contorted features of the footman. He grinned, his fingers lifting to caress her face. 'And later,' he said quietly, 'you'll see me too.'

Rebecca froze as he turned and followed his mistress along the corridor. She watched them retreat and realised, for the first time that she could see several of her fellow exhibits along the corridor. Turning her head to look left and right she saw they were at the centre of the exhibition. Below her Carina made a soft noise of pleasure and nuzzled softly at her thigh, 'You look real beautiful,' she whispered. 'Don't let her get to you, you know she's afraid. Leo's real hooked up on you.'

Rebecca sighed, 'You too?'

Carina laughed, 'I think so. Now let me show you how good you make me feel.'

Rebecca shivered as the woman's tongue tickled across her thighs.

'There, baby,' Carina whispered. 'Doesn't that feel good?'

Downstairs, Oliver Cresswell took another sip of from his brandy glass and a mask from the tray that the footman offered him. Around the smoking room the air of expectation had grown steadily since the moment they had taken their places for dinner. Beside him George was tying his mask on and grinning broadly. He glanced at Oliver. 'The game is on,' he said warmly.

Oliver smiled, glad that Isabella hadn't joined them for dinner. Fortunately he hadn't had any chance to be alone with Leo or Isabella since they'd arrived – and he was pleased. He turned the face mask over thoughtfully between his fingers. His intention was to play along – after all he didn't have to take part in any of the promised high jinx. He would watch, observe, maybe have another drink or two and then, as soon as he could, discreetly retire to his bedroom. It wouldn't be long until Monday; Monday and his meeting with Rebecca. Her face filled his mind.

Across the room, breaking his thoughts, the double doors into the smoking room opened and framed Isabella de Viton. She looked breathtaking in a sparkling silver evening dress, slashed to the waist to reveal her sumptuous curves.

Leo stepped forward and slid his arm though hers. 'Gentleman,' he said in a pleasant voice. 'May I invite you to partake of tonight's entertainment.' He glanced up at the clock. 'Later we'll round off the evening with a game of hare and hounds.' He and Isabella stepped back from the door and the first of the revellers began to trickle out into the main hallway. Oliver laid the mask back on the sideboard. George looked at him. 'What's this, Oliver?'

He shrugged. 'I think I'm going to go to my room.'

George grimaced, 'I hadn't had you down as a wet blanket, old chap.' He paused. 'No need to touch, why not just take a little look at the goods on offer – no commitment to buy, eh?' He chuckled at his own words and headed off towards the door. Oliver picked up the mask and reluctantly followed him.

What Oliver saw in the hall astonished him. During dinner the hall had been transformed. A huge four-poster bed now stood in the centre of the room, graced by identical blonde twins dressed in flowing white dresses. Either side of the stairs two coloured men stood, bearing antique pistols and tri-corn hats. Dressed as highway men their muscular torso and exotic colouring was enhanced by open white cotton shirts, in fact as he glanced around the huge room every surface seemed to be draped with an erotic masked confection. He turned to say something to George Winterton, only to discover his godfather had vanished. Around him his fellow diners began to break away to view the exhibits.

He took another pull on his brandy glass, wondering what to do next. Watching the guests he didn't hear the cat-like approach of his hostess and jumped when she spoke. 'Can you see anything to your taste, Oliver?' she purred, slipping her arm through his. She looked up into his eyes. 'George tells me you've visited several cat-houses with him – or do you just like to watch?'

Oliver couldn't find the words to reply. Across the room one of the few female weekend guests was standing beside one of the highwaymen. Her long pale fingers were cupping his crotch whilst her other hand teased across his naked chest, fingers circling the dark purple buds of his nipples. Oliver shivered as the woman sank down to her knees in front of him, her carmine lips working wet hot kisses across his flat muscular belly.

Beside him, Isabella laughed. 'Why don't you join in? She wouldn't mind sharing. If she weren't so famous I'd have asked her to come as one of our exhibits. Look at the way she uses her mouth. My God, how good that must feel.'

Oliver tore his eyes away from the woman at the foot of the stairs as she peeled open the highwayman's leggings, guiding his magnificent engorged cock between her lips. Beside him, Isabella's eyes glittered, fiery with need. 'Perhaps you'd like me to do the same for you?' She rested her fingers on the arm of his dinner jacket and bent her knees as if she would sink to the floor. Oliver gasped and stepped away from her as he saw Leo de Viton watching them from the corner of his eye.

She shrugged. 'Explore then, there are some interesting exhibits upstairs.' She turned and walked back towards her husband. Oliver was relieved to see her disappear amongst the throng of guests. Around him the others were pairing off with the exhibits. Several vanished – unlike the blonde woman at the bottom of the stairs – into shady alcoves or the maze of rooms off the main hall. Isabella turned to look at him and lifted a hand in salute, her tongue teasing sensuously around her beautifully painted lips. Without hesitation Oliver hurried past the blonde woman and her highwayman and up the stairs – at least upstairs he wouldn't have to contend with Isabella and her barely veiled desire.

At the entrance to the first landing was a bar, staffed by wenches dressed as provocatively as the exhibits downstairs. He stopped to refill his brandy glass and then turned towards the hall that lead into the rest of the mansion. He tried to get his bearings – his room was on the next floor, the staircase at the back of the house. He leant back against the bar trying to collect his thoughts. Accepting Leo's invitation had been a bad move. He let the guests move around him, some alone, or arm in arm with exotic masked men or women. Their every move betrayed a raw sensuality and sexual promise. Oliver offered his glass over the bar for a refill. Finally he stepped into the corridor that led to the staircase. The first thing that caught his eye was a huge red-headed woman on all fours. She was gloriously naked except for a scarlet corset. Behind her, impaled to the very hilt was one of the men who he had met briefly at dinner. The woman was moaning softly as her rider pressed deeper and deeper. Her ample flesh seemed to engulf her lover, seizing him, drawing him in. Oliver was so astounded he stood for an instant to watch them. They were oblivious to him, chasing their wild release. He wondered why they hadn't retired to one of the bedrooms until in the soft light he saw the flicker of metal and realised the statuesque woman was chained to the plinth, held captive for whoever might come along to take her.

He gasped and felt the first stirrings of excitement. The red-head plunged on, thrusting herself back against her rider, letting out little wild sobs of delight, her high-pitched voice at odds with her frame. He could see the slick juices of her excitement where they trickled onto her ample thighs. Ahead of him guests were finding and taking advantage of the captive exhibits. Others watched, sipping drinks, the light in their eyes betraying their own desire. Oliver could feel the heat in his belly growing. In the next alcove a beautiful young man was strapped to the wall. His pale golden body oiled and smooth . . . Behind him another guest slid an appreciative hand across the young man's naked back before picking up a delicate leather whip from a side table. The masked man weighed it speculatively in his fingers before bringing it down across the boy's flesh. His captive moaned softly, while behind him the guest slipped off his dinner jacket.

Oliver felt stunned, he had never, in all the whorehouses and parties he had been to, seen anything that matched the decadent sensual indulgence of the de Viton's house party. His intentions to go to his room were fast dissolving as he saw the next exhibit, and the next and the next . . . his mind reeled.

Callum O'Neill had really intended to leave Leo de Viton's estate. He reminded himself of that as he approached the mansion door from the bungalow complex. He was going to take one look at what was going on and then go away – clean, simple, final. He grinned to himself; he was a very poor liar. If he'd really intended to go he wouldn't have hung around getting his ass frozen in the bushes waiting for Rebecca, Carina and the rest of the people in the bungalows to go across to the main house. No, he would have got into the truck he'd borrowed and gone back to the hotel he'd booked himself into.

The door into the mansion was unlocked and the ante-room beyond in complete darkness. He stepped inside and waited for his eyes to adjust to the gloom before carefully making his way towards the door that he assumed led into the main house. Just as he got within striking distance of the handle the door opened and the room was flooded with light. To his horror he came face to face with Isabella de Viton. She looked at him in astonishment. 'Callum O'Neill?' she said slowly.

He nodded, imagining that any second a group of large men would appear to 'escort' him off the premises. To his surprise, she smiled. 'Well, well, fancy seeing you here. I suppose you've come to find Rebecca Hunt?'

Callum nodded, reluctant to speak in case he inadvertently revealed he'd not only found Rebecca but spent the night with her.

She looked him up and down thoughtfully. 'Perhaps, Mr O'Neill, you might care to join us? Presuming of course that you don't intend to cause a scene.'

'Not my intention at all,' he said casually.

Her lips widened into a predatory smile. 'In that case I'll find you something more suitable to wear. I'm afraid that you'll have to join our little soiree as part of the entertainment. I don't think we can find a spare dinner suit at such short notice.' She opened a cupboard and pulled out a soft white shirt and jodhpurs. 'I think these will fit,' she said, eyeing them and then him. 'There are boots in there too. You'll have to find a pair that fit and make sure you wear a mask.' She indicated a box on one of the chairs in the room and then paused. 'If you come to our party, Mr O'Neill, you'll have to join in the fun.'

He took the clothes from her, aware of her heady perfume and the dark sensual invitation in her eyes. 'What exactly does that mean, Isabella?'

She leant forward her lips brushing his. 'Oh, it can mean almost anything. But I think you understand that, don't you?'

Callum shivered, 'I'm not sure what . . .' he began.

Isabella traced her finger slowly across his rough cheek. 'My husband wanted to find out about you. It's quite fascinating what a few discreet inquiries can reveal about a person.'

Callum began to undo his shirt, keeping his expression relaxed and open. The last thing he wanted to let Isabella de Viton know was that she unnerved him.

'It seems that Rebecca isn't your first protegée.'

Callum let his shirt slip to the floor slowly, ignoring the way Isabella let her eyes move over his chest. 'So?' he said coolly.

Isabella grinned a sharp wolf-like grin. 'Does your little friend, Miss Hunt, know that you also like a little male flesh from time to time?'

Callum flushed crimson in spite of himself. 'I've never hidden it from her.'

Isabella laughed. 'So you haven't told her, then. Well, never mind, tonight you can indulge yourself in whatever kind of meat takes your fancy. Oh and by the way – first names only. Our guests value their anonymity.' She opened the door and stepped through before turning back. 'And then after tonight you can take your little friend away and do what you like with her. I want Rebecca Hunt out of Leo's life. Do you understand?' Her tone was cold and crisp and for the first time Callum realised that Isabella feared the effects of Rebecca on her marriage. Leo must be more entranced than he was prepared to admit.

Rebecca stretched as far as the chains would allow her and watched the masked man circle her and Carina. Behind his mask his eyes were alight with excitement and lust. Below her, Carina moaned softly, easing her tongue up against Rebecca's thigh. The delicate wet caress made Rebecca shiver. Since they had been chained together the singer had pleasured her again and again with wave after wave of teasing tentative explorations and tender kisses. Just as she was within a hair's breadth of reaching her climax Carina would pull away, leaving her breathless with anticipation and frustration. She had moaned, pleading for release while the woman below her grinned lazily. 'We've got all night, baby,' she murmured. 'Let me show you just how good this can get.'

Rebecca, panting, had fought to stay in control, only for Carina to begin again – each little foray exciting Rebecca more and more. Carina's loving caresses seemed to have little to do with the party, as if they were in a world apart. Each delicate touch was turning on the well stream of ecstasy in Rebecca's mind. She heard, in the distance, the sound of the party beginning but had ignored it as she'd dipped to press her lips to the fragrant outer lips of her companion, wanting to share and return the pleasure she was feeling.

Now the party had moved closer. The man moved around them, as if he were drinking in their mutual excitement. His eyes on them intensified Rebecca's pleasure. Between her legs Carina moaned and lifted her head, fingers opening Rebecca's sex for her tongue. As the dusky woman found the cloaked hood of her clitoris again, all thoughts of the party, even the man who was watching them, seemed to slowly ebb away in her consciousness.

She remembered the night before; Callum's hard masculine body a stunning contrast to Carina's soft curves. The images were jumbled with a stunning erotic tableau of the sexual adventures she had had since meeting Leo, Carina and Callum; the pictures flooded her feverish mind – and she knew she was slowly drowning in a sea of sensuality. She lowered herself slowly onto Carina's lapping tongue, relishing the growing joy the woman lit in her.

Around them, echoing her excitement, she heard the sounds of pleasure coming from the exhibits in the rest of the hall. She could sense that release was a few seconds away, if only Carina would guide her into the dark glittering pit of oblivion this time. Her breasts ached, her sex throbbed with pleasure and moisture. She felt Carina's mouth opening her wider, sucking and milking the delicate inner folds of her sex. The feelings spiralled out from her clitoris in growing rings of intensity and she let out a delicate sob, plunging her tongue into the other woman's sex. Carina bucked to meet her, the taste of her growing excitement flooded Rebecca's mouth, intensifying her own gratification.

Just as her mind exploded into brilliant crystal shards of pleasure she felt a finger sliding into her sex; exploratory, cool, testing her, finding a way deep inside as if they wanted to touch her orgasm, be part of it. Her body tightened instinctively around it heightening and compounding the sensations she felt. She shuddered, feeling the after-waves ripple through her and Carina's body, as if they were of one mind.

Now she felt the man's hands on her, every nerve-ending glowing – in the aftermath of her climax his touch was closer to pain than pleasure. She could feel his breath on her back and between her legs, the hot damp breaths of Carina on her throbbing sex.

'Too soon, too soon,' she managed to gasp in a thick voice she barely recognised as her own. His reply was to run his fingers down over her breasts, seeking out her nipples, nipping and twisting, sending jagged white hot flashes of sensation through her mind. She groaned, knowing it was futile to resist – even at the point of orgasm some part of her longed to feel a cock inside her, pressed home to the hilt.

The realisation that he had watched Carina tonguing her to orgasm and that he could just take her because she was there and available for his use, lit another beacon in her mind. She dropped her hips, submitting to his caresses in the most ancient of gestures.

She heard him moan softly. His hands, running over her leather-clad waist stroked the rounded arc of her buttocks, fingers dipped into her sex and across the dark forbidden button above. He seemed to take her over, stroking, nipping, spreading her gently for his explorations. One finger eased into the tight closure above her sex, other fingers stroking the delicate sensitive bridge of flesh between them. Before she had been afraid of this most intimate of caresses, now she was stunned to feel the arousal his knowing, stroking touch lit in her. She whimpered, dropping lower so that he could have access to every part of her. She heard him open his flies and closed her eyes as the scent of Carina's sex flooded her nostrils. Something brushed her face and she jumped, startled by the unexpected touch. Carina had lifted up her legs and between them stood another man, his fingers tenderly stroked Rebecca's cheek and she knew instantly without a shadow of a doubt that it was Callum O'Neill.

Before she could quite grasp how he was there, she felt the brush of a meaty phallus against her inner thigh. Her mysterious lover sought entry, fingers opening her, guiding the head of his shaft between her legs. She shivered as he slid inside, every fibre of her aching to feel him fill her. She pushed herself back onto him, driving him deeper and at the same time felt a finger open the dark bud of her bottom. She shuddered, pressing her face towards Carina's sex as the feelings of his entry overtook her.

She lapped now, aware of the solid throbbing bulk of Callum's cock where it slid into Carina's body. She sucked and kisses the junction of their bodies, running her tongue along his shaft, wet with Carina's juices and her own saliva. She could feel Carina's tongue too between her legs and without hesitation gave herself entirely to the wild rhythm of their love-making. Her rational thoughts were blotted out by the sheer power of the pleasure she felt.

Oliver Cresswell let the leather-clad girl's body engulf him, drawing him deep into the hot swollen depths of her quim. There was something achingly familiar about her body. The leather harness nipping her delicate curves excited him beyond all measure. Beneath her eager body the dark girl's tongue worked along his shaft; the ultimate addition to this erotic tableau. He worked his finger slowly deeper into the crouching girl's backside, feeling his shaft plunging deeper and deeper into her sex through the delicate web of flesh that divided her two entrancing orifices. Christ, she was tight, her body closed around him like a collar. It was all he could do to stay in control. In front of him he watched the face of his male companion, who had manfully stepped up to service the black girl. Their thrusts were in harmony, a scintillating ballet of pleasure and sensation. He drove deeper with finger and cock, while below him the crouching girl dropped lower, giving herself over entirely to his needs and the tongue of the coloured girl. He wanted to make her scream out for more. He could sense her rekindled excitement, knowing that the coloured girl was licking not only at his shaft but at that tiny bud of pleasure that drove women wild.

He started imagining the tastes, the juices mingling – the thought was enough. Suddenly he could feel the impossible undeniable press of white-hot light coming up from low in the pit of his stomach. With one hand he grabbed at the collar around the girl's neck, dragging her back onto him, pulling her closer and closer until he thought he might disappear into her sex, soaked up, drawn in, and then it was there – a screaming explosion of glorious, thundering gratification that drove away all sanity, crushing him in its roaring, white water. 'Oh, my God, oh, my God,' he sobbed, as the wave pulled him under again and again and then he collapsed down onto the girl's back, feeling her orgasm sucking the last of his seed away, an ebbing tide dragging him to the very brink of madness.

Rebecca sobbed out a wild throaty yell, words of pleasure stifled by the soft wet folds of Carina and Callum's body – and then something made her freeze. Something that wasn't possible. She eased herself into a more comfortable position, feeling the heat of her masked lover burning her back, feeling his sweat trickling down onto her shoulder blades. It couldn't be . . . Above her, the masked man eased out of her making soft tired noises of pleasure. 'My God,' he whispered again on a thick gasping outward breath and then she knew for certain. The masked man was Oliver Cresswell.

Chapter 11

Callum eased himself out from Carina's throbbing quim and turned to get the key to unlock both women. Across from him his masked companion grinned a salute.

'No,' said a sharp familiar voice from the shadows. Isabella de Viton stepped out into the light in the company of her husband and a small plump elderly man who grinned at the other masked rider.

'Changed your mind, eh lad? Can't say that I blame you,' he said in a crisp English accent. The other man laughed and began to pull on his evening clothes.

Isabella smiled thinly at Callum. 'You can let Carina go, but we have other plans for your friend,' she purred in a whisper.

Callum eyed her thoughtfully. 'Plans?'

Isabella nodded. 'Our friend, the judge, has been waiting to renew his acquaintance with your lady friend. Haven't you?' She glanced back into the face of a florid heavily-built man, who nodded enthusiastically. Callum looked down; cradled in the man's hands was a flat leather paddle.

His fingers shook as he turned to undo Carina's bonds. Rebecca looked up into his eyes and shivered. Callum felt a strange elation – he wanted to see what the judge was going to do. The glittering feral look in Rebecca's eyes betrayed her excitement. He swallowed hard, it was difficult to leave Rebecca tied and vulnerable but he had no doubt that at some level she wanted what was to follow. He stepped back as the judge moved around the plinth. From under the older man's mask a bead of sweat trickled down onto his cheek. The judge ran his hands speculatively over his plump pink target and without prelude brought the flat face of the paddle down with a resounding whack. Rebecca let out a wild throaty yell. Callum stepped forward, he wasn't sure he could bear to see her hurt.

Leo de Viton's arm restrained him. 'Watch her eyes, Mr O'Neill,' he said slowly.

Callum froze for an instant, Isabella must have told Leo who he was and he wondered what Leo intended to do about him being there uninvited. Before Callum could think about Leo any more his attention was drawn back to Rebecca as the head of the paddle exploded across her buttocks again. She wailed excitedly, straining against her gauntlets, trying to wriggle away from the electric flash of pain and then he saw the look Leo de Viton had recognised – a wild eager glint of something dark and unfathomable. The paddle rose again and he was aware of the masked man who had made love to Rebecca standing beside him, entranced by the show that was going on on the plinth. Rebecca bucked, her breasts flushed pink, her nipples erect and excited.

Callum could sense the other man's renewed excitement – and his own. The masked man had left off his jacket, his dinner shirt clung damply to the muscular outline of his waist and shoulders. Callum ran a finger tentatively along the man's spine. The masked man turned towards him, eyes alight with another familiar dark passion; one that Callum hadn't allowed himself since Rebecca's arrival in his life. His masked companion smiled and then turned his attention back to Rebecca and the judge. Callum let his fingers remain on his new companion's back, stroking the strong muscles at the base of his spine. The man leant back against his touch and sighed.

On the plinth Rebecca's mind was racing, she could see Oliver and Callum standing shoulder to shoulder watching her with barely veiled pleasure. The pain of the judge's paddle momentarily broke her concentration but she felt as if she were above the stinging hot sensation. Her thoughts were coming in a wild impossible jumble. It *was* Oliver – there was no doubt in her mind now. She recognised his distinctive stance, the way he moved. What on earth was he doing at the de Viton's party? The paddle bit into her flesh again, sending a glittering ricochet of sensation through her exhausted body – the blow seemed harder than the first few strokes as if the judge sensed she was not concentrating.

He stepped up behind her, running his rough hands over her smarting, glowing flesh. One finger slipped into her sex, and a second more invasively slipped towards the puckered tight closure that Oliver had explored with such delicacy. He must have seen Oliver at work and she realised with horror that the judge's interest lay more in that direction than in the slick open folds of her quim.

He grunted as his finger slid deeper. 'Why, little lady,' he said in a throaty voice, 'looks like you've bin opened up for me.' He stepped away, jerking his finger out of the dark flesh and let the paddle bite low, stinging the exposed lips of her sex. She screamed out this time, Oliver forgotten as the judge laid on the paddle with startling ferocity – she had no doubt what would follow. Leo de Viton kept to the shadows, his face impassive. Rebecca glanced up at him, trying to catch his eye, wanting to see if his eyes betrayed his need for her. As she did, Isabella smiled her wolfish, wicked smile and slipped her hand through her husband's arm, pulling him closer she whispered something into his ear before gently leading him away. Rebecca shivered. When the last blow fell she looked up to where Oliver and Callum had been standing – to her surprise they had vanished as well, Oliver's dinner jacket lay abandoned on the floor.

Behind her she heard the judge moving closer. He dipped his fingers into her sex, smearing her juices over the bud of her anus. 'Looks like just me an' you now, lady,' he snorted.

She heard the dull growl as he undid his zip. There was no foreplay, no electric caress of Carina's magical tongue between her legs as the judge roughly pressed his shaft into the most secret places of her body. She winced, a sharp pain echoing though her belly as her tightness closed around him. He grunted and hunkered down over her back. 'Won't you think about coming back home with me, honey?' he snorted thickly, as he pressed himself deeper. 'You'd be real welcome on my hearth rug.'

Rebecca let out a soft mewl of pain and whispered a name – it shocked her to realise it had been Oliver's. Hot tears coursed down her face as the judge fought his way towards his own dark release with no thought for her body or her pleasure. She didn't see the slim form of Isabella de Viton returning to watch, triumphantly, from the shadows.

In a bedroom just off the corridor where Rebecca was receiving her treatment at the hands of the judge, Callum O'Neill slipped off his shirt to reveal his strong muscular torso. The subdued lamp light showed his rugged masculinity off to good advantage, the shadows and highlights accentuating his enticing musculature. He turned to stroke the face of his new companion and smiled lazily, pulling the man towards him, feeling the low electric hum of excitement beneath his skin, a raw masculine throb that excited him in a way no other touch could. Their lips met in a strangely delicate, tentative kiss. Callum moaned softly, undoing the man's shirt to reveal a body as strong and rugged as his own.

The man grinned at him as Callum's lips closed around one dark puckered nipple. 'Do you think we ought to be formally introduced? My name's Oliver—'

Callum groaned theatrically, 'You Brits sure know how to pick your time, I'm Callum. Would you like me to shake your hand?'

Oliver shook his head, grinning still. 'No, I don't think so. God, that feels so good—' and made a soft throaty noise as Callum worked his lips lower, fingers struggling to undo Oliver's flies. He threw back his head drinking in Callum's attentions.

His lightly tanned skin was salty, trembling with anticipation. Oliver arched back as Callum sank slowly to his knees, cupping his companion's cock between his fingers, guiding it seamlessly into his mouth. Oliver let out a tight growl of pleasure as Callum's lips closed around him. Callum licked along his throbbing shaft, relishing the taste of Rebecca's excitement clinging to its engorged head.

Behind a two-way mirror that overlooked the bedroom George Winterton and Leo de Viton watched the two men with cool detachment. George took a pull on his brandy glass. Leo pointed to the erotic scenario that was developing in the room beyond. 'Do they know who the other is?'

George shook his head. 'I don't think so, do you? How is it that Rebecca's lover is here anyway? I'd have thought you wanted to keep her to yourself.'

Leo shrugged. 'Isabella found him wandering around the house. She thought it was better to invite him in than keep him out. No knowing what trouble he might have caused otherwise.' He looked back into the bedroom. Oliver was working his hips, flexing the heavy bands of muscles as Callum lapped at his shaft. Leo grinned. 'Under the circumstances I'm delighted that Isabella showed such foresight. She told me they'd come in here. I had no idea Oliver's tastes ran in this direction—'

George smiled. 'Are there any boundaries to pleasure, Leo, any lines which at times we don't choose to cross over? I think Oliver is just seizing the moment. Sometimes attraction has nothing to do with gender—' He looked back into the subdued light of the bedroom and felt the familiar stirring low in his belly. It was a boundary he had crossed himself on occasions, not often, not habitually, but like Oliver he sometimes chose to drink from a different well.

Leo glanced down at his watch. 'Another half hour and we'll set off the hares. Perhaps when we're done here you and I can find another spectacle to watch.'

George nodded, his attention drawn back to the muscular form of his godson fighting his way towards release; the boy never ceased to delight him. He could barely wait for Oliver to discover Rebecca. He grinned. Damned good brandy too.

Rebecca finally noticed Isabella de Viton watching in the shadows as the judge collapsed sobbing onto her back. The dark tightness was suffused with pain as he slid panting and coughing from her exhausted body.

Isabella smiled and ran her finger over Rebecca's cheeks, dipping lower to cup one of her breasts. 'I'm sure Leo's sorry he missed this,' she purred malevolently. 'It's a shame I didn't bring the harness with me.' Her fingers tightened sharply on one of Rebecca's nipples, making her gasp. Rebecca couldn't control the flurry of dislike she felt for Leo's wife and knew her face would betray her. Isabella's expression didn't falter as she knelt down and unlocked Rebecca's chains. The Italian woman smiled narrowly. 'There's a bathroom at the end of the hall. Why don't you go and freshen up before the chase begins?'

Rebecca slumped down on the plinth feeling as if every shred of energy had been sucked out of her. She looked up. 'Chase?' she said between dry lips.

Isabella grinned. 'Oh yes, we are planning on a game of hare and hounds to round off tonight's entertainment.' She looked pointedly at Rebecca. 'And you are one of the hares. Come downstairs when the bell rings. And don't forget to wear your mask.'

Rebecca hauled herself stiffly off the plinth whilst Isabella swept away into the shadows. Being confined had left her body feeling sore and stiff. Inside the small bathroom she slipped off her mask and washed her face. The judge's attentions had left her feeling used and dirty. She would like to have had a shower to wash away the smell of his body but the straps of the basque were impossible to undo without help. She ran a few inches of water in the bath, slipped off the little leather boots and crouched to wash herself, easing away the feelings of violation with gentle fingers.

She should have asked Isabella about Oliver Cresswell she realised as the water worked its magic. Oliver *and* Callum. Drying herself she looked up into the mirror, her eyes flashed in the soft light of the bathroom. How was it possible they were both there?

Somewhere in the distance she heard a bell ringing. It was important to keep away from Oliver at all costs, he mustn't discover her identity. How could she face him if he knew she was there? The irony wasn't lost on her. He could be as free as he liked, but her? She doubted, given his reaction to their first sexual encounter, that he could be so forgiving.

She dried herself, replaced the mask and strapped the little boots back on. Glancing into the mirror she smiled at her reflection, there was no doubt about it – she did look astounding. The little leather basque showed her figure off to its best advantage. Fleetingly, she thought about Carina, imagining what they must have looked like locked together on the plinth. She tucked her hair back off her face – it had been no wonder that Oliver had found them irresistible.

If only she could get through the rest of the night without him finding out who she was. She was sure Callum would keep her secret – after all she'd told him about Oliver's reaction to their first sexual liaison on the train. He knew all about Oliver. What she would say when they finally met on Monday now seemed like a great muddled, impossible, insoluble puzzle. Her mind still tumbled with contradictions and confusion as she made her way back downstairs.

At the bottom of the stairs a footman waited to direct the hares into another room. The room, below the stairs, was small and almost entirely lined with mirrors. Rebecca glanced around the masked faces trying to find Carina but she didn't seem to be amongst the two dozen or so chosen hares. At the far end of the room french windows opened onto the grounds. Outside the night was dark and star-studded. The sound of someone clapping their hands silenced everyone and Isabella de Viton stepped into the room. She waited until she was certain she had their attention and then began to speak.

'You,' she said in a low voice, 'are the quarry. If you look around the room you will see a series of mirrors. You are being watched by the pack. In ten minutes the french windows will be unlocked and you can make your get-away.' She stopped, and smiled. 'You will discover that the grounds outside have been fenced off to ensure our hounds have a fighting chance, no-one is allowed beyond the boundary fence. All the hares will change into the clothes provided. When you hear the hunting horn the pack will be on its way. Do you understand? At the second blast of the horn is the signal that the game is over.'

There were murmured noises of assent as two footmen handed out a box to each of the women. Inside Rebecca discovered a short tennis skirt, white blouse, short white socks and a pair of running pumps. A blonde girl beside her, dressed in a minuscule scarlet corset, held out the clothes and grinned. 'Not exactly the most erotic little outfit I've ever seen,' she said.

Rebecca laughed. 'You wouldn't be able to run in those,' she said, indicating the girl's spiked high heels.

The blonde giggled, 'Who says I'm going to run? Here let me give you a hand with those straps.'

With the girl's help Rebecca wriggled out of the black leather basque. She was aware of her reflection and sensed the expectation of the pack beyond the glass as she slid the soft leather down over her breasts. It added another erotic charge to know that she was being watched.

Around the changing room was a corridor where the

hounds could walk freely to observe and choose their quarry. Even those who weren't going to take part in the game walked around to admire the glorious selection of goods on offer. The multi-mirrored room revealed every secret place, every pert curve, every lithe, muscular line as the girls changed into their running clothes. Some turned to face the glass, posing and preening provocatively before their hunters.

Oliver Cresswell had given up all intentions of going to his bedroom. The revels were too compelling to miss. Dressed in his shirt-sleeves and evening trousers he watched the girls changing. His attention was drawn particularly to the slim girl who had been dressed in the leather basque. She had a delicate sexuality about her, looking ridiculously pure and untouched despite the surroundings. Her passion seemed understated and sensual rather than raw and blatant. He glanced at his watch, two more minutes and the hunt would be on – and he would make sure he caught her.

'Here, I thought you might like another drink.' Oliver glanced over his shoulder into the eyes of Callum O'Neill and grinned. 'Are you going to play?'

Oliver took the glass and nodded, their earlier intimacy and pleasure transformed easily into jovial bonhomie. 'I am. What about you?'

Callum shrugged. 'Maybe. It's damned cold out there though.'

Oliver laughed. 'The chase will warm you up.' He paused, 'Do you know many of the people here?'

Callum pulled a face. 'A few, by reputation, and I've met the de Vitons,' he said cautiously.

'What about the girls? The exhibits? Are they all professionals?'

Callum paused. 'I don't think so. Our host has a voracious appetite for female flesh—' he began. 'The coloured girl upstairs is a night-club singer, she's his mistress. I'm not sure about the others.'

Oliver pointed to the slim girl who had been dressed in leather. 'What about her? She reminds me of somebody—'

Callum hesitated. 'She . . .' he began and then looked at Oliver with a bemused expression as if something had just registered in his mind.

'Well?' said Oliver. In the mirrored room a footman opened the french windows and their quarry poured out into the night. Oliver watched the slim girl vanish into the darkness.

When Oliver turned back Callum was watching his face. 'What is it?' he said. 'You look as if you've seen a ghost.'

Callum took a long pull on his glass. 'When did you say you arrived in New York, Oliver?'

Oliver grinned. 'I thought we were supposed to remain anonymous. Monday, why?'

Callum stared at him long and hard. 'You've come to sort things out with your fianceé, right?'

Oliver grimaced. 'Yes, how the hell did you know?'

Callum's face was ashen. He stepped forward and touched the two-way mirror as if to brace himself. 'That's Rebecca,' he said unsteadily, nodding into the empty room.

Oliver felt his colour draining. 'What?' he said quietly, convinced that he had misheard.

Callum swallowed hard. 'The girl in the black leather basque, the girl upstairs on the plinth, it's Rebecca Hunt. The girl you've come to find.'

'Oh, my God—' Oliver slammed the glass down on a side table and ran towards the door that lead out into the grounds.

A footman stepped to block his path. 'You're not allowed outside until the horn . . .' Oliver threw him to one side and flung the door open. The cold air hit him like a body blow. 'Rebecca,' he shouted and headed across the grass.

Behind him, as he sprinted across the lawn he could hear the other hounds following him, as if his escape had been the signal for the game to begin. He heard Callum's voice calling his name amongst the mêlée but ignored it. The only thought that filled his mind was finding Rebecca.

Rebecca headed down through the gardens, the cold night air prickling on her skin. It was barbaric, she thought breathlessly, to arrange a chase when it was so cold. Around her other hares were darting back and forth amongst the shrubs looking for hiding places. She broke away from the main pack and headed towards a dark shape against the night sky. Her eyes were gradually adjusting to the gloom – it looked as if it might be a shed or a stable. Since she'd left the comfortable warmth of the mansion she could feel the adrenaline building, the idea of being chased lit a primeval fire in her belly. She had to find a safe place to hide where they couldn't corner her. The dark closed in around the other hares like a cloak.

As she padded towards the building she was aware of every sound and the fact that her clothes – brilliant white against the blackness – would give her away if she stayed out in the open. Pulse pounding, she hurried under the shadow of the building and circled it, behind a high fence marked the boundary of the playing area. She crouched low, letting the shadows embrace her and waited, trying to breathe as quietly as she could.

Soon, she thought, she'd hear the hunting horn and the

game would be on. Behind her along the edge of the boundary fence was a mass of dense bushes, she could slip into them if . . . she paused – if what? Wasn't there some part of her that longed to be pursued by the hunters and thrown on the grass to be taken? She shivered with a mixture of cold and anticipation. Slowly her pulse settled and now the cold felt even more invasive, she wouldn't be able to stay still too long if she wanted to be able to run away. The night sucked the heat from her body through her thin clothes.

On the light breeze came the distant sound of excited male voices – but no hunting horn, had they let the hounds out early? As the thought crossed her mind there was an unexpected explosion of light. Around the grounds hidden floodlights threw up plumes of iridescent yellow. She gasped as the glare temporarily blinded her, one light was hidden amongst the bushes behind her, cutting off her retreat.

'There,' snorted a breathy voice through the undergrowth, 'Over by the shed. You go that way, I'll cut her off—'

Rebecca was instantly on her feet, plunging out from under the lee of the shed and across the grey green lawn. Her breath came in wild explosive bursts, as behind her two men broke cover, divided, and gave chase.

She broke into a fast sprint and headed towards the next group of bushes. Looking back over her shoulder to watch her pursuers Rebecca didn't see the roots snaking across the ground. Her foot caught on something in the darkness and she tumbled headlong into a heap at the base of the tree. Hitting the ground knocked every breath of wind out of her chest. A split second later one of the hounds grabbed her ankles, collapsing in a panting heap beside her. His grin reflected the distant glow of the flood light. She wriggled to free herself, gasping for breath as her captor dragged her closer to him.

'Whoa,' he said breathlessly, 'What shall I do with you now I've caught you?'

Rebecca felt her pulse throbbing in her neck, heart beating wildly from the run as her captor pulled her blouse undone, 'Come here,' he said softly. 'Let me see what it is I've caught.'

She pulled away from him, afraid to speak in case she betrayed her excitement. He tipped her face towards his and kissed her. 'No need to panic,' he said. 'It's only a game, I'm not going to hurt you.' His breath felt hot from his exertions. His hands moved over her body with a proprietorial ease, pushing back her blouse so that he could fondle and cup her breasts. He moaned thickly as he pulled up her skirt, fingers sliding between the lips of her sex. 'Now I've caught you,' he murmured, 'I think I deserve a little prize, don't you?'

In the darkness she heard him fumbling with his flies and saw the pale outline of his engorged cock, creamy white against the dark of his trousers. Still panting, he guided her head down towards his crotch. He let out a soft mewl of pleasure as she drew him into her mouth, lips closing around the swollen throbbing head. With her face pressed against his belly she could feel his heart thundering out a wild tattoo. He groaned as she began to work on him, while his hands caressed her, his pleasure building with every stroke of her lips. He began to shudder and suddenly arched towards her, fingers locked in her hair jerking her closer, as the throbbing waves of his orgasm flooded her mouth.

'God,' he murmured, laughing dryly as he rolled down

amongst the bushes beside her. 'I don't think I'll be able to walk, let alone catch another hare. Don't suppose you fancy staying around until I recover, do you? Maybe you'd like a prize too?'

Rebecca grinned and clambered to her feet, buttoning her blouse with cold fingers, the taste of his salty offering still on her lips. Ahead of her, caught in the floodlight's glare she saw another of the hounds with his back towards her, staring through the floodlights. As she crossed a piece of open ground he glanced back over his shoulder.

Without waiting to find out whether he had spotted her or not she crouched low and plunged into an island of thick bushes, hoping he hadn't seen her. Her heart pumped like an engine. She was so intent on watching the figure in evening dress circling around that she didn't see the figure standing amongst the bushes until it was too late.

She felt a hand clamp over her mouth and a scream choked and died in her throat. 'I said you'd see me later,' hissed a dark voice. She stiffened and turned around slowly until she found herself staring into the glittering eyes of Isabella's footman. She tried desperately to twist out of his grip which closed around her like a vice. Wriggling and squirming she was no match for his strength. One meaty paw closed around her wrists; his breath coming in excited gasps.

'Little Miss High and Mighty,' he snorted thickly. 'You're no better than any of his other whores. I saw you with that man,' he whispered. 'I know what you sort are for.' He grabbed hold of her shoulders and forced her down amongst the thick cover of leaves beneath the tree. He thrust his knee down between her thighs, spreading her legs. She tried to lift herself up, force him off her – she couldn't believe that she couldn't unseat him. He pushed the thin fabric of her blouse back over her shoulders, ripping it in his excitement. She lunged up again to try and get him off her, her breath coming in miserable sobs. 'Please,' she wailed. 'No, please, don't . . .'

'Why not?' he snapped, his fingers grabbing her breasts. 'What's the difference between me and all the others, eh?'

Rebecca whined miserably as he pulled up her skirt, exposing the dark triangle of her sex. He pawed at it like an animal, fingers tearing at her tender flesh. She could feel him wrestling with his flies, grunting breathily as he fought the buttons. She made one more wild effort to get away from him, freeing a hand, she clawed at his face, tearing at his hair.

His eyes flashed with fury. 'You bloody little whore,' he barked. She saw his hand swing back to strike her and screamed as the blow exploded against the side of her head. The floodlights and his face swam, sparks fluttering across her field of vision, as her mouth filled with the coppery taste of blood. 'No, please,' she sobbed, as she felt his cock force an entry into her.

'Rebecca?' A familiar voice galvanised her into action, she began to struggle wildly, while above her the footman froze. 'Rebecca, is that you?'

Her tormentor tried to press his hand down over mouth, but too late to stop her calling out. 'Oliver! Oliver! I'm here—' she sobbed desperately, fighting the man off, hardly able to believe that Oliver Cresswell, of all people, was there to rescue her. The bushes parted and two familiar figures crouched over her. The footman scrambled to his feet, retreating out from under cover of the branches, buttoning his flies as he vanished into the darkness.

'I'll go after him,' said Callum, as Oliver knelt beside the sobbing Rebecca.

'Oliver,' she wept miserably.

He folded her into his arms. 'Shush,' he said tenderly, 'it's all right. I'm here now.'

She snuggled closer, letting his strong arms enfold her, not resisting as he lifted her face towards his, his lips gently brushing hers. 'God, I'm so glad I found you,' he murmured. 'I've missed you so much. You've got no idea—'

She slid her arms around his shoulders, returning his kiss, relishing the heat of his body close to hers. This was all she had ever truly wanted – the realisation astounded her. Everything she had ever wanted was there in her arms. She murmured his name, her voice suffused with desire and relief. He moaned, tracing a delicate path over her bruised breasts; his touch was balm, a sweet electric sensation of pure delight.

'I love you,' he whispered on a soft breath. His words lit a fire in her belly. She had been wrong to leave him, so wrong and so very very foolish. 'Let me show you how much—' He lay her gently amongst the debris of leaves and branches, tongue tracing down over her lips, pressing tender wet kisses into the pit of her throat, over her breastbone, her shoulders, her neck, circling the ripe swell of her breasts. Her whole body responded to him. Her hips arched up to meet his caresses as his tongue worked lower in a silvery starlight spiral of pleasure.

When his mouth closed over the sensitive ridge of her clitoris she almost wept with sheer joy. He whispered soft words of encouragement and love, dipping to open her with his tongue, sucking at the engorged ridges and folds, every sensation, every light touch glittering and golden inside her mind. She ran her fingers through his hair, opening her legs so that he could drink from her, have her all, any part of her was his to do with as he pleased. She wanted to submit entirely to his desire, give herself completely to him. Her excitement mingled with tender feelings of love.

He pressed his tongue deeper, making her bay with delight, smoothing her juices with his fingers over the secret depths of her body. She felt his finger circling the tight little rosebud of her backside and gasped, aware of the sensations coursing through her. He lapped her clitoris, fingers moving around every inch of her sex and beyond. She thought his touch would send her mad. She wanted nothing more than to be with him, spinning out across the frontiers of passion and desire.

He sat up to slip off his trousers. She opened her eyes slowly as if waking from sleep. 'Oliver . . .' she said softly, wanting to make everything right between them; so much had happened. He lifted a finger to her lips. 'We've both been fools,' he said softly. 'Let's begin again, shall we?'

She nodded. 'Yes,' she whispered on an excited breath, as his fingers caressed her again. 'Oh yes.'

He smiled down at her, eyes glittering with tenderness and desire as he moved between her legs. She felt the first electric brush of his cock against her cool skin and trembled. He eased closer, letting the head of his shaft nestle in the outer recesses of her sex. She whimpered softly and thrust her hips towards him, her body wanting nothing more than to feel his cock pressed deep inside her. He let out a dark throaty sob as her sex opened for him. He moved slowly deeper so that she was aware of every slick hot inch of him gliding home into her desperate body. She gasped at his tantalisingly slow progress; it was divine torture.

Just as she thought she might faint he suddenly plunged home, taking her breath away. She lifted her legs to encircle his waist, feeling her pleasure building with every thrust, every slight movement of his body against her. Eagerly she matched his rhythm stroke for stroke.

The cold night, the images of the footman and the de Vitons were lost in her mind as she joined with the man she loved, oblivious to everything except their pleasure and the mesmerising hypnotic rhythm of his body against hers.

Spirals of light and intense sensation grew and multiplied inside her mind, until it seemed as if every ounce of her consciousness was centred on the mercurial junction of their two bodies. She was aware of his breath roaring in her ears, his heartbeat crashing against her breasts and then he whispered her name. Instantly the lights of pleasure exploded in her mind, the spirals fragmenting into glittering crystal shards that swept through every part of her body.

Deep inside she could feel the throbbing heady pulse of his orgasm and called out his name again and again until they both collapsed down amongst the crush of leaves and soil, gasping for breath, their passion spent.

It seemed like a life-time before Oliver gently slipped out of her. She looked up into his familiar eyes glittering in the darkness. 'Do we talk now?' she murmured in an undertone.

He shook his head, laying down beside her propped up on one elbow. 'No, let's pretend we have just met.' He grinned and extended his hand. 'I understand you are a woman of some experience, Miss Hunt, who will make me an exciting, scintillating lover. I'm delighted to make your acquaintance.'

'Is that what lovers say?' she said unsteadily.

Oliver shook his head. 'No, I don't think they do. All I know is that I want you more than anything else on earth. Will you marry me?'

Close by she heard Callum laugh and then the rustle of leaves as he clambered back into the bush. 'You limeys sure have got a funny way of behaving. You're meant to share a cigarette now—'

Rebecca blushed. 'How long have you been standing out there?'

Callum hunkered down onto his hands and knees. 'Long enough to hear Oliver here say he understood you were a woman of some experience.' He mimicked Oliver's educated English accent and then grinned at him. 'Why don't you just tell her you're wild about her, she's a great lay and you wanna spend the rest of your life screwing each other senseless.'

Oliver looked at him thoughtfully and Rebecca wondered for an instant if he might hit him, then Oliver threw back his heard and began to laugh. 'Works for me,' he said between snatched breaths. He turned to Rebecca. 'What do you say, Becky? Shall we spend the rest of our lives in bed together?'

Rebecca smiled. 'Yes,' she said quietly.

They walked back to the house arm in arm with Rebecca between the two men. At the door they were met by George Winterton, cradling a large brandy balloon and obviously a little the worse for drink. He lifted a hand in salute. 'See you found Rebecca then, Oliver,' he said heartily.

Oliver nodded. 'Yes, George, I'd like to know how long you knew she was here?'

George grinned. 'Leo's idea, old boy,' he said. 'Better have a word with him.'

At the doorstep Rebecca hesitated and turned towards Callum as Oliver and George went inside. He took hold of her hand and lifted it to his lips. 'It seems as if it ends here,' he said with more than a trace of sadness in his voice.

'Oh, Callum,' she began.

He pressed his finger to her lips. 'Hush, not a word. I only have to look at the two of you together to know that what you've got is the real thing. He loves you.'

Rebecca looked into his eyes. 'Will he ever be able to forgive me?'

Callum snorted. 'Don't even ask. It makes it sound as if you're owning up to being guilty and you shouldn't be guilty. I promised you an education when we met on the ship.'

Rebecca laughed. 'So what was Leo de Viton?'

Callum thrust his hands into his pockets and pulled a face. 'I'd look on him as finishing school.'

Rebecca hesitated. 'What do you think I ought to say to him?'

Callum grinned. 'Who, Leo? I'd recommend "Goodbye".' He caught hold of her elbow. 'Come on, let's get inside before we freeze to death. Don't want your fiancé falling prey to one of those wild hungry women in there.' He turned back towards her. 'Do you think Carina was serious about wanting a white knight?

Rebecca kissed him gently on the cheek. 'Why don't you go and ask her?'

* * *

Every carriage was packed with bustling busy passengers. It was impossible to find a seat so Oliver and Rebecca stood shoulder to shoulder in the corridor, the movement of the train bringing them too close to each other and too close to those around them. It was a relief when they finally got to London and changed onto the little branch line that would take them home to Norfolk.

At Cambridge they'd finally found an empty carriage

and she'd curled up beside him. 'I'm so glad we're home,' she said softly, looking up at him.

Slowly, he turned towards her and for an instant their eyes had locked with an electric and desperate longing. He pressed his lips to hers and murmured, 'Rebecca, my love,' between hot, sweet kisses.

Her body responded at once, aching for his touch, for his warmth, for the smell of him. 'Oh, Oliver,' she whispered and returned his kiss fervently, feeling his tongue slip between her lips. She'd groaned as his hands lifted to cup her breasts, her nipples hardening under his caress, a tiny crystal ripple of pleasure coursing through her.

Something like a sob trickled from his lips and she knew then that they were lost. His fingers moved frantically, fighting with her buttons, whilst his other hand pushed eagerly between her thighs. Gasping with pleasure she opened to him, letting his fingers slide across her stocking tops towards her knickers, letting her desire guide her. She lifted to let him have greater access and suddenly, almost before she realised it, his fingers were pushing aside the thin fabric and plunging into her.

She was wet for him, moist, fragrant – a wild longing bubbled up inside her and her tongue sought his. She heard him whimper and felt his fingers move deeper, exploring every delicate crevice and fold.

Gasping, he moved nearer, his breath ragged and excited. Rolling her onto the dusty carriage seats he lifted her skirt and dragged down the thin material of her knickers. She didn't resist him, in fact her hips lifted unconsciously to meet his touch. His hand fumbled with his flies and suddenly his cock sprung towards her, aggressive, hot and needy. She didn't hesitate, instead she guided him back into the seat and mounted him.

The merest fleeting brush of his erect shaft against her inner thighs sent a great coursing plume of desire through her. She knelt over him and helped him guide the raging bulbous head into the soft inviting heat of her inner lips. Sinking down slowly she felt him slide home. For a few seconds her body resisted his assault and then he was there, filling her, opening her. She cried out at the hot electric sensation and pressed herself onto him relishing the wild compelling ache she felt inside. She wanted to possess him, to reclaim him for herself.

He bucked against her, filling her to the brim. Tears of pain and excitement bubbled up behind her eyes and she whimpered as he began to move in and out of her – a slow, smooth stroke – impaling her again and again. She felt a trickle of liquid on her thighs and looking down saw a glistening smear of her excitement, clinging to his shaft. She had waited so long for this wonderful special moment when they would be together. Her body was her gift to him.

The juddering rocking movement of the train added to their fervour. Oliver thrust deeper, grasping her hips, dragging her closer. Instinctively she moved against him, enjoying the sensations of his fingers exploring the delicate contours of her sex where it wrapped around his shaft. His finger tips brushed the swollen bud of her clitoris and she gasped. He stroked it knowingly, rhythmically, as if he totally understood what she needed to fan the glow of excitement between her legs into a roaring flame.

Against her neck he murmured soft, sweet words of love, whilst his other hand moved to her breasts, desperately trying to free them. Finally the buttons gave under his insistent fingers. Pulling her nearer, his lips worked over the sensitive areas of her shoulders and collar-bone. His mouth pressed hot heady kisses into her tingling flesh, whilst the rhythm of his fingers and cock kept up a driving relentless force. Sliding her blouse down, his lips closed over her dark puckered nipples. Sucking one between his lips he let his tongue tease round it.

Rebecca felt as if she was losing all control; between her legs the tiny glowing circles of sensation blossomed and grew. Her hips ground instinctively into Oliver's body, pressing down onto his fingers, pressing down on his cock, chasing the feelings even though they threatened to drown her.

Suddenly she felt Oliver straining up under her, in the same instant she felt the same desperate force within her, as her muscles tightened around his shaft. The intense circles of light shuddered up through her body and mind making her cry out in astonishment. Throwing back her head she let the great waves of pleasure and light engulf her again and again. Beneath her, Oliver bucked like a wild animal. Growling deep in his throat he pushed into her once more, joining her in an all-consuming, shuddering orgasm. Sobbing, Rebecca collapsed down onto his chest and wept hot tears of joy and relief.

'I love you, Mrs Rebecca Cresswell,' he murmured breathlessly, kissing the pit of her throat.

Rebecca moaned and ran a finger across his broad chest. 'Would you like to show me again just how much?' she whispered mischievously.

Oliver grinned. 'Oh yes,' he said and pulled her down towards him, his lips closing on hers.

A Message from the Publisher

Headline Liaison is a new concept in erotic fiction: a list of books designed for the reading pleasure of both men and women, to be read alone – or together with your lover. As such, we would be most interested to hear from our readers.

Did you read the book with your partner? Did it fire your imagination? Did it turn you on – or off? Did you like the story, the characters, the setting? What did you think of the cover presentation? In short, what's your opinion? If you care to offer it, please write to:

> The Editor
> Headline Liaison
> 338 Euston Road
> London NW1 3BH

Or maybe you think you could do better if you wrote an erotic novel yourself. We are always on the look-out for new authors. If you'd like to try your hand at writing a book for possible inclusion in the Liaison list, here are our basic guidelines: We are looking for novels of approximately 80,000 words in which the erotic content should aim to please both men and women and should not describe illegal sexual activity (pedophilia, for example). The novel should contain sympathetic and interesting characters, pace, atmosphere and an intriguing plotline.

If you'd like to have a go, please submit to the Editor a sample of at least 10,000 words, clearly typed on one side of the paper only, together with a short resumé of the storyline. Should you wish your material returned to you please include a stamped addressed envelope. If we like it sufficiently, we will offer you a contract for publication.

Adult Fiction for Lovers from Headline LIAISON

SLEEPLESS NIGHTS	Tom Crewe & Amber Wells	£4.99
THE JOURNAL	James Allen	£4.99
THE PARADISE GARDEN	Aurelia Clifford	£4.99
APHRODISIA	Rebecca Ambrose	£4.99
DANGEROUS DESIRES	J. J. Duke	£4.99
PRIVATE LESSONS	Cheryl Mildenhall	£4.99
LOVE LETTERS	James Allen	£4.99

All Headline Liaison books are available at your local bookshop or newsagent, or can be ordered direct from the publisher. Just tick the titles you want and fill in the form below. Prices and availability subject to change without notice.

Headline Book Publishing, Cash Sales Department, Bookpoint, 39 Milton Park, Abingdon, OXON, OX14 4TD, UK. If you have a credit card you may order by telephone – 01235 400400.

Please enclose a cheque or postal order made payable to Bookpoint Ltd to the value of the cover price and allow the following for postage and packing: UK & BFPO: £1.00 for the first book, 50p for the second book and 30p for each additional book ordered up to a maximum charge of £3.00. OVERSEAS & EIRE: £2.00 for the first book, £1.00 for the second book and 50p for each additional book.

Name ....

Address ....

....

....

If you would prefer to pay by credit card, please complete:
Please debit my Visa/Access/Diner's Card/American Express (Delete as applicable) card no:

| | | | | | | | | | | | | | | | | | | |

Signature .... Expiry Date ....